ONE KILLER PROBLEM

**Also by Justine Pucella Winans**

*Bianca Torre Is Afraid of Everything*

# ONE KILLER PROBLEM

## JUSTINE PUCELLA WINANS

An Imprint of HarperCollinsPublishers

HarperTeen is an imprint of HarperCollins Publishers.

One Killer Problem
Copyright © 2024 by Justine Pucella Winans
www.epicreads.com

Library of Congress Control Number: 2023944103
ISBN 978-0-06-332448-0

Typography by Chris Kwon
24 25 26 27 28  LBC  5 4 3 2 1

First Edition

To all the gay girls with bad attitudes
and even worse digestion.
This one's for you.

# ONE

## A Mystery Club That Can't Solve Mysteries

**THE WESTBRIDGE HIGH** Mystery Club has many talents, but solving mysteries is not one of them. It's not exactly their fault. There aren't a whole lot of mysteries to solve, other than who is screwing whom in questionable school locations, what the hell goes on in AP classes after they take their tests in May, and who thought it was a good idea to keep a mandatory swimming unit even in the dead of Northeast Ohio winters. It doesn't stop them from trying, though. But this time, they're going a little too far.

"What are you two doing in Mr. Ford's room?" I ask.

Mari, one half of the club, answers first. "I know this is your Friday study session time, Gigi, but he's not even here yet, and we'll only be a minute." She pulls an old phone and a roll of duct tape out of her bag, like that's normal. "We have as much of a right to be here since he's our math teacher too."

"Yes, but I'm not duct taping something to the bottom of his desk," I counter.

She crosses her arms over her chest. Her brown eyes somehow manage to catch even the smallest rays of sunlight

1

through the windows to sparkle. Her curly black hair falls gently over her pale skin as she tilts her head toward me. God, she's so pretty. Her whole aura is just like sunshine and butterflies.

With the smirk she gives me, maybe it's me that has the butterflies.

Regardless, I'm not the kind of sapphic that makes a habit of really disagreeing with hot girls. Especially not Mariela de Anda, not only because she's been my older brother's best friend since they were in first grade, but because I've had a major crush on her for almost as long. She adjusts her skirt before sliding underneath Mr. Ford's desk and my face heats as I look away to avoid seeming like the pervert I currently worry I am.

"Sean?" I ask the other half of the Mystery Club. "Do you want to explain what's happening right now? I'm not the type to snitch, but this is really weird."

"Official club business," he answers. Sean's my best friend and a total sweetheart, but he looks intimidating as hell. Like if you took Timothée Chalamet, put him in that machine that made Captain America, and then made him live in a postapocalyptic world for a minute. Despite being the same age, I look and feel so much younger.

I roll my eyes and unzip my backpack to grab my lunch sack and math book. Mr. Ford will give me shit if I'm not ready to go when he gets back with his own food from the teacher's lounge. "You can't have official club business if you aren't an official club."

Mari slides her head out from under the desk. "That's the whole point. We're trying to become one so Ethan can't kick us out of the club room."

"He's trying?" I ask.

Their club room is big . . . for a storage closet. It literally just has a table, a few chairs, a whiteboard on the wall, and bookshelves for the English department that have titles so old the pages are dehydration-pee yellow and have more penis drawings in the margins than not.

Sean unfolds a paper and slides it toward me. EVICTION NOTICE is printed across the top. Jesus Christ, our student council president is so extra. "But will he even approve it? Mystery Club is hardly even a club so much as a community service group."

Given the lack of mysteries, their tip line is mostly requests for cleaning and random odd jobs from other clubs. Mari and Sean seem to be fine with it, mostly because the two are so overworked from being top of their respective classes, the twice-a-week meetings are like stress relief sessions for people like them that don't know how to actually relax.

Mari almost slams her head against the desk from sitting up so quickly. "First off, we're not called *Mystery Club*, our club is called the Mystery and Thriller Literary Scholars. You know this."

"Literally no one calls you that."

"*Second*," she continues pointedly, "we are developing critical thinking and problem-solving skills by giving back to the Westbridge community through the impassioned and craftful solving of their day-to-day mysteries while connecting them to great works of fiction with literary analysis." With a smile, she flips me off. "That official enough for you?"

So they're a book club that does bitch work.

I can't lie, though, the way Mari puts it, it does sound pretty official. Now I know why her college app essay was about founding the club. Plus it's cute when she shows off how smart she is. "Ten out of ten," I reply. "I'm sold."

"Thanks, Gigi." Mari rolls her eyes.

"Happy to help."

"We just need a faculty advisor and ten members, then we are good to go," Sean says. He slides an interest form toward me. With his sharp features and size, I feel like I'm being offered hush money from a mob boss. "What if, instead of making fun of us, which is not helpful, you join us, which is? At least in name?"

"Do I have to actually read books that aren't gay YA fiction or gay YA graphic novels?" I ask.

"You don't have to read anything," Sean says. "Not even this document. Just sign away your soul because you love us."

"Fine." I add my signature (G scribble R scribble) and then print the full Gigi Ricci next to it. "Merry Early Christmas."

"It's April," Mari says.

"Happy Early Easter."

"You're atheist," Sean comments.

"Screw you both, you're welcome." I slide the paper away from my textbook. Shit, what chapter are we on? Sean seems to read my mind and opens it to chapter eighteen. He's right. I do love him. I look back toward Mari, currently dusting off her butt as she steps toward us. "Okay, but why did you duct-tape a phone under Mr. Ford's desk?"

She shrugs. "We figure solving a real mystery might help, so we want to find out why everyone thinks this classroom is haunted." I open my mouth, but she beats me to it. "No, we don't think it's actually haunted. But we can find out if someone's doing shady stuff in here, so I have a recording going on my old phone."

I internally cringe. It wouldn't take two amateur detectives to solve that case. I could do it right now. As Taylor Swift would say, "I'm the problem, it's me." And by problem, I mean the ghost of Classroom 212. Not in a spooky plot twist, *Gigi Ricci? She's been dead for forty years!* kind of way. More in a Gigi-Ricci-is-a-little-shit kind of way. Since I've been spending every Friday lunch with Mr. Ford for extra help, I've occasionally moved stuff around or left the occasional creepy note. Mr. Ford thinks it's hilarious. I also find myself hilarious, which is probably why I continue to do it.

Almost like he telepathically heard me thinking about him, Mr. Ford appears at the door. He looks between the three of us, holding a Dave's Cosmic Subs bag in his hand. "Are you two helping Gigi so I don't have to?"

"That sounds annoyingly hopeful," I comment. "You wound me, Mr. Ford."

"The fact that you are friends with two of my best students and still only do about half of your homework on time wounds me."

It's got to be more like sixty to seventy-five percent now, he's just being moody.

"Don't forget my brother," I add, since Luca is also high in the rankings. "I'm surrounded by nerds."

He scratches his chin. "Have you tried some kind of brain cell osmosis?"

"Why are you using big science words when this is a *math* study session?" I snap.

Mari and Sean just watch our banter, trying not to laugh. Most people hate Mr. Ford, since he's a tough teacher and sarcastic to the point of almost seeming mean. I can't trust anyone who isn't at least a little bit of a bitch, so I like him. Plus, he's really into watching the UFC, so my mom and I often run into him and his wife at the local sports bar when fights are on.

"Anyway, what do you two need?" Mr. Ford asks, dropping his lunch on his desk, clueless of the hidden phone secretly recording us all. Which is probably not legal, but what am I? A saint?

"We wanted to ask if you'd be our club advisor," Sean says. He holds out another form. "If we don't become an official club, they'll take away our club room."

"Club closet," I say, causing Mari to shoot me a glare.

"Do I have to do anything?" Mr. Ford asks.

"Just sit in on some of our meetings," Mari says quickly. "You can work on other stuff. It's very low-key."

Mr. Ford shrugs. "Sure, maybe there's a slight raise or something if you're a club advisor. I'll look into it." He signs the form.

Sean and Mari smile like they won the lottery at Disneyland. They give a bunch of thank-yous. "Did you want to stay and study?" Mr. Ford asks.

As if those two even need to study. I don't think I've ever seen either of them use flashcards or pore over their textbooks. With the amount of Pokémon Sean plays with me on weekends while procrastinating on homework, I'm pretty sure the jerk was gifted with brilliance. Or a really solid memory. Either way, he's a perfect student without even trying, despite looking like he beats freshmen up for lunch money. Mari's the same. While she gives off the appearance of a bubbly, kind, straight-A student, I've never seen her read a single book for class, but she always has some cozy mystery or thriller on hand. It's annoying they both do so well with low effort while I can try to sit down and study for hours yet barely retain three words.

"Nah," Mari answers. "We have to bring this over to Emma in student council. See you in class, Mr. Ford. Bye, Gigi!"

I'd be lying if I said my heart didn't skip a bit when that bright smile turned toward me.

I open my brown paper bag. I'm responsible for my own food, which means it's whatever slim pickings are left in the fridge and pantry. My sandwich is as dry as my love life, with only some questionably aged prosciutto and cheese my aunt left after her last visit. With the addition of a small baggie of Goldfish and dinosaur fruit snacks, I am both a seventy-year-old nonno and a five-year-old child on a one-day road trip.

Mr. Ford crosses his arms, giving me the most dad look someone who isn't your dad can give you. In fact, probably even more of one than my dad could give, since my dad looks more like a hipster lumberjack Jesus than someone who has two kids in high school. Mr. Ford has the whole stable, I-have-a-401(k) vibe with his button-up shirts and khakis.

"So," he says. "Heard you got detention again. From another fight."

My stomach drops despite myself. I had been so focused on thinking he was disappointed in me as a student, I didn't even consider *that*. How had he even heard about the fight? My teeth dig into my lip as I attempt to come up with an excuse that doesn't entirely sound like one.

Mr. Ford sighs. "Gigi, aren't you supposed to train martial arts for *self-defense*? Isn't the whole thing that trained fighters are supposed to be strong enough to know when to *walk away* from a fight?"

Damn, he's good at that *I'm not mad, I'm disappointed* emphasis. He knows I train jiu-jitsu and have trained

Muay Thai, and he's trying to use that against me. I already got the talk from mom about *how I'm not representing my academy well*, like the whole point isn't to be able to defend myself from bigger, hateful jerks like Kenneth Wright.

It's almost worse coming from Mr. Ford though. Like he had been rooting for me and this was just another event to prove him wrong. I'm no stranger to being a disappointment, but it hits different when it's a teacher who seems to believe in me.

I try to swallow away the pooling guilt by pushing down on my stomach to help me expel the sinking feeling like trapped gas. Mr. Ford's not being totally fair. He just stated the fact that I got in a fight without hearing my totally reasonable *why*.

"Yeah, but this was self-defense. Kenneth shoved me into a puddle, totally unprompted."

Mr. Ford raises his eyebrows. "Unprompted, huh?"

My face flames. He's too good at knowing when someone is guilty.

"He started it. He said I looked like a guy." And it was the way he said it, with a sneer, that told me that he wasn't really commenting on my short hair and slight muscle definition, but the fact that I look queer, and to him, that's a bad thing.

"And what did you say?"

I can't meet his eyes. "I said 'then call me daddy like your mom did last night, fuckface.'"

While he would never admit it, I swear he had to bite back a laugh. "That's kind of a prompt, Gigi."

"No excuse for him to get physical," I mutter.

If Mr. Ford could cross his arms harder, he would right then. "But that's an excuse to break his nose?"

I'm not going to lie, it felt good to shove Kenneth down and smash my elbow into his face. Just once. After that, I got up and walked to Principal Daniels's office before Kenneth could go there and cry about it. Still, I stand by my decision. "I got some bad scrapes and I could have snapped my wrist if I didn't train break falls all the time. And worst of all?" I grab the Eevee keychain from my backpack, stained in mud and torn at the neck so he's one shake away from being beheaded. "Look how they massacred my boy."

Mr. Ford sighs, taking a seat at his desk. "Okay, Marlon Brando, how about you tackle those chapter eighteen problems instead?"

I bite again into my sandwich and all my saliva instantly drains. I could probably live on prosciutto and cheese if it wouldn't require a daily double dose of MiraLAX, but a little giardiniera or condiments would go a long way right now. Besides, the last thing my IBS needs is to pendulum to the constipation side.

"I have plenty of time to finish it later in detention," I mumble. I look back up at him. "You wouldn't happen to be running it today, would you? In case I need help?"

"On a Friday? Absolutely not." Mr. Ford pulls out his own lunch, a beautiful-looking sub sandwich. While my lunch is fancier than usual thanks to my aunt, I would kill for some of those condiments. He sighs, dropping his voice like he's mostly talking to himself. "I've got another annoying meeting that will keep me here late though."

"Looks like both our weekends are off to a great start." I suck down half my water bottle before being able to go back to my sandwich. "At least we have something to look forward to with the pay-per-view fight tomorrow. Will you and Mrs. Ford go out to watch?"

"Of course. That card is *stacked*." Mr. Ford rolls up his sleeves, voice brimming with excitement. "Where are you all watching it? Usual spot?"

By you all, he means me, but mostly Mom and the other jiu-jitsu coaches they watch the fights with.

"I'll ask my mom and let you know if I catch you after detention." I finish off my sandwich and dig into the Goldfish. "You happen to see any of the weigh-ins yet?"

"No, but since this is the first time you could have watched them considering you've been in class all morning, including my own, I'm assuming you haven't either."

I smile under his pointed look. "Of course, Mr. Ford. I always pay total and complete attention in all my classes."

He sips his drink. "Honestly, I never watch those. Everyone looks so sad and hungry."

"Some of those weight cuts are brutal," I agree.

He leans back in his chair and tosses his hands up for emphasis. "I know I'm no fighter, I'm only a fan, but it seems so unnecessary. Those aren't even the weights they'll be fighting at anyway. Like can't everyone fight at their natural weight? And I'm pretty sure the origins of weight cutting were from mob bosses having a boxer weigh in at one fifty and fighting at one eighty or something. If it started as cheating, why is it still in practice?"

I can't exactly fact-check him on that nor do I really care to. He has a point. Besides, I know Mr. Ford can't stand any kind of cheating. I copied from Sean's homework *one time* and he went off, talking about how life is already unfair enough and I shouldn't play into it when I could apply myself or something.

He didn't get me in real trouble, I'm good enough at doing that myself, but we did have to spend the next Friday extra help session doing the whole assignment together.

"Anyway," he says now, "stop distracting me and solve for $x$ on page 198, problem 1a, then let me know what you get."

I didn't even glance at the page yet. I turn over to the first question. The fact that question one has parts all the way to h is a freaking scam. Mr. Ford probably laughed at the faces of relief when he said the homework was only problems 1, 4, and 8.

I read the problem a few times and already feel frustration rising. I look up. "We can use calculators on the test right?"

"Of course," he says. "I'm not a total monster."

I search through my backpack, but I can't find it. "Shit," I mutter. "I must have left mine at home."

"Want me to call back Sean and Mari for the Mystery of the Missing Calculator?" Mr. Ford teases. He's already reaching in his desk for one to let me borrow.

"Ha-ha." I stand to grab it. "Maybe the ghost took it."

Mr. Ford rolls his eyes. "Hate to break it to you, Ricci, but we're the only ones haunting this classroom."

# TWO

## When Things Go from Bad to Worse

**MY DETENTION IS** held in the library, which is better than a classroom because at least people walk in and out of the library and give me a distraction. I'm telling myself I'll get ahead on my homework, but I know I'm a liar.

On my way to the library, I double-check my backpack for my discreet bag of flushable wipes, hoping I didn't forget them like I did my calculator. Since I was diagnosed with irritable bowel syndrome, which seems to be the diagnosis you get when your intestines fall apart at the slightest sign of stress or certain food triggers and they are *pretty sure* it's not anything worse, I've made sure to carry them around.

I refuse to rely on the point-five-ply paper the school thinks is passable, and it's not like my intestines care whether or not I'm in detention.

My belly gives a slight grumble of a warning. Maybe I should stop by the nurse's office for Gas-X or something? Nurse Maria knows me by name, but I'm pretty sure she'll quit if I joke one more time that *I really want to try harder in school, but I've taken so much Imodium here, I just can't give a shit.*

14

"Hi, Gigi!" a voice says. "Can I interest you in any chocolate?"

I jump as the sound pulls me back into the world around me. I'm staring at the table set up outside the library, where the Peace Studies Club set up chocolate sales to raise money for Westbridge High's Spring Fest. It doesn't make sense that they run a festival that has absolutely nothing to do with peace, but everyone knows that club is just a way for popular kids to hang out and pretend like they give a damn for colleges. I'm not actually sure they do anything else. Spring Fest is like their main thing. They tried to organize a walkout earlier in the year, which would be more in the direction of what one would expect a Peace Studies Club to do, except instead of any actual issue affecting humans, the walkout was against the dissection of frogs in science classes. I'm all for skipping class, but I'm not down for public embarrassment to that degree.

Suddenly, I'm looking right into the eyes of Westbridge's own golden boy, Kyle Sinclair. He's an objectively hot star-quarterback, blond-haired, blue-eyed, freckled stereotype. But he's also ridiculously nice and knows everyone's name, including mine apparently, which makes it hard not to like him.

That's saying something too because I personally think the Peace Studies Club has so many reasons to be unlikable.

"Hey, Kyle. I don't have cash . . ." I start, but looking at the chocolate bars has my mouth watering. Maybe the sugar will help me get through detention. Or trigger my IBS, but either way, that gives me something to do for the next few hours. "Do you take Venmo?"

They do, of course.

"What flavors?" Emma Galligan asks from next to Kyle.

I almost didn't notice her. She's the president of the club to Kyle's vice president, so they spend a lot of time together, but their personalities are completely different. Emma has kind of that stick-up-her-ass, image-is-everything rich-girl attitude. I guess she can at least back it up, since she's always put together, manages club relations for the student council, rivals Mari in grades, got into a bunch of top colleges, and is basically a Northeast Ohio celebrity. She wrote this award-winning essay that got her a fancy scholarship, put her on the local news, and even had a line that was quoted in a congressional hearing. It basically became her entire identity, to the point where it's in all her social media bios. Cringe, yes, but I can't really judge as I'm pretty sure colleges would want to pay me *not* to read any essay I crafted.

Emma and Kyle make a weird but logical match. Sean and I were trying to figure out if they were dating last year, but they look a little too similar, so it would be borderline strange. Like with her straight blond hair and gray-blue eyes that are a shade or two off from Kyle's, they could easily be cousins.

I'm an indecisive bisexual stereotype and can't decide on a flavor to pick, so I give Emma a wink. "Surprise me."

Emma frowns, not making a move. Kyle recovers by flashing his own Crest white smile. "My favorite is the cookies and creme bar and you strike me as a caramel kind of girl, so I think those two would go really well together."

He winks, and my bisexuality almost takes a sharp turn to the straight. It's not like I'm into Kyle—I could never be emotionally attracted to someone who sincerely thinks they are nice and would list their biggest flaw as "caring too much"—but I can't deny that he's hot.

"Sounds good." I take the chocolate bars and send over the four dollars to the Peace Studies Club account. "Thanks."

Might as well support Spring Fest. Once Mari told us she'd be going to Columbus for college, I decided to use the romantic, tropey setting of our school festival to finally confess my feelings. I'm not expecting a whole sapphic *Love, Simon* deal—I know she'll probably let me down nicely—I just feel like I should get it off my chest and use the rejection to move on so it hurts less when she leaves.

"Of course, I'll see you around?" Kyle asks it like a question.

I open my mouth to answer, but Emma responds first with an eye roll. "Well, yeah, weirdo, she also goes here."

Kyle's pretty face is in conflict as his eyes glare at her but his mouth maintains that easygoing smile. Huh. Well, I don't know what's going on with them, but I want no part of it.

"Yeah. See you both."

I awkwardly sidestep away from the table and walk into the library. Despite the fact that I refuse to read any book assigned to me in school and our librarian is not exactly trying her best to get more queer books in the

Westbridge catalog, the library is one of the nicer places on campus. It's close to the front entrance and has plenty of windows, so there's natural light instead of the horrible yellowed, sometimes-burnt-out hallway lighting. The books are stacked up neatly, which is oddly satisfying, and there's plenty of tables set up for studying.

Or for detention, I guess.

Ms. Ruby, the younger teacher who is supervising, sectioned off a few tables. As a real overachieving delinquent, I either arrived early or only two of us are supposed to be here today. I'm at one table, and some other brunette white kid I don't know is at the other. Maybe a freshman? Regardless, Ms. Ruby doesn't seem to be paying attention yet, as she's deep into some historical romance book, so there must be a few minutes until we start.

The freshman boy looks over at me.

"Are you Gigi Ricci?" he asks, kind of in the same voice you'd ask someone if they are a murderer or a Michigan fan.

"Yes?" It isn't supposed to come out as a question. I just don't understand why this child is talking to me.

His voice drops to a whisper. "Is it true that you broke Kenneth Wright? I heard he almost died."

I make a face. "I broke his nose. He's fine."

I open my mouth to explain how Kenneth totally started it and it was basically self-defense, but I don't get the chance.

"Badass," the kid says with wide eyes.

A new voice speaks up. "That Gigi's giving free nose jobs? Totally."

Oh no. I'd recognize that voice anywhere—school, invading the comfort of my own home, the occasional nightmare.

Sure enough, my nemesis, Cedar Martin, slides into the chair right next to me despite there being another table open. She's the third wheel of Luca and Mari's friendship, so I've known her forever. And she has relentlessly teased me the entire time.

We just don't get along. She's fake, with her faux-witchy white-girl fall-but-year-round aesthetic and disgustingly rich family. It's definitely all of that and has nothing to do with the fact that it's obvious she also has a crush on Mari. And maybe I shouldn't assume every girl that carries around an oracle deck is gay, but I do.

Even now, she's wearing an oversized black sweater with a neckline that falls off her shoulder in an annoyingly hot way. Cedar's curvy, and always seems to dress in a way that suits her perfectly.

"What are you doing in detention?" I snap.

Much like my brother and Mari, Cedar's a total geek.

"I was coding in class when I should've been doing the work that I already finished." She shrugs, her sweater falling that little bit more off her shoulder, and I have to make a conscious effort to keep my eyes locked on her face. "I'm pretty sure Ms. Meyer doesn't like me."

"How is that possible when there's so much to like?" I deadpan.

She takes it in stride. "I know, my beauty, charm, intelligence, humility . . ."

I snort.

That's when I remember the freshman, but his back is already turned.

Cedar doesn't even give him a second glance, just continues. "I'm assuming you're sitting here because of the whole broken nose incident and not because you can't resist spending time with me?"

She's insufferable.

"At least now it's an actual punishment," I retort.

"I didn't know you were into that, but I can punish you if you'd like." Cedar winks.

Against my best efforts, my face goes completely red. I know she's teasing me to get a reaction, but I can't help myself in giving one. It's not like I'm a prude or anything, but I'm hopelessly inexperienced.

I've only been kissed two times. My first kiss was when Mom and Dad made me accompany Luca to a theater camp because they didn't want him to go alone, and me and one of the guys in the ensemble kissed backstage before we both immediately broke away and said, "Sorry, I think I'm gay." My second kiss was the universe making a fun callback because Sean and I went to the *Cinderella* cast party last year, and the now-graduated Lacey Stevens kissed me before saying, "Sorry, I don't think I'm gay."

So, yeah, I don't exactly have a lot of romance under my belt despite the fact that I would absolutely love to. Like a real kiss. With someone who actually wants to kiss me.

And then, you know, more than that.

At least I'm already blushing.

I'm once again saved when Ms. Ruby looks up from her book to take attendance. The freshman boy is first, then Cedar.

"Gianna Ricci?"

"Here," I call out.

"Matt Russell?" Ms. Ruby asks.

He doesn't answer, as he isn't here. I know Matt Russell. He made a homophobic comment to Luca my freshman year and shoved him up against the wall by his shirt, so I jumped Matt's back and locked a rear naked choke. Causing him to pass out in the hallway got me a suspension, but also made me sort of famous at Westbridge.

Basically, Matt Russell is a conservative dickwad. I'm shocked he's skipping detention though. Maybe he couldn't miss spreading misinformation online or posing for dating profile photos with a dead fish or whatever guys like him do for fun.

"Too bad," Cedar says. "I read this book where a group of teens are at detention and one of them died. We could have taken him out as community service."

"As long as we pay off the Mystery Club so they don't solve it."

"Don't you mean the Mystery and Thriller Literary Scholars? Aren't you also officially a member in name or did they not track you down yet?" She stifles a laugh before looking away. "Haven't seen you with Mari as much lately."

I turn to her. Is this some kind of casual way to see if

anything happened between me and Mari? Is Cedar trying to determine whether I'm a rival or not?

"I—"

"Ladies, no talking," Ms. Ruby calls without looking up from her book.

Well, I didn't really know what I was going to say anyway, so that's fine.

I open my textbook. I'm supposed to read a chapter for history. I try to focus my eyes on the page and read. I'm about halfway through it when I realize I didn't absorb anything that I read. I'm technically seeing the words, but they are refusing to register. Even if I try to focus, it doesn't help. It just makes me feel brainless.

But I would listen to the entire audio version of this boring, confusing textbook before tearing up in public, so I look around for a distraction.

Next to me, Cedar reads a book that I doubt is for class because it's obviously queer fiction based on the cover. At least, I'd be upset if it wasn't queer, given how the two girls are almost brushing fingers. If they aren't lesbians, I'd throw the book across the room and never read again.

Maybe I'm thirsty for my own love story. Would be nice. Even with my whole confession plan, I can't see it going well. I'm not the kind of person that shows my emotions and acts all rom-com embarrassing. I probably won't even get out all my feelings for Mari, so I'll turn the confession into a joke, and she'll laugh like she always does. Well, that wouldn't be all bad. At least then, no one gets hurt.

My phone buzzes in my pocket, and for one ridiculous moment, my heart jumps in my chest like it would be a notification from Mari. Trying to be sneaky, I pull it out and look down at the screen.

**Mom:** hey kiddo—got the address for the bar tomorrow

**Mom:** *family friendly sports bar

**Mom:** :)

They really didn't need to clarify, I figured, but okay. Another text with the address comes through.

**Gigi:** cool—I'll tell mr. ford

**Gigi:** he and mrs. ford are gonna watch

**Mom:** sounds good hun, they're always welcome:)

I'm always ready to leave detention as soon as possible, but now I have a legitimate reason. Hopefully I'll catch Mr. Ford before he leaves.

It goes by slowly enough, but finally, Ms. Ruby looks up from her book at us.

"All right, thanks for being quiet and mostly productive." She looks at me at that point. My zoning out and constantly checking my lap for the time must have been obvious. Whoops. "Have a nice weekend and try to stay out of trouble."

The freshman boy immediately runs off without missing a single beat.

"Love that spirit," Cedar says from next to me, "but I wouldn't even have that energy if my life was on the line."

I gather up my things and humor her. "What? You're not a runner? What would you do then, fight?"

23

"Absolutely not. Do I look like I'm prepared to fight or flee?" She gestures down at her heeled boots.

I snort. "Okay, so you'd just die, then." I stand up and pick up my backpack. "Let's hope we don't have to run from a killer anytime soon."

"I wouldn't die if I had you," she says, all smiles.

My face is on the brink of heating again. She's doing this on purpose.

"You're strong but small, so I can push you in front of the killer and get some more time to safely speed walk away," Cedar continues.

And any small spark of hope for her is extinguished.

"Thanks," I say. "Maybe I'll see you around, but I hope not."

"Oh, I'm sure you will." Cedar grabs her own backpack and stands up. In her shoes and my sneakers, she's much taller than me and I have to bend my neck back to meet her eyes. "On Monday, this weekend, in your dreams."

I roll my eyes. "Bye, Cedar."

I walk off in the opposite direction of the front doors before she can say anything more. She's the one person that always gets me like this. It's so annoying. We're literally a year apart and she acts like I'm a little kid. I see the way she is around Mari, and it's totally different. Around girls she likes, Cedar's a little more reserved and chill.

I, on the other hand, seem to be hopeless around girls whether I like them or not.

Unless we're fighting. But that's not usually the case.

I pull out my phone to shoot a quick text over to Sean.

**Gigi:** I'll be a min, let me know when you're done with mystery club

**Ace Pokémon Trainer:** sure thing <3

He also earns his contact name by sending a happy Sylveon GIF, because he knows it's my favorite Eeveelution, with Vaporeon as a close second.

It's late enough that the hallways are almost scarily empty. Like *I'm* the clueless girl about to fall in front of the killer. Technically, that might be better for me, grappling wise. Unless they have a gun or something, but then I'm dead anyway and the chance of that happening after school, when everyone's gone, is way lower than when the school is crowded.

I should stop thinking about all this. I'm going to get myself worked up over nothing because I'm by myself walking through the halls. Being alone anywhere you're not usually alone is always creepy; that doesn't mean anything bad is going to happen.

Or maybe the universe is foreshadowing me running into student body president Ethan Mitchell or something.

I climb up the steps closest to Mr. Ford's classroom to get to the second floor, which is somehow even creepier because there aren't the distant sounds of clubs that are still hanging around. Mr. Ford's classroom door is open, but not all the way. Enough of a sliver to make it seem like he wouldn't mind me walking right in, but not so much that it's inviting. I can't hear any voices, so whatever meeting he had must have been long over.

"Mr. Ford, I got the address for the sports bar tomorrow . . ."

My words trail off and get lost in the air. I'm not sure what I'm seeing at first. It's enough to momentarily shut my brain down.

When I do manage to comprehend what I'm seeing, it's a piercing kind of horror. One that overwhelms the senses and has my thoughts and heart uncomfortably racing. Mr. Ford is in the room, but he's on the floor against the side of his desk. His neck is bent at an impossible angle, and he's surrounded by a large pool of blood.

# THREE

## How to React to Dead Bodies

**A SCREAM CATCHES** somewhere between my throat and the brief moment when things were still okay. I rush forward to him. Maybe he fell and needs help. Maybe this is an elaborate prank he set up that was wildly messed up but will give me a taste of my own medicine for pretending there's a ghost in the room.

"Mr. Ford?" My voice starts quiet but rises in intensity because, while his eyes are uncomfortably open and looking into the distance, that doesn't necessarily mean he isn't just a great actor. "Mr. Ford! Come on, this isn't funny. Get up."

His arm is too stiff. My eyes and throat burn. This can't be happening. This can't be fucking happening.

"Hey. Asshole. Wake up." The fact that my swearing does nothing is a worse sign.

Shit. This is fucking happening.

With a shaky arm, I reach out toward his neck. The pale skin under his stubble looks bruised. I check for a pulse.

There isn't one.

"Holy shit." A voice says from behind me.

I turn, still shaking and now with Mr. Ford's blood on my

27

knees and shoes, to the completely shocked and horrified faces of Sean and Mari.

Sean rushes forward. "Is he okay?"

"He's dead?" I say. The words shouldn't come out like a question, but they do. I don't want to believe it. I mean, how can he be dead here when he was just alive and laughing with me a few hours ago? My brain seems to catch up on everything and then speeds ahead. "He's dead. He's *dead*. Oh my god."

"Gigi . . ." Mari's voice comes out soft, careful, and she steps toward me like she's approaching a wild animal. "Did you kill Mr. Ford?"

"Are you *kidding* me?" I scream. "Why would I kill one of the few teachers who doesn't hate me?" I'm shaking. I need to calm down. Of course it looks bad. They weren't here. "I just got here from detention, I was going to ask him to come to watch the fights tomorrow, I . . ." Tears are leaking now and my stomach hurts, but not the usual IBS cramps and pains.

"Shit," Mari says. "I'm calling for help."

I don't understand what happened. Eyes blurry, I try to look around for some sign of someone, *something* to explain this. There's a stepladder placed behind his desk. There's a large white poster draped next to it. Did he fall off of that?

As I both hear and don't hear Mari call 911, I move toward the poster, slightly stained with Mr. Ford's blood. I can't bring myself to touch it, so I kick it over with my

28

shoe. It's a poster of two cats, forming an L. The text above reads PURR-PENDICULAR and underneath it says MEOW-THEMATICS IS FUN!

My eyes start to burn. "What the fuck?" I don't know what to do. My hands tremble as I look back. "What the *fuck*?"

Sean doesn't know what to say either. He looks like a ghost himself as he takes in the scene. Our eyes meet.

"Please tell me this isn't real," I manage to say.

It can't be. There is no way Mr. Ford would even *buy* a math poster with a cat pun, let alone *die* trying to hang one. My body seems to reenter a state of shock as it hits me all over again that he's dead. He's dead right here, and I can't look down at him again. I can't.

"Paramedics are coming, Principal Daniels is also on the way," Mari says. Her voice is strong but trembling. She also seems to be keeping her eyes away from the floor.

I step away from the worst of the crime scene, keeping close to the wall in case I fall over. I glance over at Sean and Mari. "How did you two even know to come here?"

It takes Sean a second to respond, but he holds his phone screen up for me to see. It's open to an email, sent to the tip account the Mystery Club has. The sender is someone called *Miss Mystery*.

There's no subject, and the body of the email only reads *Classroom 212*.

My stomach drops and a chill passes over me.

Someone knew about this before me.

In that moment, everything feels horribly still. Then time fast-forwards in a whirlwind.

The school officer and Principal Daniels arrive first and take us out into the hallway until the paramedics come soon after. Luckily, they don't make us stay near the classroom long enough to have to see them move Mr. Ford. I already saw enough, and tears keep threatening to come every time I get a moment of clarity to think about it.

Principal Daniels escorts the three of us into the main offices, where we wait for our parents.

I think he stops himself from making a comment about finally seeing me for something that isn't my fault. But that would be a little awful given the death and everything.

My calm mind still pushes everything away. It's all too fast. I was kneeling in front of Mr. Ford's body, and now I'm sitting in the office with the secretary's floral blanket draped across my shoulders and a Capri-Sun from the cafeteria in one hand. The police quickly got our version of events; even though I probably could have asked to wait until our parents arrived, I just gave responses. More than anything, I want to get out of here.

Principal Daniels and Ms. Leslie don't look at us. Although I suppose students finding a teacher dead in his classroom is uncharted territory, and it's not like either of them would really know what to say.

I take a sip of my juice, the metallic pouch shrinking against my fingers. I don't taste it.

"Can we go?" Mari asks.

She and Sean have their own juices, but for some reason I'm the only one with a blanket. I guess I looked the most in shock, or they know I was getting extra help from Mr. Ford. Sean is unmoving next to me, still understandably frozen. Mari wipes at her eyes on occasion but at least seems relatively held together. She's always been reliable in emergencies.

"Once your parents arrive, you can leave," Principal Daniels says, glancing at us for only a moment.

The police came to investigate the scene, but it was quickly determined to be an accident. There was no other reasonable explanation, and everyone agreed that it was just an unfortunate tragedy of Mr. Ford hitting his head the worst possible way when he fell, so we were all allowed to go home.

Since my parents are both supposed to be working, I'm not sure who's coming to get me. I know someone is. I mean, they wouldn't leave me alone after this. And both Mom and Dad have the main office number saved since they've gotten quite a few calls about me.

At least this time, it's not my skipping classes, intolerable personality, or choking out another kid for bullying my brother.

Sean is picked up first by his mom's current boyfriend. He's not exactly the friendly, sensitive type, so he basically rushes Sean out as quickly as possible, like it's some kind of an inconvenience to pick up a teenage boy who accidentally came across his teacher's body.

31

What a dick.

I tell Sean to come over this weekend as much as he wants. It will be better than in his apartment.

Mari's dad arrives not long after. They have a soft conversation in Spanish as he hugs her. While they're Spanish the same way my family is Italian, Mari's dad at least taught her enough of the language to be conversational. As if that wasn't enough reason to be jealous, she chose Italian as her language requirement in school and speaks that better than me too. Before they head out, they both turn toward me.

"Lo siento, Gigi," Mr. de Anda says. "¿Cómo estás?"

He pulls me up and in for a hug. Mari's parents know me well because they have the hangout house, and Luca would constantly bring me along when he was supposed to be in charge, or when Mom and Dad had work and Mrs. de Anda agreed to watch us both. Instead of awkwardly being a third or fourth wheel and embarrassing myself in front of my crush, I often hung out with her parents.

I was thinking about the long game of getting the family approval, and they are basically second parents, like my parents are to Sean and Mari.

"No estoy bien, pero . . ." I try to think of the words. "Voy a vivir?" My Spanish is unfortunately limited and doesn't really dive into the confusing emotions I'm currently drowning in.

Mr. de Anda reaches out to squeeze my shoulder. "You're allowed to not be okay. Just let us know if you need anything, ¿entiendes?"

"Entiendo," I say. "Gracias." It's not much, but it gets him to smile.

"I'm going to warm up the car," Mr. de Anda says, sensing that Mari might want to tell me something. He looks between us. "Don't be long."

We both nod. When Mari turns to me, her expression is both soft and serious.

"Seriously, though. Are you okay?" She frowns a little. "I mean, obviously you aren't okay, but like . . . how not okay are you?"

I shrug. "You seem to be handling it better than me."

Mari winces. "I'm glad I seem that way because I feel . . . I don't know. This is really shit and I'm sorry, Gigi."

"Me too."

"Text or call if you need anything, okay? Or if you just want to talk." She reaches out to squeeze my hand. "I'm here, all right?"

Her brown eyes and hand are both so warm, it almost makes things feel okay again. My heart flutters in my chest.

"Okay," I say. "I will."

With one last soft smile, she steps away to follow her dad. I'm left alone with my depressing thoughts and the echo of what happened. I mean, death is supposed to be this far-away thing. Sure, I've been to a funeral or two of extended family, but I didn't have to see them until after they were cleaned up, and that was bad enough. I wasn't close to them or anything either. I definitely wasn't expecting someone I saw nearly every day to die, just like that. An accident. One moment fine, and the next . . .

I don't want to keep thinking about the Mr. Ford that is not quite Mr. Ford. I don't want to think of him that way. I want to somehow see him show up tomorrow and listen as he goes on about the fighting odds and stats that I don't care about and have the coaches try to convince him and Mrs. Ford to come for a jiu-jitsu class.

Oh god. *Mrs. Ford*.

"Gigi!"

I look up at Mom's voice. They are barely taller than me but practically barrel into me as they rush into the office. Their arms still strong around me, they check me over like I've been assaulted.

"Jesus, Mom," I mutter. "Are you going for a hug or a double leg?"

They ignore me. "Are you okay? How are you feeling?"

"I've been better," I say. My eyes threaten to burn, but I've already been too vulnerable in front of people today. Even if it's just Principal Daniels, Ms. Leslie, and some police officers left, I don't want to cry.

Mom pulls me in for another hug. "I'm so sorry. This is all so fucked up, but I'm here now, sweetie. I've got you."

As much as I don't want Mom to treat me like a kid normally, there's a part of me that just wants to sob into their shoulder and have them make everything okay. I can't though. I'm not all emotional like Dad and Luca.

"Can we just go home?" I ask.

34

"Of course." They brush a few strands of hair off my forehead. "Let's get you home."

The drive back starts out pretty silent. It's clear Mom wants to speak, but isn't really sure what to say, and I can't really blame them.

"Do you want to talk about what happened?" they ask after a while.

"Not really."

"Do you need to punch something?" they ask. "We can stop at the gym, or I think I have pads at home."

I don't know what it says about me that it's the first thing they thought I'd like to do after talking, but they aren't necessarily off base. "No, that's okay. Maybe this weekend." I don't like seeing them so concerned and worried, so I throw on a smile. "We can drive around and look at the rich people houses before class."

It is one of our favorite mother-daughter bonding time activities, other than training. Commenting on the houses, the features, the dream of not having to worry about money like those faceless owners.

Mom gives a little smile back. "Whatever you want, kid. I'll try to make it happen."

The rest of the ride passes in silence, but it's not quite so uncomfortable. I try to focus on the passing streetlights and setting sun to keep my thoughts occupied. It works well enough, and after a few minutes of it, we're pulling into the driveway of the little one-story house we call home. It's a world away from the dream homes we'd drive by, with its peeling shutters, grown-out grass, and the one window with the broken screen that we never fixed but simply don't open, but I've never been so happy to see it in my life. We start to walk in.

"When the school called, they said there would be a counselor for you on Monday, but maybe you don't have to go in that day. We'll figure it out." They bite their lip as we enter through the side door. "You'll be okay?"

I nod. "I'll be in my room, but I'm fine. Really."

They don't look like they believe me, but they're not exactly an emotional person themself, so they don't press it either. "I'll call you when it's dinner."

I'm not sure I entirely want to be alone, but I'm not sure what to say, so I head down to the basement. Since it's a two-bedroom house, Mom and Dad converted the basement to a bedroom so Luca and I wouldn't have to keep sharing. I volunteered to take it. It's bigger and he's too scared of spiders.

Plus, it's furnished and nice, so it doesn't give off *basement* vibes. I turn on one of the lamps next to my bed and curl up in the mound of plushies I sleep with nightly.

Turns out, never getting over a love for plushies comes in handy when things feel particularly shitty.

"What the hell happened today?" I ask Amber, the golden-eyed cat that's squeezed to my cheek. She doesn't respond, obviously, but I also bring Gingersnap the Dragon into the cuddle.

In front of them, I finally allow myself to cry.

Mr. Ford was a good teacher. A good person. He always helped me and never judged me for being poor, or queer, or occasionally violent. He judged people on their behavior, the kind of person they were at heart, as one should.

I just don't understand.

How could it have happened so suddenly? He mentioned having a meeting, and maybe that was about decorating his room a little more . . . but seriously? He just had to fall off a stepladder and *die*? It's not fair.

I wipe at my eyes. How could he slip up like that? And for a freaking cat pun poster? Mr. Ford didn't even like cats. Sean and I would constantly show him pictures from the shelter Sean volunteers at, and he'd ask to see the dogs instead.

I sit up, making a face. Wait. Why *would* Mr. Ford even try to hang up a poster like that? Even if someone did tell him to decorate the room, he would have got some basic yet informational math poster. Even if he got the cat poster as a joke, that's not something he'd do on a Friday night. He'd wait to make me or the Mystery Club do it for him on Monday.

And even if, for some ridiculous reason, he did decide to hang that poster then, what was with the email Sean and Mari received? If someone saw him, why wouldn't they call for help? It doesn't matter if someone didn't like him. It could be Kenneth Wright or Ethan Mitchell bleeding out on the floor and I'd still call 911. I just wouldn't be sad about it.

"Something's not right," I tell Gingersnap and Amber. "Something's really fucking not right here."

Because if someone knew Mr. Ford was dead and didn't do anything to help, that has to mean that they were responsible. The police and Principal Daniels aren't going to look into it— they were absolutely positive it was an accident, and I don't think my word alone would convince them overwise. Mari and Sean have made me read enough mysteries to know that authorities won't give any attention to cases that seem to have a clear explanation. The truth usually only gets out when either the criminal gets cocky and messes up, or when the person who discovered the body vows to get involved and solve it.

Whether I like it or not, that's me. I have to find out who sent that message to the Mystery Club, because something in my gut tells me this wasn't an accident. But how the hell can I figure it out? I don't know shit about solving a murder.

My phone buzzes. There are texts from both Sean and Mari, checking in on me.

I can't help it. A bubble of laughter escapes from my lips.

I might not know the first thing about solving a mystery, but I happen to know two people that do.

# FOUR

## A Planned Gay Confession and a Prayer to a Dead Man

**MY MOOD ON** Saturday is in general . . . not great. It still feels unreal, and I kind of want to curl up in a ball and be sad, but I can't allow myself to do that. Instead, I stress baked an entire tray of lasagna and a whole container of cookies to take to Mrs. Ford. Since I've met her at fights before, Mom assured me it wouldn't be weird and even let me put the ingredients on their backup, emergency-only credit card.

Maybe I'm not great with emotions, but food is one way I can show her that some of Mr. Ford's students really cared about him. I wipe my face. Not gonna cry. I'm fine. It's so damn weird to use the past tense with him, but I'm fine.

Maybe even one short step above fine, considering that Sean and Mari agreed to use their supposed mystery-solving skills to look into Mr. Ford's death. I also used my status as a semi-official Mystery Club member to convince them to help me bring food over to Mrs. Ford, but I'm pretty sure they would have done that anyway.

A knock sounds from the door, but when I open it, it isn't Sean and Mari.

It's my brother. And, because of course, Cedar.

"I forgot my keys," Luca says, waltzing past me to get into the house because he's the kind of gay that walks like that.

"Hi," I say. "I'm doing good, thanks."

"Hey, Gigi," Cedar says. "I'm sorry about Mr. Ford. The whole thing . . . I'm sorry."

The fact that she of all people thought to say something only makes my brother look worse. "Thanks."

Cedar stands at the doorway, not moving. "I just can't believe an accident like that would . . . Again, I'm really sorry."

An awkward moment passes as I question whether to tell her that it probably wasn't an accident. I don't really want to talk about it now. It's practically uncomfortable that she's looking at me with concern and not cracking some awful joke at my expense.

"You don't need an invitation to come in," I say, "unless the goth vibes aren't just a phase and you actually believe you're a vampire."

I make a point of eyeing her heavy eyeliner, black dress, and black lace-up boots with heels.

"I'm more of a cryptid goth than a vampire goth," Cedar says. "Perhaps an eldritch god goth if we're feeling fancy."

I roll my eyes and step aside so Miss Cthulhu can enter.

Luca has already grabbed a can of ginger ale from the fridge and draped himself over one of the kitchen chairs. "I can't believe I was in the building and had no idea he fell. It's terrible."

His brown eyes are wide as he looks between Cedar and me. He almost looks a little guilty, like he fully believes he should have sensed what happened on the other side of the building and stopped it somehow.

Everyone says Luca and I look exactly alike, but that's probably because our hair is basically the same length and color, even though half of my head is shaved in a fade and he hasn't even come near clippers. I don't see the resemblance, really. He's soft and delicate, where I'm sharp. Plus, I have a scar on my left eyebrow, which looks totally badass. (Never mind that it wasn't from a fight or even jiu-jitsu and was instead from when I accidentally slipped on some ice a few winters ago. People never salt their sidewalks.)

"At least you didn't have to see him," I say.

He winces, looking a little pale. "Yeah, sorry."

I don't think I drank any fiber today, so I pour myself a cup of water from the sink and stir some in. The flavorless kind saved my life after trying one mix that tasted like a sad, melted orange Popsicle. Reluctantly, I give Cedar a look. "Want some water?"

"Sure."

I take out another cup. "I'm shocked that you would actually be okay drinking from the tap," I say. "Your mom might disown you for consuming water that wasn't sold in a bottle for five dollars."

"Five dollars?" Cedar widens her black-lined eyes. "That's peasant water."

I refuse to laugh. I might *respect* her for playing along

with my teasing but that doesn't mean I *trust* her. What starts out as fun banter can turn embarrassing in a heartbeat. I can only keep my cool for so long in front of pretty, popular girls. Even ones that are annoying and look like a hot cheerleader who got lost in a cemetery and had to blend in with the Satanists to survive.

Luca glances between us before settling on Cedar. "I'm going to set up the movie." He scurries off to his room. I hand Cedar the glass of water.

"No ice?" she asks.

I glare at her.

"I'm teasing, it's cold. Although that glare might have made it colder." She takes a sip through a smile. "Mari said she's coming over with Sean?"

I nod and point to my neatly wrapped food trays. "We're gonna check in on Mrs. Ford."

Cedar nods. "That's really sweet of you."

I shrug. There's another pause between us. "I would rather just talk about other stuff."

"Can I ask you something personal, then?"

I sigh, bracing for some question with a punch line.

"Do you . . ." Cedar blushes slightly. "Do you still have feelings for Mari?"

I don't even know what to think about that. I'm both a little disappointed and annoyed.

"Why?" I ask. "Are you jealous?"

I'm almost surprised when that deepens her blush before

I realize we're talking about Mari, and Cedar's totally different where that's concerned.

"I . . . I mean . . ." Cedar starts.

"I've been planning to tell her I've liked her at Spring Fest, but feel free to jump in before then. Who knows? Maybe it will work out for you."

I hate how the surprised, hopeful look in her eyes crushes my chest. "Seriously?" she asks. "You mean that?"

I shrug. "Yeah."

Something like a laugh escapes from her lips. "I thought you had no idea how I felt."

"Everyone knows you like Mari, Cedar. It's obvious."

Her expression falls all at once. "I don't think I need *you* telling me what's obvious. You're the most . . ." Jaw set in frustration, she lets out a sigh. "Whatever. That gives me until Spring Fest to try to win her over, so. I'll see you around." She starts to step away before giving one look back. "I am sorry about everything. Seriously."

I don't respond, just wait for her to walk away.

I'm glad Sean and Mari are both here with me because the moment Mrs. Ford opens the door, I'm one sad sentence away from falling entirely the hell apart. Her black hair is up in a ponytail, her eyes are rimmed in red, and a lack of sleep hollows her otherwise smooth skin.

"Hi, Mrs. Ford," I say. "I'm so, so sorry for your loss. We, um . . . we brought some food for you."

In addition to my lasagna and cookies, Mari has brought a container of gazpacho, so we're all carrying food.

Mrs. Ford gives me a little smile. "I appreciate that, kids. That helps a lot." She looks between us. "Why don't you come in for tea? I have this whole charcuterie board and I don't want it to go bad . . ." She squeezes her lips together and releases them. "My parents are on the way, but I wouldn't mind some company."

We all awkwardly step into the house. Mrs. Ford has us set the food down on the table, where there is already the largest board of cheeses, olives, and who knows what else resting on the table.

"It's already been picked at by guests, so please help yourself," Mrs. Ford says. "With the wake tomorrow . . ." She clears her throat before looking up: "You are all welcome to come to that as well. The address is there on the table. I'd love to see some of his students there. I'll get that tea. I already had water going."

Mrs. Ford moves over to the kitchen, leaving us in the dining room. It's probably just because I know what happened, but it feels like the air in the house is different. There is a general kind of fog to it, feeling heavier than the air outside, like the building itself knows what happened and aches because of it. I almost have to wonder how much grief was etched into the wood of these walls just overnight.

My eyes catch a large photo on the wall. It's Mr. and Mrs. Ford on their wedding day, years younger and smiles huge, with golden text underneath the photo that reads *Arthur and Priya Forever!*

Forever never felt fucking shorter.

Mrs. Ford brings in two cups of tea at a time before joining us at the table. I don't even know what kind it is, and caffeine is usually a bad poop trigger for me, but I don't have the heart to decline, so I sip it anyway.

"How are you holding up?" Mari asks. "Considering, I mean. Do you need help with anything? Chores or tasks or . . . anything so you don't have to worry about it?"

Old Mystery Club habits die hard. But Mrs. Ford waves the offer aside.

"No, no. I just appreciate the food, thank you." She sips her own tea, fingers tense around the cup. "It just . . . It's hard to believe. I still feel like he'll walk through the door at any moment."

The three of us are all silent, but I guess it's hard to know what to say. Personally, I think I'd want to hear more about positive things when everything is so . . . horribly not. I clear my throat.

"I was thinking . . . one of my favorite Mr. Ford moments happened a few weeks ago in class," I start. "When Jaime Morton didn't have his homework completed because he said he was practicing for the drag show and no one could possibly think of math while in heels, Mr. Ford not only bought a ticket to the show but borrowed Jaime's heels and taught in them for the rest of the class." I can't hold in my laugh. "It was truly iconic."

Mrs. Ford laughs. "That sounds just like him."

"I think my favorite moment was when Principal Daniels came in to watch the class last year," Mari says. "He questioned why Mr. Ford went off topic from the curriculum to go into a lesson based on questions we had, and he put Principal Daniels on the spot to solve the problem. I was legitimately secondhand embarrassed when he couldn't, and Mr. Ford said *that* was why he wanted to teach us the concepts as a whole and not just what we needed to memorize for the test."

Mrs. Ford smiles into her tea. "He really loved all his students." She bites her lip. "Well, maybe not all of them."

"Definitely not Ethan Mitchell," Sean says. "When he took time away from class to talk about the student council election, Mr. Ford did an impersonation of Ethan from his desk, and I almost peed my pants I was laughing so hard."

"I remember hearing about that." Mari giggles a little. "I'm pretty sure about twenty percent of the ballots for the senior class president said *Mr. Ford*."

"Artie had the best sense of humor," Mrs. Ford agrees. Her smile falls. "I don't understand why he would fall like that. Over a cat poster? I can just see him making fun of the whole situation, but . . . it doesn't make sense."

I nod, probably too enthusiastically for the subject matter. Taking a breath, I try to control my voice. "I don't know if this is okay to say, and I swear I don't mean any insult, but I really don't think Mr. Ford hung that poster. There's no way."

Mari and Sean share a look. Mari's voice is soft and considerate. "He really didn't like cats. Or puns."

Probably his most major flaw, but she really is right. And she would know, considering how both she and Sean tried to convince him to read their favorite cat-pun-filled cozy mystery series.

Mrs. Ford shakes her head. "I know. I *know*. But the police said it was a tragic accident, cut-and-dried. I know something isn't right. I really believe there is something . . . something they've missed. But what am I supposed to do? Get a private autopsy?"

"You could if you want to," Sean says. "Even if it was just an accident, it could give you peace of mind."

"But the wake is tomorrow, and family is already coming into town, so I'd hate to delay it."

"I think everyone would understand," I answer. "If anything, there can be a memorial tomorrow instead. Something to honor him."

Mrs. Ford looks thoughtful. "That's not a bad idea."

"And we can look into it, while you wait on the report," Mari says.

Mrs. Ford holds up a hand. "No, I don't want any of you getting involved in anything. I can handle it." She gives us a reassuring smile. "You're doing enough by being here. It is really nice to see you. He really loved having you all in class. I mean, Mari, he worked so hard on that college recommendation letter, you'd think it was for his own kid. And he would always talk about you being a genius, Sean, even if he was a little concerned about . . ." She shakes her head. "He was a little nosy, wasn't he? He just cared too much about you students." She turns toward me. "I swear, he was half convinced you should become a comedian, Gigi, but he had been talking about how much you're improving in class . . ."

I blink. My skin is itching and the air feels even harder to breathe.

"Can I please use your restroom?" I ask.

Mrs. Ford points me down the hallway, and I practically speed walk around the corner so I can splash cold water onto my face and get it together. I can save my tears and this budding panic attack or whatever it is for my bedroom.

My cheeks are blotchy with shades of pink and I look paler than normal, but otherwise good enough. I step out of the bathroom and start to head back when the door to the right catches my eye.

It's Mr. Ford's office. The number of math books stacked on the desk clearly reveals that, since I remember Mrs. Ford saying that she's a painting instructor and never really liked any classes in school besides art. I probably shouldn't go inside.

I do anyway.

It's not like Mr. Ford can say anything. Plus, I don't know, maybe there will be something in here that confirms our suspicions and could help the Mystery Club investigate. Sure, Mrs. Ford asked us to stay out of it, but that's because she's an adult and it would be irresponsible for her to say we should find out the truth. Doesn't mean we have to listen. She won't be mad if it turns out we're right that someone was involved in Mr. Ford's death and we get proof to back it up.

Plus, there's something about the way his desk is set up, a textbook still open, papers in the middle of being graded. It almost makes it seem like a pause rather than an ending. Like he just stepped away, and I'm waiting to ask him for help on solving for $x$.

Only he can't exactly help when $x$ is potentially the person who killed him.

"How do you even talk to a dead person?" I whisper to myself like he can hear it. "Ouija board? Seance? Prayer?" I look around. There aren't any haunted board games or candles, so prayer it is. I start with the sign of the cross. "In the name of the father, the son, and our lord and savior, Stipe Miocic." I pause, but the room is silent. I throw my hands down. "See, I know you aren't here because even your ghost would have laughed at that shit." I turn toward the surface of the desk. He was grading quizzes from last week. I flip the pages to find mine—eighty-two percent.

"Of course you have to leave the one quiz I actually do well on at home," I mumble. If there is some sort of afterlife, he's making fun of me from there.

To the left of the quizzes sits an open planner. It's all business, unlike the Pusheen-themed one I bought to write my homework in, as if I'll open it up again at home. It's still on this week, and I check what he had planned for yesterday.

There're two things written.

*3 p.m. - office hour :(*

Despite that being his actual time of death, I'm more concerned with the earlier note. It's enough to make me pull out my phone and snap a picture because it's not something you would normally expect to see written in the daily planner of a teacher.

*Get evidence flash drive from BW*

# FIVE

## The Wrong Week to Quit Drinking (Coffee)

**DESPITE ME GETTING** the photo from Mr. Ford's office, there wasn't time to actually get into any investigation for a while. The Mystery Club helped Mrs. Ford with the memorial, and between that and Mom and Dad allowing me to take time off school but refusing to leave me alone during my break, the investigation fell to the back burner. Mari also had to drive down to Columbus for a campus visitation day, so by the time we were all able to get together and get back on track, a week had already passed.

While delaying the investigation made me nervous, it did give us all a little more time to process what had happened and feel like shit about it, plus confirmation that authorities wouldn't do any investigation at all. Nearly every Cleveland news outlet that reported on it called it a tragic accident.

On the bright side, maybe that caused anyone who was involved to let their guard down.

Now in our first (not so) official Mystery Club meeting, we decide to meet at my house. Only Sean and Mari want to get coffee first. Considering Mari just drove back this morning, I couldn't say no.

At the drive-through, I lie and say I don't want anything, and after they get their drinks, we head back home. I really don't have spending money at the moment anyway, and while I know Mari would probably offer to just buy my drink, I don't want her to waste like five dollars on an *okay at best* herbal tea. We get back to the house and crowd around my kitchen table, while I try not to cast too many longing looks at their drinks.

"Do you want a sip?" Mari asks.

My face heats. Tried and failed.

"Nah, I had to quit," I say, like I'm a seasoned forty-year-old who has to meet at a bar while still in my first year sober.

I love coffee. The smell, the taste. I liked it even when I was a kid and my nonno let me try espresso before my parents could stop him. But caffeine is a major IBS trigger for me, coffee especially. I'm already more stressed than usual. I don't need yet another reason to risk shitting my pants in front of my crush, even if I am at home.

Mari pulls out a notebook as I try to find any snacks to make me feel better about the lack of caffeine. I'm already getting a little hungry. I manage to find some sciadone my aunt made and a pack of spring Oreos because I'm a slut for seasonal treats.

I take my first bite and feel a lot better. Sciadone is definitely my favorite part of spring.

"All right," I say after swallowing. "So what do we know

so far? Mr. Ford had the meeting that day and also collected evidence from someone."

I pull up the photo of his planner on my phone.

"We have to figure out who BW is," Sean says.

"But who the hell still uses a flash drive?" Mari asks.

"People doing shady shit," I answer. "Criminals. Murderers, probably. Which means this BW is a definite person of interest."

"You should have joined the Mystery and Thriller Literary Scholars earlier," Sean comments. "You're a natural."

I still refuse to call it that, but maybe Sean has a point. With my nosiness and tendency to act before really thinking about the potential consequences and their understanding of mysteries, maybe we can figure out what really happened to Mr. Ford. It almost makes me feel better about the situation. Instead of just sitting back and crying like I've been on the brink of doing the past week, I can direct my anger toward finding out who did this and making them pay. It's a way healthier emotional response, I think.

I take an Oreo. "Maybe we should write this all down?"

Mari nods. "We know that Mr. Ford died sometime between three p.m., the end of the day, and five p.m., when detention ended and we received the email." She makes note of the window on the blank page. "As of now, we have three persons of interest, although it's possible that they might all be the same person . . ." She notes them down next to the time of death.

Miss Mystery — sent email to MTLS at 5:00 p.m.
Unnamed Student — whoever Mr. Ford planned on meeting during office hours
BW — has evidence Mr. Ford was looking for?

It's hard to believe that an accident would have so many strange details surrounding it. I can't believe the police really aren't looking into it any further.

"So we just have to figure out who these three people are . . ." I start.

"And one of them is the murderer," Sean finishes.

That word seems to fill the room, like the sound of it alone formed something big enough to take up space and breathe the air. My mind has been skirting around it, but that's what we're all saying. This wasn't an accident. There was a murder in the math room.

And we're the only ones who will do anything about it.

"If Mr. Ford had met with this BW earlier in the day, which would make sense since he wrote it above the three o'clock office hour, that means BW is likely another teacher or a student . . ."

"We also know the killer is a Westbridge person too," I interrupt, "since there were no guests signed into the school at the time of death."

Someone released that detail, which, along with the fact that no one was seen leaving the classroom on hallway cameras, the police just used to yet again confirm that it was a simple accident and not worth the time an investigation would take.

Apparently, they weren't able to recover footage of the classroom, but they didn't care about that part.

Mari nods. "Right. But it also means that before he was killed, Mr. Ford might have had the flash drive."

"That's a potential motive for the killer," Sean says quickly. "Whatever is on the flash drive might have looked really bad for someone."

"Which means we need to find it." If the killer didn't already, which is definitely likely, but I'd rather focus on the possibility of something working out. "Where do we look?"

"The classroom," Mari answers. "Where else would he put it without the time to take it home?"

She has a point. He didn't leave at lunch, only went to get his food from the teacher's lounge. I doubt he would leave anything with evidence in there, so his desk makes the most sense. The time he was gone wouldn't even be enough to get to the math office on the other side of the building. It was barely enough time for Mari to get away with hiding her phone.

"Oh shit, the *phone*." I twist toward Mari with my hands pressed to the table and my torso leaning over like I'm trying to emulate Luca when he did a creepy-ass production of *Cats* at theater camp. "It could've recorded what happened."

Mr. Ford didn't know it was there, which means whoever had been with him might not have even bothered looking.

Sean winced. "It's been a week. I know the police may have skipped stuff since it was deemed an accident, but do you really think it could still be there?"

I shrug. "I mean, there's a chance, right? Who would want to go into a room where someone had just died?"

While I know it's a long shot, and I'm mentally hitting myself for not remembering it earlier, it's not something we can just ignore either.

"You're right. Can we try to sneak in tomorrow?" Mari asks. "We can ask Luca if they're having a *Joseph* rehearsal over the weekend to get in. I think he mentioned that set builds were happening."

Tomorrow's Sunday. Right. Since I've been doing school-work from home all week, it's been hard to keep track of the days. I shake my head and slump against the seat. "I have to help Mom tomorrow. There's a jiu-jitsu competition for the kids, and there's like twenty of them signed up."

While I haven't competed since eighth grade, I have the experience to help coach the kids, and it's fun to be around. I can't exactly let them down by skipping, especially not when Mom has been understanding of me all week and not pressing me to go back to school right away. But with the competition in Sandusky, we'll be gone the entire day.

"I have a shift at the shelter tomorrow," Sean adds. "I really can't miss it either, as we have two people coming in for kitten adoptions."

Mari shrugs it off. "We can go Monday. If it's still there

now, it will still be there then. Besides, it would probably look way weirder if we walked into the room where he died on a weekend when no one has business being there. It makes more sense to go during the school day."

Before we can agree, the doorbell rings. I stand up from the table.

"Are you expecting someone else?" Sean asks.

"No."

"Then why the hell would you answer the door?"

Fair, coming from a member of the Mystery Club, and not a bad point.

"I'm gonna check the window first. I'm not a babysitter in a horror movie."

I attempt to discreetly check the window to see who is at the front door. I'm just able to put the large box of chocolates and the handsome blond together when Kyle Sinclair is suddenly waving back through the window.

Well, shit, I have to answer the door now.

I open it and try a small smile, but I'm not sure it looks right. "Y'all are really pushing the hell out of this chocolate fundraiser, huh?"

He opens his mouth to answer, but a redheaded girl next to him responds first. "Wait, aren't you the one who found that dead teacher's body?"

I blink. "What?"

"I'm sorry. But is that the Mystery Club?"

Did I hear her right? Turning behind me, I realize Sean and Mari are clearly in view with the front door open.

I'm assuming she's a Westbridge student, as she's wearing the Peace Studies Club shirt, but I have no idea who she is. Maybe a freshman or a sophomore?

"Yeah?" I don't know why my answer comes out as a question. The Peace Studies Club has requested Sean and Mari before, so it makes sense they would know them.

The girl's face lights up. "Aren't you looking for new members? I'll join. I'm, like, so into true crime."

"We're actually called the Mystery and Thriller Literary Scholars, and we only really study *fictional* murders," Sean starts, but Mari gives him a shove as she moves toward the door.

"Of course we would love to have you join. What's your name?"

"Aimee Rhodes." The girl perks up, giving a wave.

"You can't be serious . . ." I direct my snide comment at Mari along with a death glare, but she's all rainbows and cupcakes as she gives Aimee her number with the promise of getting her to sign up on Monday morning.

"We'll talk more then," Mari finishes, "but we already bought chocolates, thanks." Kyle starts to say something, but she's closing the door. "Thanks!" It shuts on the two of them.

"What was that?" I whisper-yell. "We can't have new members coming in while we are *secretly investigating a murder.*"

"We don't have to keep her involved at all. We just need more members."

I throw up my hands. "What does that matter when the teacher who signed on to be your advisor is dead? It's not even a real club and we need to focus on the crime that happened!" Immediately as the words leave my mouth, I regret them. I know how much the club means to Sean and Mari. Besides, that's just all the more reason why they want to find out who would go so far as to kill Mr. Ford. "I'm sorry," I add. "I'm just not handling the whole murder-mystery thing well. It's a lot more fucked up than books make it seem, isn't it?"

Sean nods. "You can only put so much trauma in three hundred pages before it would become just too depressing to read." He frowns. "Turns out there is nothing cozy about finding a body. I can't imagine it'd be different even if we owned a bakery or lived somewhere with small-town charm."

Mari gives a small smile under her glassy brown eyes. "Honestly, our favorite cozy series, *The Purrfect Meowder*, is on its tenth book. Feline vet assistant Miranda Morgan should be way more messed up. I've only seen one body and I'm already falling apart."

A long sigh escapes Sean's lips. "We'll never be feline vet assistant Miranda Morgan."

"No one will," Mari agrees. "But that does remind me . . ."

Mari steps over to her bag and pulls out a book. It's worn and clearly loved, and I recognize it as book one of the series. Mari's cheeks redden slightly as she continues. "I know it seems a little silly, but maybe this could help. I found these books when I really wasn't doing well mentally and they kind of saved me? It's a great escape and there're some cool themes about believing in yourself. Since you're now officially part of the club and we're actually solving a murder, I thought it might help."

Despite the fact that a bad cat pun was found with Mr. Ford's body and I should be averse to them now or something, the gesture really means a lot. I knew Mari and Sean were both obsessed with the books, but I didn't really ask why. My heart skips a little at how open and vulnerable Mari looks. Can I really do something like that by admitting my own feelings?

"Thank you," I say, taking the book. "We're going to get justice for Mr. Ford. And we're going to save Mystery Club in the process."

"Mystery and Thriller Literary Scholars," Sean amends.

I roll my eyes. "Yeah, whatever."

Mari reaches out to squeeze my hand. Her soft and warm touch has my heart pounding in my chest. "Even if it means being nice to very energetic freshmen?"

"What are you talking about? I'm always nice."

Sean and Mari both nearly pee themselves laughing.

But, whatever. We've got a meowder to solve.

# SIX

## Guidance Counselors Are Like Fiber Powder: They Give All the Shits

**WALKING INTO WESTBRIDGE** on Monday morning feels like I've accidentally stumbled into a parallel dimension. It's still the same building, still the same general faces, still the same *Go Wildcats!* posters because Westbridge is oh so original. But there're those few things that are off. Students still murmuring about what happened, some even slipping out a few tears despite none of them being at the memorial last weekend. I'm getting some strange looks from having been home all week after finding Mr. Ford's body.

Not to mention the morning announcements, which discuss the extra counseling sessions students clearly haven't been taking before Emma comes on.

"Hello, Westbridge. It's Peace Studies Club president and Peaceful Leaders of Tomorrow Scholarship Honoree Emma Galligan."

Ugh. She's the worst.

Her chipper voice continues despite my prayers. "While we are all grieving the passing of Mr. Ford deeply, I wanted to announce that the school board decided Spring Festival will still happen as planned next Friday. It's what Mr. Ford would have wanted. We're holding a raffle at the festival to raise money for his family in these difficult times. Show your Wildcat spirit by giving what you can. Thank you."

Well. While I'm not necessarily upset that Spring Fest isn't canceled, since my confession plan hinges on it and it is cool that they are fundraising for Mrs. Ford, there's something about the whole thing that seems . . . off, to say the least.

I can't think about it too much, because once the first bell rings, I am summoned to the guidance counselors' offices. My homeroom teacher had the slip waiting for me and everything. I don't really want to drop by, but it's an excuse to miss class, which I will take. I arrive in the empty waiting area.

A thin older woman with a friendly expression immediately walks out from the nearest office. She has large earrings in the shape of donuts and a sweater and pants in two different shades of pink.

"You must be Gianna," she greets. "I'm Mrs. Goode, the grief counselor employed by the school. Would you mind talking for a minute?"

"It's Gigi," I say.

"Gigi, wonderful." She seems to take that as consent, as she walks back into the office.

I awkwardly follow. It's clear that Mrs. Goode started last week because the office has absolutely no personality. The desk is all but empty aside from the computer, which is probably pulled up to my (likely extensive) file. There is one succulent on the other side. The walls only have generic posters about mental health and goal setting.

"I just wanted to check in," Mrs. Goode says. "See how you are doing. We've been a little in touch with your mom as you had the week to process at home, and I'm here to make sure your adjustment back to your regular schedule goes as smoothly as possible. I know it's difficult, and I wanted to say that this office is open to you at any time. I'll write any passes you need. What's most important is you. You can say as much or as little as you are comfortable with."

"In that case, I'll say little, and we can end this." I don't even bother sitting in the plush chair in front of her. "I appreciate the intro."

She leans back. "That's completely fine. You went through a traumatic experience, Gigi, and you are allowed to deal with it in a way that makes you feel better."

"Don't say that unless you mean it because breaking another asshole's nose would make me feel better."

She gives a knowing look. "And would you like to talk about why you feel such anger? I am happy to listen."

Trying to trick me into opening up. Cute. I'm sure she was already warned about anger issues or aversion to authority issues or chaotic bisexual issues or whatever the hell problems they decided I have without actually talking to me.

My phone buzzes in my pocket. That has to be Mari.

She has first period study hall, so I bet we're on for the investigation.

"As much as I'd love to hear you use fancy words to describe everything wrong with me, I've got major diarrhea right now and I'd hate to stain your nice furniture here." I pat the back of the chair, looking down at the fabric. "Or stain it more at least. Regardless, thank you for the offer to cry about feelings together, but no, thank you. I'm fine."

To Mrs. Goode's credit, she takes it all in stride. "My door is open for whenever you need it."

"Oh, wonderful," I say. "But don't hold your breath. Now, if you'll excuse me, I have to repent for my sins in the bathroom."

"The all-gender restrooms on the second floor seem to be the most private."

That almost makes me crack a smile, but I don't want to give her the satisfaction. Instead, I give a thoughtless wave and walk out of the office. I almost have a full-on jump scare when I run into Mari in the hallway.

"How'd you know I was here?" I ask. "Weren't we supposed to meet by room 212?"

She holds up her own pass. "I have mine toward the end of this period but got away with leaving early. I saw you weren't in class, so I told Sean to meet us here. How's the grief counselor?"

"She's fine. You'll like her."

Since Mari's not an asshole like I am, therapy will probably be great for her.

Before she can respond, I glance up past her shoulder to see Sean speed walking down the hallway, glasses nearly falling off his face. We both turn toward him.

"I thought Gigi was the only rule-breaker," Mari teases.

I grin. "I know, such a bad influence. Look at Sean skipping class."

He immediately holds up a blue hall pass. His isn't even for a counseling session; it's just because he asked for it, I guess.

"Wow," I say. "How does it feel to be God's favorite?"

"More like Mrs. Choi's favorite," Sean says. "Are we ready?"

It's not like I'm *eager* to go back to the room where Mr. Ford died, but if we can find the evidence he mentioned in his planner on Mari's phone, it's definitely worth it. Worst case, I got Mrs. Goode practically foaming at the mouth to unpack my trauma, so hey.

"Let's go," I say. "I have a pretty good feeling the phone might still be there."

The phone isn't there.

"Are you sure that's where you put it?" I ask Mari, who's lying on the floor under Mr. Ford's desk like a mechanic. I try to keep my vision directly on her, and not the corner where his body was slumped. They did a good job of cleaning everything up though. If I hadn't been there to see the body, I wouldn't have guessed anyone died here at all. Even the stepladder and cat pun poster are gone, which is nice.

The room wasn't even locked or anything. They just moved all math classes to one of the portable classrooms. It's weird but works out for us, so we can't really complain.

"Do you really think I'd forget where I put it?" Mari slides back out from the desk, sitting up. "The killer probably found it. I only taped it to the bottom of the desk; it wasn't that inconspicuous because I didn't have a lot of time." Mari gets back up to her feet. "We still have the flash drive to look for."

"It's not in his desk," Sean says, closing the last drawer. "Nothing of interest here really."

Mari taps her chin. "Maybe he hid it?"

"How are we supposed to tear through the entire room?" I ask. "We don't have that much time before you have the meet-and-grieve with the counselor and Sean and I get in trouble." I sigh. "I already have three more weeks of detention lined up, I don't need four."

"Don't be mad," Mari said, "but I called for backup in case."

"What?"

The door creaks open and my excuse for Mrs. Goode almost comes true as I nearly shit my pants.

But it's not Principal Daniels, a murderer, or even a ghost. It's so much worse: my brother and Cedar Martin.

They look comically opposite, with his pastel pink shirt and light gray overalls and her black hoodie, black jeans, and heeled Doc Martens.

"Are we late for the investigation?" he asks.

"You told them?" I snap at Mari.

"As of this week, we signed up as Mystery Club members," Luca counters. "So yes." I catch him noticing Sean in the back of the classroom and adjusting his hair. He probably asked Mari if he could come, knowing she'd agree.

Mari's already walking up to Cedar and pulling her inside. "Did you find the phone's location?"

Well, that explains why Mari got Cedar involved. Unlike my brother, she's at least useful.

"It must be dead. I can't track it," she answers. Her eyes flicker over to me. "You okay, Gigi? Scared of ghosts?"

I scoff. "Please, I'm not afraid of things that don't exist."

"Like what, your love life?" she teases.

I take a deep breath. She really can't go five seconds without being annoying. Do all of them think this is some kind of joke? I'm already feeling bad about being in this classroom. I don't want to deal with this.

"At least I've had some contact with other people," I snap.

"Fighting doesn't count," Cedar says.

"In Gigi's defense, jiu-jitsu is weirdly erotic."

I glare at my brother. "Luca, you're not helping."

He mouths *sorry* before stepping toward the back of the room to *investigate* close to Sean. Cedar slides out her laptop, apparently satisfied with getting the last word in our exchange. Mari leans in close to her to look at the screen.

"See? There's nothing. Whoever took it must have turned it off."

They are so close together, and they look *good* together. It sends a little pang through my chest. I'm embarrassed and left out and seeing them together makes me feel like nothing's changed from when I'd be the odd one out and better off hanging with Mr. and Mrs. de Anda.

Like I'm just a kid.

"Okay, whatever, fucking fine." I say. "At least help us look for the damn flash drive."

Cedar lets Mari take her laptop and steps toward me.

"Gigi, come on. You can't seriously be upset that we're trying to help."

She's calm, but that just pisses me off more. They don't understand. She and Luca are just using this as an excuse to get close to their crushes and that's messed up.

Plus, it's so much easier to shove aside my weakness and my pain and be angry instead. I know it's wrong, but I don't care.

I step toward her, so close that she immediately backs up toward the wall. She almost bumps into the trash can between us and the door. "One of the only people in this shithole to care about me was killed and *I* had to find his body. This isn't some excuse to skip class and make heart eyes. Fuck off."

Our faces are only inches apart, and her cheeks are entirely red. "You don't even know what you're saying. We're literally helping, stop being so angry."

I laugh. "Angry? This isn't me angry. This is annoyed. Disappointed. Pissed." I put my hands on either side of her, palms touching the wall. "You want me to be angry?"

Sean gently grabs me and backs me up. "Hey. You're being a lot."

He's right. Biting my lip, I look back at Cedar. "Sorry. Fine. But this isn't a game. It's cool you don't care about anything, but I care about this. So either actually help or stay out of it and focus on your own shit like spending Daddy's money and pretending to be someone you're not."

With this, Cedar's eyes start to water, and she rushes out of the classroom.

Mari sighs. "That was too far, Gigi." She runs after her.

Shit.

Luca gives an apologetic smile. "I'm not saying you aren't valid in your grief and being in your feelings, but I should probably go comfort her." He's halfway out the door when he turns back. "Try to go easy on Cedar though. She's going through shit and to hear that from *you* when she's been in l— Like, a bad place." His expression is awkward, like he almost said something he shouldn't. "I'll see you two later."

Sean turns to me. "You good?"

"Yeah," I say. "I overreacted. Just give me a second to cool down. I'll keep looking."

He knows me well enough to get how I am. When I'm this annoyed, it's better to be alone and breathe through it. "I'll keep watch outside," he says before exiting.

I sigh. I know I'm a bitch sometimes, I know I'm a little aggressive sometimes, but other people do the same shit and act out and lash out and it's *fine*. But I'm expected to be the bigger person and always apologize? I'm tired. I'm tired and I'm sad and I want to punch something and cry. But no, I'm supposed to go on like everyone else and pretend it's all good and I'm not now even more fucked up than I already was from seeing Mr. Ford.

I cross the room, not seeing anything out of place, and back against the windows to wipe my eyes before they can get red. I can't let anyone see me crying. I count my breaths, inhaling and exhaling on a count of eight. I'm strong. I'm strong and I'm not going to cry. Who cares if Cedar thinks I'm mean? She doesn't like me anyway.

More rumors will spread, probably saying I threatened or attacked her. Adding to my image of being unstable, wild, generally funny and cool—until I snap like the delinquent I am. Which is fine.

No one can hurt the strongest person in the room. Doesn't matter if I actually am as long as everyone thinks it's true.

Feeling a little better, my eyes drift over to the glass behind and next to me. If anyone has seen me at my worst, it's Sean, but it's too bad I can't just climb out the window to avoid everyone. It's not that far of a drop, so I probably wouldn't die.

Although Mom would be really mad if I broke a leg and couldn't help them with some classes when needed. Plus, training has been the one thing keeping me from having a complete breakdown.

Wait. There wasn't evidence of anyone entering or leaving the room when Mr. Ford was murdered, but is it possible that someone left out the window? It seems like a person could fit through.

I glance outside.

There isn't a lot to hold on to, but there is a tree nearby. Maybe the killer could have jumped there? I nearly press my forehead to the glass trying to see the building. There's a small ledge in the design. Could they have gotten there and jumped?

You'd have to be fearless. And very athletic.

But it isn't impossible, I don't think.

"What are you doing out here?" a voice asks from the hallway.

Sean's response is abnormally loud for him—he must be trying to give me a warning. "Principal Daniels, I was standing outside here to pay my respects to Mr. Ford."

There's no way I can make it out and not be seen. What do I do?

"In the middle of class?" Principal Daniels sounds annoyed and a little incredulous, and I can't really blame him.

"It's my study hall," Sean says quickly. "And it's part of my religion." A long pause. "To pray for the soul of our dearly departed in the place where their soul . . . departed. Dearly."

Can I hide under the desk? It seems a little too obvious because there's no way I'll fit with the chair. It's not like there are curtains or anything. Do I test out my window theory?

"Wait! Don't go in now. I have to finish my blessing," Sean says desperately.

"Mr. Ryan, I am not saying you can't practice your religion, whatever that may be, but we have to discuss what is being done with this room."

My heart jumps to my throat. I don't have time for the window. I keep backing up until I press into something solid.

I spin around to face the storage cabinet.

The doorknob starts to turn.

Well. I've had worse ideas.

# SEVEN

## Being Short Can Save Your Life

**FOR A WHILE** in jiu-jitsu, and still sometimes now, I would constantly wish I were bigger. I would generally be one of the smallest on the mats, and while size doesn't mean skill, when you are facing someone at a similar level, it makes one hell of a difference. I'd have rounds that were five to eight minutes of being stuck on bottom, my hip escapes and frames simply not enough to compensate. Cheeks still hot from frustration and stinging from the gi's friction, I'd spend the ride home fighting back disappointed tears until I could safely let them out in the shower.

It took a long time for my technique to really improve, and while I still have those days, I learned the advantages of my size and opportunities where being small became a strength.

This is one of those moments. The storage cabinet is split by a shelf, and with mostly just the top full, I am able to squeeze into the bottom among the textbooks. I'm practically kneeing myself in the face and my ass hurts, but the doors are shut, and that's what matters.

As long as I don't think about being in a dark cabinet of a possibly haunted classroom where Mr. Ford recently died.

"Get back to class, Mr. Ryan," Principal Daniels says as the door clicks open.

The space between the cabinet doors is a sliver enough to let light in but not actually big enough to see through. It feels like there's always enough space in the movies.

I lean forward to get my face right next to the crack, but pain shoots through my neck from the awkward angle, so I instantly sit back. I was only able to catch a glimpse of the speckled tile floor anyway.

Footsteps fall into the otherwise-silent room. I manage my breaths so they don't make any noise.

"It looks basically back to normal," a second voice says. "Can't we just have classes in here with the sub?"

I recognize the voice as Mr. Maplewood, the vice principal.

"I don't think students are comfortable having class in here," Principal Daniels says. "At least not for a little while. Maybe we can use it for desk storage?"

"Or hold detentions here and maybe kids won't act up because they don't want to hang out in a classroom haunted by a dead teacher."

Neither Principal Daniels nor I laugh at that joke. I never liked Mr. Maplewood. Now I know why. He's a sadist who hates teens and has no business being in a school.

"Did you hear the rumors though?" Mr. Maplewood continues. "Teachers are talking."

While I can't see the annoyance on Principal Daniels' face through the tiny crack of light, I feel like I can imagine it well.

"What rumors?"

"Apparently, Artie was looking into a bunch of students cheating. Interesting he was doing that right before he died." Mr. Maplewood makes some kind of sound effect that must be from a crime show.

I didn't know that Mr. Ford was looking into a whole cheating scandal, but that definitely sounds like him. What if he uncovered something that really pissed someone off?

Although . . . killing someone because they caught you cheating? That's like some elite private school, dark academia shit. Not Westbridge, where ninety percent of the student body ends up at Cleveland State, Miami University (the Ohio one), or Tri-C.

Although that would make sense in terms of the evidence he mentioned. Maybe BW is a snitch?

"Enough of that. You're watching too many true crime documentaries," Principal Daniels chastises. "It wasn't some scandal or murder. It was a tragic accident. Plain and simple."

There's a beat. It's still the middle of a class period, so everything is near silent. There's muted speaking from whatever class is next door, but if I make any sound, I'm screwed.

My muscles are close to cramping, but I force myself to keep still.

I guess I was too preoccupied with squeezing myself in here as quickly as possible to think about getting in a comfortable position. My shirt rode up and the corner of a textbook is pinching the skin right above my pants.

I bite the inside of my lip as I gently slide the book over. I hold the last breath I took in my chest, but the footsteps don't move in this direction. They stay where they are for now.

I exhale.

How long will they be here?

"I'm sure we can make the storage thing work," Mr. Maplewood says finally. "At least until the kids get over it."

My neck is sore from the position I've been stuck in; my foot is bent at a weird angle. I'm not sure how sustainable this is. I've been partially in the closet for years as a kid, so you'd think I'd be used to it by now, but no. This will be my most relieving coming out yet.

Suddenly my toes cramp up, and without thinking, I reach down to grab them and start rubbing over my boot. In doing so, I lose my balance. I try to catch myself on the side of the cabinet and hit something sticking out of the metal side. It smacks against the cabinet door and while I manage to not fall out of the cabinet, I also knock into the books and both sounds echo throughout the classroom.

Despite the pain, I bite my lips harder and stay quiet.

"Did you hear that?" Mr. Maplewood asks.

Footsteps. Coming toward the back.

No no no. If they find me here, I'm screwed. Thinking about it now, hiding was a way shittier idea. Hiding makes me look guilty. I should have made up a prayer and pretended I'm part of Sean's improvised religion. And now I listened in on their entire conversation, which adds to the Gigi-getting-expelled outcome of this plan.

The footsteps are close. I can hear them right on the other side of the door.

Still holding on to my foot like that can pause the pain, I press down on my throat. Maybe I can shove my heart back down. It's beating so loud in my ears that, unreasonably, it makes me think he can hear it too.

A shadow passes over the crack. He's right outside.

I hold my breath. This isn't good. Once the doors are opened, I'll be in plain sight.

It's completely dark. All I can hear is my heart pounding. My hand, tight against my boot, shakes.

"I wouldn't worry about it," Principal Daniels says. "This room is always making noises and shifting. That's why students think it's haunted."

Mr. Maplewood chuckles, footsteps growing lighter. "After that *accident*, maybe it is."

I let out a breath the same time the door opens and shuts behind them.

It stays silent for a moment, and I don't move, almost too afraid that they stayed behind. But muffled voices drift in from the hallway, and the room seems lighter without the presence of others.

My foot hurts so bad, I'm ready to risk it all, so I tumble out of the cabinet. The object against the door falls out, sliding across the floor, but I can't pay it any attention yet. Quickly undoing my boot, I rub the toes that seem stuck together. I practically rock back and forth on the classroom floor until the pain calms a little and the cramp isn't so bad.

What the hell did I just do?

And what fell out of the cabinet with me? After tying my shoe, I step over to it. It's a small lockbox, like the kind people keep outside to hold a house key. I can't pull it open but it has a dial for a four-digit code. Shit. What would Mr. Ford use? All I know about him is that he loved his wife, math, and the UFC, probably in that order. That makes me think of Mrs. Ford and the big wedding photo in their dining room.

Wait. Wedding. Anniversary. That's a start.

Pulling out my phone, I search for *Priya Ford* on Instagram. Thankfully, I find her, and I'm able to scroll back to their last anniversary photo. October twenty-ninth.

I try it on the lock. 1–0–2–9.

It pops open.

I want to burst out laughing in relief. Or maybe cry. Potentially both. Thank bisexual Jesus he was such a wife guy.

"Arthur Ford, you whipped son of a bitch," I say with a smile. "I'm gonna solve this thing."

And when I pull the flash drive from inside the small container, I really believe it.

It's hard enough to have to wait until lunch to be able to look at the flash drive, but it's even harder when I have to deal with Math 3 in the depressing portable classrooms trailer at the back of the school with Ms. Wilcox, an ancient skeletal substitute who refused to call me Gigi even though "Gianna" is only used when I am in some deep shit with my mom. "Gianna Rosa Ricci" means it's probably my last day on the earth because I'm in so much trouble they want to take me out of it, which really only happened the two times I got caught fighting.

Three, technically. But one wasn't at Westbridge, so does it really count?

Point is, by the time I meet up with the rest of Mystery Club in the library, I feel like I've aged five years. Mari is already at a table with Cedar, who's on her laptop. Shit. I wasn't really expecting to have to deal with Cedar already.

Mari leans over her to look at the screen, resting her head and palm on Cedar's shoulder. I know that the two of them and Luca are touchy people, but there's still something about it that sends an annoying pang through my chest. Of course I'm jealous.

But am I wrong for still wanting to tell Mari how I feel?

I'd say that Mari spots me first, but even after she waves and calls my name, Cedar doesn't look away from her screen, so it's safe to say she's avoiding me as best as she can while still being available to help the girl she actually likes.

Great. I'm feeling great and not at all bothered by any of this.

"Did you bring the flash drive?" Mari asks as I arrive.

I fish it out of my pocket and toss it to her. She passes it to Cedar to put into her laptop right as Sean arrives.

"Did I miss anything?" he asks.

"No," I say as I notice that *both* Mari and Cedar greet him.

"Damn," Cedar says. "It's password protected."

"Does that mean you can't get into it?" I ask.

She doesn't look up at me. "I *can*, but decrypting it will take a while. So it's not something we can look at right now."

"At least we have it," Sean says. "Even if it takes some time, it's better than nothing."

I'm tempted to ask Cedar how long a *while* is, but something tells me she wouldn't give a helpful answer anyway. I glance around the library. There aren't really a lot of students in here and the ones that are probably won't be able to overhear. Still, I feel a little exposed.

If the killer really is a Westbridge student or teacher, they could be anywhere. And if it's possible someone murdered Mr. Ford because of this flash drive, we really don't need anyone else knowing that we have it. I already got in one fight last week. I'm not sure Principal Daniels will let anything else slide, even if it is an actual threat.

"Didn't you mention you overheard something else?" Mari asks.

I lean forward on the chair, keeping my voice low. "I'm not sure if it's just rumors, but apparently Mr. Ford had been looking into some big cheating scandal. With a lot of students involved."

Both Mari and Sean have matching shocked expressions.

"Like some kind of cheating cult?" Sean asks.

Mari nods excitedly. "That's just like book three of *The Purrfect Meowder: The Catnapper Craze*. It was a whole Satanic Panic thing but with a cat demon. Not a real demon. The point is, it's a total guidebook on dealing with murderous cults."

I look between them. "No. I don't think it's a cult. I think it's people cheating and not wanting to get caught."

Sean leans in toward Mari. "I think we're dealing with a book six kind of scenario."

"Oh . . ." Mari nods. "*Curiosity Killed the Cat Doctor.* Miranda's boss was blackmailing this client because he was cheating on his wife and got killed because of it. The motive is there."

"Blackmeowling," I say, but then shake my head. "Whatever. The point is Mr. Ford might have actually had something on students cheating."

"Well, it's probably Big Willy," Cedar says.

The three of us turn to her.

"What?" I ask.

"Big Willy," Cedar repeats. So I did hear her correctly. She brushes hair out of her face. "It's a Westbridge student who you can pay to write essays. I'm assuming they're a senior, because apparently they'll sell old test and quiz answers and targeted study sheets, but I've only used them for an essay once."

I can understand why Sean and Mari wouldn't have heard of them. They are nerds and don't need any help. But I'm kind of offended that no one told *me* about this service since I definitely do.

Then again, I don't think I'd be able to afford it. All the money to my name is stored in a tampon box under my bed that I'm trying to save for after graduation. And even that is a truly laughable amount.

Cedar pulls up an email, which is an essay being sent from bigwillywestbridge. The bottom has a logo that looks like Shakespeare in sunglasses.

It was bad enough that everyone thinks Mr. Ford died trying to hang a bad cat pun poster. Knowing that he might have been killed by someone who combined Shakespeare and a dick joke is not better.

Although, honestly, he'd probably find it kind of funny.

"Big Willy," Sean mutters. "BW. That's who Mr. Ford was getting evidence from."

"But why would Big Willy give Mr. Ford evidence against themself?" Cedar asks.

I shrug. "It probably was just to gain a sense of trust so they could meet with Mr. Ford alone later in the day and kill him." I cross my arms. "BW, the office hours person, Miss Mystery. They're clearly all just Big Willy."

"We should message him," Mari says. "We can use the Mystery and Thriller Literary Scholars email."

"It's not like that makes it anonymous," I mutter. "Everyone will know it is you two at least. And I don't think Big Willy will believe that the valedictorian is *actually* trying to request an essay. They'll know you're trying to figure out who they are."

Mari bites her lip, which I have to admit is adorable. But she knows I'm right. Even if Cedar tries to send a message, they might figure she's trying to help out the Mystery Club now.

"What if they don't think we know about their connection to Mr. Ford?" Sean says. "Technically his death was an accident, right? We can pretend that Miss Mystery is a different person and try to get on their good side. They'll probably agree to help with the investigation of finding Miss Mystery to make it look like it isn't them." He shrugs. "It's a long shot, but if we get close to them in any way, we might be able to figure out who they are."

It's not a bad idea. "Worth a try," I comment. "Nice thinking, Sean."

"Thank you, although I have to admit, it is inspired by what Miranda Morgan did in book four: *Killer Claw Enforcement*."

Mari crosses her arms, looking very proud of herself. "See? We may be more of a book club, but I told you it helps us with actual mysteries."

"Well, fine." I say. "Let's get this Big Willy." I immediately frown. "Pretend I didn't word it like that."

From: mysterythrillerlitscholars@gmail.com
To: bigwillywestbridge@gmail.com
Subject: To Be or Not to Be . . . the Hero That West-
bridge Deserves

Hi Big Willy,

Hope you are doing well. We at the Mystery and Thriller Literary Scholars (aka Mystery Club) were hoping to get your help with an investigation, as you are a trusted pillar of wisdom and puns at Westbridge High.

We were sent an email from a Miss Mystery (a fellow alias) and have reason to believe this person is actively trying to hurt you and other Westbridge students. We clearly, as other Westbridge students, do not want this to happen!

Since you are so intelligent and brilliant at a variety of subjects, plus you clearly are a giving person of the people, would you be able to help us in this investigation? Do you already happen to have any idea of who this person might be? We would appreciate any and all help you can give.

What we are trying to say is . . . we could really use some Big Willy.

Sorry not sorry,

The Mystery and Thriller Literary Scholars

(Mystery Club)

# EIGHT

## Family Dinners and Responses from Killers

**FAMILY DINNERS ARE** kind of an event at the Ricci household. We're a seventy-five-percent-queer Italian family but it's only once in a blue moon that everyone's schedules line up. Since Luca gets a day off from rehearsal, Dad isn't working the night shift today, and Mom had morning classes, it is essentially the word of God that we can't have other plans this evening. Well, the word of Mom, but that's scarier than God, because Mom for sure exists and can heel hook me.

The actual dinner isn't anything special, just pasta e fagioli, but Mom and Dad let me have a small glass of red wine (probably because they don't know what to do about the whole favorite teacher dying thing).

I sip the tomato broth and feel the heat travel down into my chest. Normally, I try to get the pasta and bean mixture without a lot of broth but made an exception for today because it's cold out and this is cozy. I swear, Cleveland weather makes me seem stable.

"This show you're in . . ." Mom turns to Luca. "What's it again?"

"*Joseph and the Amazing Technicolor Dreamcoat.*"

Mom makes a face. "It's about religion? I had to go to a Catholic church for eighteen years growing up. I did my time."

"It's a musical," Luca says. "Not a sermon."

"How much singing?" Dad asks.

"It's *all* singing," I say before Luca can respond.

Both Mom and Dad cringe.

"We can slip out during intermission," I add.

Luca shoves me over that one.

It's not like we don't support Luca and his acting, and the boy does have a ridiculously great voice, but none of the rest of us particularly like musicals. If he'd join a band or something, I'd be happy to watch the performances, but there's something about theater that directly opposes my already limited attention span.

Dad lifts his glass of wine to toast to my point. "There's always intermission," he says.

Luca takes a big spoonful of his pasta. "This is homophobic."

"Come on, Luca. We love you. We would just love you more in movies or even a concert than musicals," Mom says. "Not everything is for everyone and that's okay. I still have nightmares from that production of *Cats*, hon, I can only take so much more."

He twirls his spoon around the broth. "It wasn't that bad."

"It was a cat-astrophe." Dad jokes. When he gets groans, he oh so gracefully changes the subject. "We should talk about your teacher dying. It's been over a week, it's almost weird that we haven't been talking about it at this point."

Mom not so subtly kicks him under the table.

"It's really okay if we don't," I mutter.

"Gigi, you're *grieving*," he says, rubbing his shin. "I get it. People grieve in different ways, and we don't have to talk about that if we don't want to. But we can talk about safety. Sharing your location, not going out alone, being very careful on stepladders." He makes a pointed look at me, the shortest one in the family.

I have to bite back a retort that Mr. Ford didn't die from slipping.

"Sure," I say. "Better yet, I'll have Sean reach everything for us. Then I'm not alone and no extra height needed. Problem solved. Now we don't have to talk about this again."

There's a small lull in conversation as we go back to eating, but after another swallow of wine, Mom's eyes get almost glassy. "Pretty soon we won't be able to do dinner like this at all," they say.

"Because we'll all fall off stepladders and die?" I ask.

They glare at me. "No." Mom turns to Luca. "You're going off to Chicago, and then what, I have to talk with only Gigi and your dad?"

"Ouch," I say, and take another bite.

Mom smiles. "Don't take it badly, love. It would be even worse if you left because then who the hell would I train with?"

"I'm shocked Luca wouldn't jump at the chance to roll

87

around with sweaty guys." Dad adjusts his glasses. "Seems right up your alley."

"Ha-ha." Luca rolls his eyes. "You're so funny, Dad. They should give you a Netflix special."

"At least then I'd have money for your college," Dad says. "How are you supposed to afford the Chicago cost of living?"

Dad's not quite the serious type. I mean, he mostly dresses in bright V-necks and patterned socks, has a color tattoo sleeve, and his beard is grown out like a mountain man. But he is a very honest kind of guy, sometimes to the point of coming across like an asshole. Most people don't want to bring up money around their kids, especially when they don't have a lot of it, but Dad isn't one for beating around the bush.

Not that he and Mom can lecture about saving money or career choices. He can make pretty good money bartending, but it's hit or miss. Like making the mortgage payment in one Saturday night or having a dry week and needing to max out the credit cards again.

Luca shifts in his seat and the area around his nose grows red. "I'm fine."

"What does that even mean?" Dad asks. "You can't pay rent with *fine*."

Usually, Dad and Luca are the ones to get along better. Despite looking like a literal lumberjack and having height the rest of us don't, Dad isn't very into sports or fighting. Luca's so extra, I feel like he naturally gravitates toward the most seemingly chill member of the family to restore the balance of the universe.

But Luca looks weirdly uncomfortable. "Just don't worry about it, okay? The school has programs for work-study, and that gives you a paycheck."

"I don't think it's so unreasonable to make sure you're okay," Dad continues off Luca's attitude. He sighs. "I know I'm not always the best at expressing it. I'm just worried about you."

"Oh my gosh, just let it go," Luca snaps. "I'm fine. You may have forgotten, but I am an adult now, and I have it all together."

He slides his empty bowl across the table, stands up, and struts out of the room.

"You forgot your phone," Mom calls after him.

There's a short pause.

"I don't want it right now," he snaps before his bedroom door shuts.

Mom rolls their eyes, picking up his phone. "I'll go talk to him." They give a look toward Dad. "Maybe cool it on the money thing? He's probably stressed about it."

Pretty sure we all are. At least I'm not planning on going out-of-state for school and making it worse. But I don't want to say anything and seem like I'm taking sides.

"Fine," Dad says in a way that implies this is a temporary promise.

Mom walks off after Luca, and I go back to my dinner.

I don't care about my brother's dramatics right now. He's worried about the college he *chose* to go to while I'm trying to keep it together while solving the potential murder of my teacher and planning to confess to my crush in like a week.

I turn to Dad, who also resumed eating as if we didn't lose half the table. "Dad, can I ask you something?"

"Sure," he says.

"How did you get girls to like you?"

"I didn't." He says it simply, not embarrassed in the slightest. "Not for lack of trying."

"Okay, well, how did you get Mom to like you?" I ask.

"Honestly, still not sure," Dad says. "Perhaps I saved a kitten from a burning building in a past life? My brother was the one training jiu-jitsu with them. I only showed up to give him a ride home, and your mom came right up to me and said, 'You're cute, you should get dinner with me sometime,' and I was sold." Dad smiles wistfully. "Not only were they hot as hell, but I also saw them get Pasquale in a nasty choke. Seeing someone beating the shit out of my older brother was incredible but they also could theoretically have kicked my ass if I said no to dinner."

I sigh. "I'm not as smooth as Mom."

Dad puts a hand on my shoulder. "You don't have to be. You just have to take a chance." He smiles. "Your mom was actually my first serious relationship," Dad says. "But it worked. I'm convinced we're soul mates. Before that, even my parents thought I was gay."

"So you did the gayest thing a straight guy could do," I say. "Marry a queer person."

Dad laughs. "Exactly." He finishes his bowl and gets up to start cleaning the table. "I may not be the suavest guy, or anything close to it, but I think you should tell Mari you like her."

My jaw drops. "Who said anything about Mari?"

"I was born in the morning but not *this* morning." He brings the three empty bowls over to the sink. "Luca's too self-absorbed to notice, and I think your mom just wants you to marry Sean so he can be their son." He thinks for a moment. "Even though I feel like Luca would be down to take your place on that one."

That tracks. My dad is more observant than I thought. I'm still embarrassed though.

"Long story short . . ." Dad flicks on the sink. "I'm rooting for you, and she'd be lucky to have you as a girlfriend."

Even though that's what a parent should say, it feels really nice.

"Aw, thanks, Dad."

He gives a big smile. "Now, do the dishes. It's all you, Casanova."

I glance at the pots still sitting dirty on the stovetop.

"*This* is homophobic," I mutter, taking my own bowl to the sink to add to the mound I'll have to tackle.

My fingers are all wrinkly by the time I get through all the dishes, and the area between my shoulder blades aches.

I'm like sixteen going on sixty, and I one hundred percent blame the fact that I competed in jiu-jitsu until I started high school. Or maybe I'm allergic to doing dishes. It's not like Mom and Dad can afford a dishwasher right now, but at the very least, the prima donna can handle half before he goes off to college.

Lying down on my bed is the best feeling ever tonight. I stretch out before resting my head on Gerard, the gray pillow cat, and hold Amber in the crook of my arm. Scrolling through Instagram, I pass random pictures like Kyle and the Peace Studies Club fundraising for the Spring Festival and popular girls like Jane Neal posting thirst traps, and spend more time on the random cat videos.

Okay, I might spend a little time on the thirst traps, but girl makes them look like an art form.

Creepiness aside, I want a cat so bad.

Especially with Sean sharing pictures of the cats up for adoption, I'm smitten with nearly every one I see. I like cats because they are adorable assholes and I really relate to that. Plus, it could give Mari a reason to come over, since she and Sean are obsessed with those cat lady cozy mysteries.

I sigh. Spring Fest is next Friday. Hopefully being in the Mystery Club and trying to figure out this investigation together will make her at least not uncomfortable with my feelings. I'm not expecting her to date me or anything, not when she's about to go off to college in the fall. I just want to get it off my chest.

That's all.

My phone buzzes with a group FaceTime request from Mari. I try to fix my hair as best as I can and push my plushies out of frame.

"Hey," I say casually as Mari's and Sean's faces appear on my screen. They must be hanging out at Mari's house because I recognize the artwork of her dining room behind them.

"We got a response from Big Willy," Mari says quickly.

My heart leaps into my throat, but for a different reason than seeing her in a thin tank top with her curly hair tied in a loose bun and showing off her shoulders. While it doesn't give me anywhere near the same feeling, even Sean looks handsome with his hair neatly parted and his glasses on. Why am I the only one who looks like garbage?

I swallow the desire to put Amber over my face.

"What did he say?"

Mari reads from the open laptop next to her. "'Boys' locker room. Number sixty-nine. One p.m.' Of course it's sixty-nine."

"The good news is this means Big Willy is someone who uses the boys' locker room," Sean says. "The bad news is I have a physics test at that time so I can't go."

"Luca and I both have presentations for AP Lit that period," Mari says. "But . . . isn't it when you have gym?"

Now I get what's going on. They need me to break in. I guess it makes the most sense. I just need to come up with a reason that doesn't make me look like a pervert or give me a suspension in case I get caught.

"No problem," I say. "I'll do it."

Mari and Sean are all smiles, which makes it seem worth it.

Just have to sneak into the boys' locker room for Big Willy.

Wait.

Fuck. Whatever.

# NINE

## Will the Real Big Willy Please Stand Up?

GYM CLASS, AS usual, doesn't have a great start. Sure, I wasn't really planning on participating anyway as I have a locker to break into, but I couldn't if I wanted to since someone stole my uniform. I don't know who the hell accidentally took a Westbridge cotton gym top with *Ricci* Sharpie'd on the front, but maybe I do have more enemies than I thought.

Or it was Coach Phil getting revenge for me skipping more than I should have.

Since I can't change, and I'm already getting some looks from the other girls in the locker room for being in there without getting into my uniform, I walk right back out into the gym. Coach Phil scrunches his eyebrows together as he holds his hands out.

"Where's your uniform?"

I shrug. "Seems it has been misplaced."

He gives an eye roll and points to the benches. "You're getting docked points, but you're here, Ricci. I'll give you that."

I follow the tip of his finger to the bleachers. I sit back

and wait for the locker rooms to clear out again and give my reluctant "here" when Coach Phil takes attendance. He actually makes everyone clap afterward, which is so extra considering I've missed *maybe* five classes. I'd have to miss nine to fail, so it's not a big deal.

"All right," he says. "Someone grab the ball cart. We'll head out and start with passing drills."

I almost forgot we're on the soccer unit. Finally, some fucking luck. If the whole class is outside, I can easily sneak into the locker room. I casually check the time on my phone. I have ten minutes.

Skipping over to Coach Phil, I make a show of clutching my stomach. "Coach, can I use the bathroom first and then meet you on the fields? It might take some time, if you catch my drift."

He narrows his eyes. "This isn't an excuse to get out of class?"

"Technically, but my IBS is a valid excuse, according to that doctor's note I gave you. Plus, what can I do without my uniform? Maybe I can check for a spare in the lost and found?"

He sighs. "Tell you what, you can stay in here and use the period as a study hall, but you have to make up the class by coming to a wrestling practice. And if you're not here tomorrow, in as close to the appropriate attire as you can get, I'm dropping you down to a D."

"Coach Phil, you are a hero," I say. "I'll work singles and doubles with the boys happily. When's practice?"

"Tomorrow, six fifteen. I'll meet you here."

"Six fifteen in the evening?"

He laughs. "Nope."

Ugh. Now I'm going to have to set my alarm before six, which doesn't even feel like a real time. I'll have to buy Luca coffee for a week to convince him to drop me off early.

Those problems are for Tomorrow Gigi to deal with. For now, I rush into the girls' locker room bathroom to keep my story at least somewhat believable. When all the voices and shoe scuffing fade and it's two minutes to go-time, I step back out into the gym. It's completely empty.

I sneak over to the boys' locker room, hiding outside the door as I peer in.

It doesn't look like anyone is left inside. I can't hear any noises either. The coast should be clear.

I step inside, keeping my steps light, just in case. I have my excuse at the ready. Sean had his gym period in the morning, so I'm going to say that he left medication behind in his locker he needed me to grab. The only pills I have are my birth control pills for my ridiculous periods, but I don't think anyone will really look too hard. Besides, how many high school dudes *actually* know what birth control looks like?

Sean also knows in case anyone asks him after, but I'm hoping that I'll get in and out without being seen and won't have to worry about it regardless.

I quickly scan through the lockers until I get to sixty-nine. There's a Post-it Note on it, which only says *Happy birthday to me*. And a combination lock.

"What is this escape room bullshit?" I mutter.

The birthday message has to be some kind of clue. But whose birthday would Big Willy mean?

Wait. Shakespeare.

I have to pull out my phone to quickly Google that one because who the hell knows his birthday off hand? Supposedly it's April 23, which happens to be the day of Spring Fest next Friday. Which reminds me to stress about my planned confession.

Ugh. I try 04-23-64 and pull. The lock doesn't budge.

Okay, well, a few websites said while it is celebrated on the twenty-third, the specific date isn't known. So technically, the main answer given is April 1564 without the specific date.

04-15-64.

It snaps open. Big Willy, you pretentious weirdo. That's not even how normal people put dates in combination locks.

Inside is a small packet of paper, clipped together. It doesn't make any sense either, because why would things go smoothly for me, I guess. It's lines of random numbers.

**1 3 15 19 20 1, 18 1 13 15 14**

**1 4 1 13 19, 3 12 1 21 4 9 1**

**1 20 11 9 14 19 15 14, 14 15 18 1**

And on and on for three pages. All the rows have a random comma, and the first number increases while the rest of them are all random.

Is this some kind of math thing? Is Mr. Ford's killer

98

seriously going to make me do *math* to try to solve this case? I sigh. It would honestly be easier to just beat the shit out of Big Willy until they confess, but Mari and Sean wouldn't like that.

Besides, I still have to figure out who they actually are.

There's a thump from somewhere else in the locker room.

My heart freezes in my chest. Is someone else in here? Is it Big Willy? I pat my pockets, but I don't exactly have anything to defend myself. Between three pages of printer paper, my phone, and a packet of birth control pills, I'm a sitting freaking duck.

A shower starts.

Shit, okay, it's someone weirdly just taking an after-lunch shower. Whatever. I got the ridiculous clue, so I can slip out without them seeing me.

I walk around the wall of lockers separating me from the open area by the entrance and immediately freeze in my tracks because in front of me is a completely naked Kyle Sinclair.

"Oh my god," I blurt.

This was not the Big Willy I was expecting to see today.

Face entirely flaming, Kyle puts his towel in front of his crotch. "Gigi? Um . . . what are you doing here?" His voice comes out like a full octave higher than usual.

With my cheeks equally hot, I look up at the ceiling, which probably makes it even more obvious that I'd been looking at his body before. Jesus Christ. It's not even that he's ridiculously hot, although I'm not gonna lie, he is. It's just hard not to look at a penis when it's like right there in front of you.

"I'm so sorry," I start. "I was grabbing medicine for Sean . . ."

"No, I'm sorry!" He wraps the towel around his waist. "I work out during lunch sometimes and I was a little late in using the showers today. I'm guessing you saw . . ."

"Um, yeah, I mean, I didn't mean to. I wasn't expecting . . ." It's like neither of us can speak anymore. "I'm really sorry for walking in on you like this."

This is certainly not how I expected my first time seeing a naked guy to go. Although it could've been worse. While the towel at least covers the more embarrassing areas, his toned upper body is still in complete view, and there's something about the sweat that works aesthetically for me. I take a deep breath and force my eyes back up. Clear thoughts, Gigi, clear thoughts.

Kyle throws on a little smile. "This is not normally how I get naked in front of girls. I promise."

"Really? This is exactly how I've seen all my naked guys."

His expression shifts to something authentically light. "Spend a lot of time in the men's locker room, huh?"

"This isn't a strip joint?"

He makes an exaggeration of a seductive face, biting his lip and running a hand through his hair. "It can be, for the right price."

"And what's that?"

"My dignity. I'm a terrible dancer."

I snort. I didn't realize that Kyle was funny. I guess I assumed he was like Emma and the other Peace Studies Club members, who seem like they wouldn't know a joke if it showed up to their previous Spring Fest and slapped them in the face.

"Is it cool if we keep this between us?" I ask him. "I'm not exactly supposed to be in here."

Kyle makes a motion of zipping his mouth shut. "Not tell people about one of the most embarrassing moments of my life? Sounds good to me."

Of course it's at that exact moment that the fire alarm blares. I swear, I see Kyle's soul leave his body.

"Well, I better stop dicking around and go." I hold up my hands. "Not making a joke because I just saw your, I mean . . . I'm leaving so you can get dressed. Sorry again."

Before I can embarrass myself even further, I rush out of the locker room and don't look back until I'm out the doors and heading in the direction of the fields. Normally, that's where everyone ends up anyway during drills. We literally just had our fire drill for the month though, so while I don't know why we're doing it again, I can't say I'm mad about it when it saved me from an incredibly awkward situation. At least today is actually sunny. It's still chilly enough to cool my heated face, which is an added bonus. There's way too many people to push past in order to get to the soccer fields, so I try to spot a random line I can join.

It's not exactly easy to find a teacher that doesn't hate

me, but I luck out by seeing Mr. Mora, my English teacher. He's the only other teacher I like besides Mr. Ford. Well, I guess the only teacher I like now. He's the super-friendly, nice, younger English teacher that queer kids can't help but flock to. Sean's like his favorite student ever, especially after he helped Mr. Mora and his husband adopt their cat. He wanted to sign on as the faculty advisor for Mystery Club but already had his hands full with the Latinx Student Union and QSA. Since Sean, Mari, and Luca are all close to him, I'm likable by proxy.

As I approach his class, I can practically hear Mr. Mora's sigh above everything.

"What class did you skip, Gigi?" he asks.

I hold up both my hands in defense. "I'm not skipping," I say. "I got separated from my class."

"Who's your teacher?"

"Coach Phil."

Mr. Mora looks up toward the heavens like he needs that strength to deal with me. "Did you get separated from your gym uniform too?"

"Actually, yes, someone took it."

He doesn't seem to believe that, and I'm being honest for once.

"Someone took your gym uniform? With your name on it?"

"People are into weird things; I don't know what to tell you."

Mr. Mora rubs the side of his head in a way that implies *if you fail your junior year of high school by flunking gym class after all the help I've given you in English, I will scream* without the need to say it aloud.

"All right. I'll let him know."

"You're the best," I say with the sweetest voice I can muster.

I fall into line with the rest of his class, none of whom I recognize. They must be freshmen or sophomores or something. I easily blend in since most of them are still taller than me.

"Gigi!"

Oh no. I turn toward the sound of the voice, landing on the freckled face of Aimee. She has way too much energy for a fire drill.

"I'm so excited to be a part of the Mystery Club. Is there a mystery yet? Once we start an investigation, I'm thinking of writing a paper on it. Ooooh, or I can do a play-by-play of it on my podcast. You can even be a guest!"

I match her smile. "I would rather break both of my own arms than go on your podcast."

A high-pitch laugh escapes her throat. "Oh my gosh, Gigi, you are so funny. I love your sense of humor."

Normally, that's a comment that would flatter me, but I wasn't joking.

"What's that in your hands?" she asks.

"It's none of your godda . . ." I swallow the rest of my

sentence. I don't necessarily have to tell her what this is *from*, but since she's really into true crime or whatever, maybe she could help me figure out what the code on the paper means. Then I don't have to look so clueless in front of Mari. "I mean, it's this clue for a mystery Mari's working on. I'm sure you'll get all the details at the next club meeting, but I'm a little stuck, if you want to take a look at it."

"Of course!" Aimee grabs the paper from my hands too enthusiastically, but I let it slide. She bites her lip, skimming through the number lines. "Do you think it's code?"

"Probably," I say.

"Oh, duh," she says suddenly, making a show of bopping herself in the forehead all cute-like. "None of the numbers are higher than twenty-six, so they correspond to letters. Easy."

Am I supposed to be following?

She seems to read on my face the fact that I'm not. "So 1 is A, 2 is B, 3 is C, and so forth . . . Hold on." She borrows a pencil from Mr. Mora before turning back to me and starts writing a key in the margins, with each letter of the alphabet getting its respective number. "So that makes the first line . . . Acosta, Ramon. Isn't he a senior here?"

He is. And if all these lines are names, which would make sense with the formatting, that probably means they are Westbridge students. Which means . . .

Holy hell, did Big Willy give me their client list?

My stomach gives a sickly rumble. Oh no.

"Great job, Aimee, you're a genius." I grab the list and fold it to fit in my pocket. "But I'm going in now. Bye."

"What?" Aimee asks. "Why?"

I want to place my hand over my belly button because it hurts, but this isn't my first rodeo. I've been in cars before and had to hold it through the sweats and praying to a god I only care to contact when I'm in pain. I turn away from her and step back up to Mr. Mora.

"Mr. Mora? All the excitement is triggering my IBS," I joke, even though it's fair to say and all my teachers should know my intestines are a failing game of Jenga to begin with. This is probably the universe getting back at me for lying about having to rush to the bathroom so much recently.

"All right," Mr. Mora says. "Let me see if I can get the all clear to go inside the building."

That seems a little extra for a drill, especially when I'm on the brink of potentially shitting my pants. But he gets the approval. The teacher next to him agrees to keep an eye on both classes, so Mr. Mora escorts me inside. There is a bathroom right by the entrance, but I shake my head.

"I have to stop at the locker room," I mumble.

I didn't think to bring my bathroom kit of flushable wipes to a fire drill. My mistake. But I really don't want to go without it and risk the dangerous lack of ply the available toilet paper has. If it doesn't tear, it will definitely give me a butt rash and that is the last thing I need while already trying to solve Mr. Ford's murder. Big Willy is enough of a pain in the ass themself.

Mr. Mora nods. "That's fine, I just have to keep escorting you."

Yeah, probably not a good idea to wander the halls alone during the drill. Principal Daniels would have a stroke if he saw me.

I walk past the boys' locker room. I pray that Kyle doesn't choose this moment to leave the locker room. I don't think I can face him again yet. Thankfully, I'm able to get my backpack from the girls' locker room and rejoin Mr. Mora in the hall without any issues.

"Why did we even have another drill?" I ask. "Aren't we due for like a lockdown or active shooter or tornado drill instead?"

Mr. Mora makes a face. "It wasn't a drill. There was an actual fire."

Holy shit. How did that happen? Was there an accident with one of the Bunsen burners or something? Did anyone get hurt?

"Where is it?" I ask. Since Luca, Sean, and Mari all had reasons they had to be in class, I'm sure they were able to get out safely. There wasn't enough panic for the fire to have trapped people inside.

Now all the clearance makes more sense though. Are we even allowed to be in the building? Shouldn't there be a lot more smoke?

"They put it out already," Mr. Mora says. As if he can read my mind, he adds. "It's at the other edge of the building. I think most of the smoke escaped."

"Which room?" I ask.

Mr. Mora looks uncomfortable, almost like he's not sure if he should tell me. We stop, now outside of the nearest bathroom.

"I don't know if you'll be comfortable hearing it."

I think back on the events of the day. "I'm pretty sure it's impossible to be more uncomfortable than I've already been made today."

Mr. Mora sighs. "I'm sure you'll find out anyway . . . It was in the math office," he says. "Right at Mr. Ford's old desk."

I thought my stomach hurt before. I didn't even think about checking the math office after we looked at the classroom. We were focused on the flash drive and Big Willy and didn't even think of the office as a place to find evidence. But if nothing was there, why would it get burned down? What was in the math office that is now likely up in flames?

It might make sense as to why Big Willy gave a specific time for the locker room.

It was a distraction.

My lower intestines groan along with me. "Oh," I say, biting back a few swears. "I see."

Then I rush into the bathroom. Once I'm safely on the toilet, I shoot some emergency texts off to Sean and Mari.

**Gigi:** BIG news

**Gigi:** i think we got a list of clients from big willy

**Gigi:** but also someone set THE MATH OFFICE on FUCKING FIRE?!

**Mari:** where are you now?!

**Gigi:** . . .

**Gigi:** why don't you tell me where you are and I'll meet you there?

# TEN

## If Your Life Isn't Threatened, Are You Really Training Jiu-Jitsu?

**AFTER CATCHING UP** Mari and Sean on the list of clients and the two of them promising to go through and decode it all before the Mystery Club meeting tomorrow, the rest of the school day passed in a blur. Mom called me to come straight to our jiu-jitsu academy to assist her with the kids' class. Despite everything, I can't pass up the opportunity for a little extra cash.

I decided to stay around for Mom's advanced adult class too, despite them using me to show the technique and people asking to see the choke again a few too many times for me to think they needed it.

It's nice to have the distraction. While I'm training, I'm not thinking about everything that's going on with my life off the mats. I'm in the moment and in my body.

I'm currently trying to create space between me and Skye, a blue belt in her late twenties, who has me in side control. Her pressure's killer, even though she's even smaller than I am, but I push up on her neck and create enough space to slip my knee in between us. I can tell she's tired, as it's almost too easy to hit a scissor sweep and land in mount. She defends against my Ezekiel choke attempt, but I'm able to transition to s-mount and slide into an arm bar. She taps twice and I release everything. The buzzer goes off before we can reset.

She groans, pushing up to a seated position. Her brown hair falls into her face, and she reties it. For everyone with long hair, it's pretty much guaranteed to fall every round if you don't braid it back. Yet another reason I cut mine short.

Skye reaches out a hand to fist-bump me. "You're too good. A great roll but damn."

I gesture to the loose belt now barely keeping my gi closed and then start to retie it. "You're doing great. That cross face was hell. And I'm a blue belt too."

She gives an exaggerated eye roll. "A sixteen-year-old blue belt is a totally different beast. You've been training since you were, like, a fetus. Us adult blue belts are still only on our first belt promotion." She stretches her arms. "Not to mention I have an office job, which basically saps energy like a corporate parasite, so between that and my shit neck and back, I'm always operating at like no more than fifty percent."

I snort. "You're talking like you are seventy. What are you, twenty-three?"

I know she's nearing thirty, but what can I say? She's hot and I'm a kiss ass.

"Cute." She stands first and helps me to my feet. "I can't

wait until they promote you to purple and I can feel better about getting my ass kicked by a teenager."

It's the end of class, so we all line up at the wall by ranking. Skye stays next to me, as neither of us have any stripes yet. Mom gives some announcements about a new morning class, and we bow out. I step off the mats and remove my gi top.

Moving sweaty hair away from my eyes, I check my phone. Considering I haven't been checking it at all since school ended, there's not that much. Some cat and Pokémon memes Sean tagged me in that I immediately like, the meditation app I've never used once telling me to get on my shit, and a new email. I swipe down to look at it.

Weird. It's from some account called watchyourbackwestbridge. I'm kind of over all these fake email accounts. It has to be Big Willy, but how do they even have my personal email?

There's no subject line, but I click on it anyway.

*Stop investigating or someone else will get hurt.*

My body grows cold. This is a threat. I've just been threatened. At the same time, it's like my blood boils. Big Willy is threatening me now? If they were going to threaten me, they should at least have the balls to do it to my face so I can hit them.

There's a link under the message. When I click it, a private video pops up. From the thumbnail, I can already tell it's Mr. Ford's classroom. My stomach drops to my uterus as I press play.

Thankfully, or unthankfully, it's not from the day of Mr.

Ford's murder. The recording is from when we searched the room on Monday. The camera clearly captured me, Sean, Mari, Cedar, and Luca. I scroll through and of course, it has full view of the cabinet and me grabbing the flash drive.

Which means not only does Big Willy know we have evidence and are lying to them, but they're saying one of us is the next person on their hit list. It also means that if I go to Principal Daniels or the cops with this, they'll know that we were searching through a potential crime scene and that I not only eavesdropped but also stole something from the room.

Shit.

"Um . . . Gigi?"

I glance up, probably unable to bite back the stress and scowl on my face. Which immediately makes me feel terrible, because I'm looking at Benji Denver, an orange belt who happens to be the one Westbridge freshman I know. He's small for his size and wears glasses that practically take up half his face. He looks like the last person you would expect to train in combat sports, but that's the thing about jiu-jitsu. The small, nerdy guys are often the ones who are the most technical and deadly, and while Benji's only like fourteen now, in a few years, he'll be a real problem.

He's already allowed in the adult classes, which is saying something.

I force a smile on my face. "Sorry, Benji, what's up?"

"I'm just, I'm like a huge fan," he starts. "Of you. Like in jiu-jitsu, but also just as a person. Like I heard you kicked Kenneth Wright's ass and that's the most epic thing ever because that guy is the worst."

This is both endearing and very strange. I'm not sure how to respond. No one ever told me they were a fan of mine before. Am I secretly Westbridge High famous or something? I'm definitely not famous here. I haven't competed in jiu-jitsu tournaments since middle school, so I'm mostly just known as Coach Dani's kid.

"Thank you?" I manage to say.

Between the threat and this, my brain and emotions are in overdrive.

Benji shifts on his feet, still in his gi but wearing sandals. "I heard you joined the Mystery Club. Are they accepting new members?"

I raise an eyebrow. It's kind of weird he's asking about that. Usually my life at Westbridge and my life at this academy are extremely separate. Does Benji know something?

Still. Mari would kill me if I said no. "Desperately, are you interested in joining?"

"Yeah, I want to spend more time with you. You all. Solving mysteries."

My heart is still pounding in my chest and I feel a little bit of pain in that area, so I'm possibly dying, or it's just sore from training. This threat has me messed up. I feel like I can hardly focus on Benji's face and I have to sit on my hand to stop it from shaking. Sure, it's possible Benji's being a little suspicious, but he's been doing privates with Mom for a while, so we've known each other for years, even if we aren't close.

I can be a little cautious without being totally paranoid. Or at least save that energy for people who weren't training in class with me while the threat was sent.

"Sorry, I'm a little distracted right now," I admit. "The next meeting is after school tomorrow. It's in room one twenty-three. If you accidentally go in a room that looks like a glorified storage closet, you found it. Sound good?"

He quickly nods. "Yes, thank you!"

Benji scurries away before I can say anything else. It can't hurt to have him show. Aimee's been bugging Mari about going to a meeting, so we'll be careful about what we say there anyway.

My phone vibrates in my hand. For a moment, my stomach lurches, but it's just a call from Luca.

"I'm outside and freezing my ass off. Hurry up," he says as a greeting.

Mom still has two classes to teach tonight, but I didn't feel like sticking around late, so I asked Luca for a ride. I have to at least pretend I'm catching up on homework. After hugs and goodbyes to everyone, I slip outside. My chest is still hurting and I feel dizzy. What the hell is happening to me?

Luca waits in the car, hazards on. Even from outside, I can see that he's holding his hands to the vents in order to warm them up. Luca pops the trunk and I stuff my gi in before joining him up front.

"I'm dying," I tell him.

Luca winces. "Training was that hard?"

I strap in. "No, seriously. Something is wrong. My chest hurts and I feel like I need to keep moving my hands but I kind of want to pull at my hair? I'm also a little light-headed and all my senses are like on steroids."

Luca turns toward me, putting a hand on my shoulder. "You're not dying. It sounds like it might be an anxiety or panic attack. You'll be okay, I'm here. Let's breathe, all right?"

I frown. "No, I'm not like that."

"Like what?"

"Soft, like you." I clutch my chest and wince. "I didn't mean it like that. It's just, I don't have anxiety or panic or any of that shit. I'm fine."

"There's nothing wrong with having anxiety or feeling panic." Luca keeps his voice soft, still breathing slow like I'll match it off peer pressure alone.

I slide my hand through my hair because for some reason I feel like if I don't move I'll drop dead or something.

"It's not *soft*," Luca continues. "It's normal. I mean, Jesus Christ, Gigi. You saw a dead body a week ago. This is normal, and we'll get through it together. Now, breathe with me, dammit."

This time, I listen. I follow his breaths on a count and

focus on the pressure of his hand on my shoulder. It helps me feel like I'm back in my body and not so much in my head. Was that really a panic attack? Shit. Like I need another reason for Mrs. Goode to track me down and add onto my already extensive file. I'm glad only Luca was around to see that.

"Did something happen to trigger this?" Luca asks once I'm calmed down. "Sometimes my panic attacks come out of nowhere, but if this is because of . . . you know, what happened, maybe there is something you can identify as a cause?"

Yeah, I'd say there's a pretty freaking big one.

"I was sent an actual threat from Big Willy," I admit. "They know we're looking into Mr. Ford's death and lying to them about it and they basically said one of us is next."

Luca's eyes go wide. "The Big Willy email account sent you a threat?"

"No, it was a new email but come on. It's obviously them. Their whole thing is making anonymous burner emails."

It's hard to read Luca's expression, but I guess it's not the kind of thing you expect to hear from your sister. "I'm just surprised," Luca says finally. "Isn't Big Willy helping you?"

Of course Mari or Cedar told him all about that. I guess it's only fair since he is technically involved. Big Willy saw him in the classroom too.

"They want us to think it's someone else," I say, "to get us off their track obviously. But it's them. What we need is to find out who this person is." I lean back against the

116

car seat. My eyes are starting to burn. "I feel like if some-one had threatened me like this a week ago, I'd threaten them right back, saying to fucking try to hurt me, you know? I'll break their knee or some shit. But . . . I don't know, Luca. After seeing Mr. Ford like that? Hearing this feels different. Like this is an actual murderer, not just some school bully. What if they hurt you or Sean or Mari or even freaking Cedar and I can't do anything about it? I couldn't save Mr. Ford and that was bad enough, but if I can't save any of you . . ." I wipe away my tears, looking at the passenger-side door.

I shouldn't be telling him all of this. I give him shit, but Luca has enough to worry about without me bringing down the mood like this.

"It's totally understandable you're feeling that way," he says. He tosses on a smile. "But we'll get through it. I can even help look into who this Big Willy person is."

"Yeah?"

He nods. "Of course. And literally nothing bad is going to happen to me."

"That sounds like what people say in a movie right before something bad happens to them."

Luca rolls his eyes. "Well, good thing we aren't in a movie because I highly doubt someone called Big Willy is going to try and kill me." He starts the car. "Now, let's go home. Someone brought slutty brownies to rehearsal today and I snuck you extras."

That's the best thing he's said yet.

"Did I ever tell you how much I love you?"

He gives me a look. "Rarely."

"Well, you are officially my favorite sibling."

"I'm your only sibling, asshole."

"Now you're also my least favorite."

Luca starts in the direction of our house and while he mocks an annoyed look, he's still smiling. It's not exactly the thank-you I probably owe him, but he knows I'm not exactly the best with this kind of thing.

I think, for now, it's enough.

# ELEVEN

## Find Your Light and Exit Dramatically

**THE SCHOOL DAY** passes slowly, with me paying more attention to the other people who could possibly threaten me than class, but after the final bell, I head over to the Mystery Club closet. While I thought I was relatively fast, a quick stop at the bathroom apparently caused me to be the last to arrive. Even Benji Denver is already sitting at the small table, a plate of cookies in front of him.

"Hi, Gigi!" he greets. "My moms made cookies when I told them I was joining a new club."

I pull out the leftover seat across from him and next to Sean. "You're already the freshman MVP of this club, Benji."

I don't know if that comes across as a dig at Aimee but I don't care. Benji's moms own a bakery together, so I am more than happy to take advantage of that. I snatch one from the plate.

"So where were we?" I ask.

"Shouldn't you introduce yourself, Gigi?" Mari asks pointedly.

I give her a look as I take another bite of my cookie. "I think everyone knows me."

"We all did introductions. Your favorite mystery book and a fun fact."

Ah. She wants this to really seem like a real club. I guess I can't blame her for that. Besides, I am trying to stay on her good side. With Spring Fest fast approaching, I want my rejection to be as painless as possible.

"Hi," I start, "I'm Gigi Ricci. Pronouns she/her and a junior here at Westbridge. Let's see. My favorite mystery book is . . ." I hate being put on the spot. I swear, I forget every book I've read in my life. What's a book? "The next one I'll read because my favorite moment is always the big reveal at the end. And a fun fact is . . . uh . . . Eevee is my favorite Pokémon."

I was going to say something about the number of times I've broken my nose (twice) was catching up to the number of times I've broken someone else's nose (three, but once was a total accident), but I feel like Mari would want something a little less scary for the new freshmen.

"Now that we wasted time with that, what did I actually miss?" I ask.

Mari rolls her eyes and draws out a sigh, but in the way she does when she's not really mad at me. "We're going through the list of clients to see if there are people we can discreetly ask about their experience buying from Big Willy."

We ultimately decided to let the new club members know we're trying to figure out who Big Willy is but in a watered-down way. We're not going to mention that we think Big Willy is connected to Mr. Ford's death, or anything more than a harmless curiosity about the mysterious Westbridge antihero.

"Did Cedar get the flash drive content yet?" I ask.

"Not yet, but she'll have it soon."

I feel like I haven't really seen her since we got into our little fight or whatever. She's definitely still mad at me. "Did she mention me?"

Sean blinks. "Why would she mention you?"

My entire face heats. "She wouldn't. I mean, whatever. Let's focus on the mystery."

"I'm so excited," Aimee quickly adds, at least blissfully changing the subject. "This is kind of like true crime since it's a whole cheating ring and that's a crime, right? I've already started—"

She's interrupted by my phone buzzing loudly on the table. I forgot I put it on vibrate in case Mom or Dad called. Any embarrassment is immediately swallowed by the chill that runs down my spine at the sender.

"Oh shit," I say. "Watch Your Back emailed me again."

It's like my heart stops. Mari's eyes widen. "What does it say?"

"Who's Watch Your Back?" Aimee asks.

I don't bother answering that. My fingers shake, but I open the email. There's no message though. The body of the email only contains a picture. Of Luca. Onstage. But not from the audience. It's a near bird's-eye view.

Dread falls over me and my stomach drops.

It's a relatively normal picture, but not something you want sent to you by a killer.

"I think Luca might be in danger," I manage to say.

"Danger?" Benji gasps.

Sean is the first to take off, with Mari and me at his heels. To their credit, Benji and Aimee follow close behind despite probably not knowing what the hell is happening.

What if something happens to Luca? Something bad?

We race into the theater, where they are in the middle of rehearsing some number. Luca's practically center stage, just like he was in the picture. It had to have been taken today. My palms sweat as we sprint up the aisles to get closer to the stage.

I scan the theater, but I only see the rest of the musical crew and cast that isn't backstage giving us weird looks and clearly confused

Then there's a crack.

I don't know how Sean senses exactly what's happening or has the reflexes to react to it, but he hoists himself on the stage effortlessly and tackles Luca out of the way the same moment one of the stage lights crashes in the spot where he was standing.

Glass breaks, people scream.

I should run to Luca. But once I see his surprised face looking at Sean on top of him, skin so red it practically matches the discarded gel coloring the broken light, I know he's safe.

I run to the back of the theater, vision narrowing. I nearly trip as I power up the small spiral staircase that leads to the catwalk, but my rage gives me enough balance to keep going.

I stomp onto the platform, not seeing how high I am in the air, not feeling what should be a burn in my thighs, not hearing any of the commotion below.

The catwalk is empty.

My phone buzzes again. This time with a call from an unknown number. Shaking from my own rage, I answer.

"You were warned," the voice says, using a voice changer like we're in *Scream* or some shit. "Next time, I won't miss."

My angry swears are lost in the sounds of the dial tone and my own pounding heart.

I have no choice but to head back down to the chaos onstage, weighted by my defeat. Mr. Jones, the director of the musical, struggling to dial his phone and call for help, is practically hyperventilating trying to figure out what exactly happened.

Making my way back to center stage, I watch Sean get Luca back to his feet. A nurse or someone will likely check over him, even though he seems okay. If anything, Luca probably passed out from the excitement of body contact. I try to maintain my composure as I walk up to them.

"Thanks for saving me, Sean," Luca says. He looks star-struck. "I don't . . . I don't even know what to say."

"It's no problem," Sean says. "I have to rescue cats all the time. It's no different really."

I love Sean more than life itself, but sometimes he can miss out on some nuance and be a little too blunt. He's so book smart, but he struggles a little in social settings. Or in seeing when someone is clearly in love with him.

Luca nods with a smile that's too tight. "Catzoned," he mutters. "I've been catzoned."

Maybe I should talk to Sean.

"You okay?" I ask Luca instead.

"Physically, yes, I'm okay," Luca says. "Mentally? I wish I were a cat."

My chest feels tight, and I press my hand down over it. I keep swallowing, nausea not quite escaping me. "It had to be Big Willy. They sent that threat and . . . I should've done something. Stayed closer to you . . . I'm sorry."

His expression softens. "It's not your fault, Gigi." He looks back over at Sean. "Plus, I got to feel Sean's abs through his shirt, and I don't think he noticed my half boner."

I lift my eyes to the heavens, as if I can summon another stage light to fall and finish the job.

"You almost died, pervert."

"His face was like an *inch* from mine. I almost died twice."

I shove him, but at least he has me smiling again.

"Are you okay?" Mari asks, pulling Luca in for a hug before he has the chance to answer.

He squirms a bit and shrugs her off. "Yes, I'm alive. The assassins fail once more. Now, get off. You're going to wrinkle my costume and I do not have the brain capacity to stay late and steam it."

Benji rushes over to us. "Is everyone okay? Can I get any-one anything?"

"Yeah, Benji, all good." I have to suppress the desire to ruffle his hair. He's fourteen, not ten, but with his size, it's easy to forget. Still, I of all people know how annoying it is when people make a big deal about being small.

"So eager to help," Luca says. "You're perfect for the Mystery Club."

Mari's face drains of all concern. I can see the *It's the Mystery and Thriller Literary Scholars* rage burning in her eyes. "I'm going to smack you."

My brother has many talents and getting people to com-pletely lose all concern over him with his sense of humor is one of them. Thinking on it, I'm probably the same. The Ricci family loves to complain but suppress all real emotions with jokes and teasing. It's in our blood or something.

I pull Luca over to me. "I'm glad you're okay. Seriously."

Principal Daniels has arrived, and he's talking with Mr. Jones. I hear them say something about the light being old and likely falling on accident. Anger boils in me. "It wasn't an *accident*. I literally got a call that confirms someone was targeting Luca."

They turn to look at me. Shit, I must have been louder than expected.

"Do you have a recording?" Principal Daniels asks. "Any proof?"

"No, but . . ." I look at my call log. "I can call them back." I dial back the number and put the call on speaker.

"Willy's Concert and Event Lighting, how can I help you?" the voice asks.

Principal Daniels frowns. "Is this a joke, Ms. Ricci?"

I gape at the phone. This wasn't who called. How is that possible? I hang up. *Willy's* Lighting?

They're freaking rubbing it in our face.

"I . . ."

"We'll look into this of course," Principal Daniels says, "but it seems likely that we'll just need new equipment."

"But I'm not—"

Luca laughs. "So funny, Gigi, always the jokester." He gives me a harsh whisper. "We need the budget increase, let them think it's the old-ass equipment."

God, I really hate him sometimes. But I let him lead me away. If they aren't going to believe us and want to write off everything as accidents because it's easier, we're better figuring it out on our own anyway. I step back toward where the rest of Mystery Club waits as Luca is shuffled off by other theater kids to the nurse.

"I just don't understand why Big Willy would act this soon," I say. "I just got the first threat last night, and we haven't even reached out to anyone yet."

"Well, Aimee did mention Mystery Club was looking into Big Willy on her podcast," Benji says.

"She *what*?" I snap at the same time Aimee excitedly blurts, "You listen to my podcast?"

"What the fuck is *wrong* with you?" I ask her.

"Gigi, stop—" Mari's voice comes from behind me. I ignore it.

"My brother could've gotten seriously injured or killed." I grab the front of her shirt and pull her close to me. Her eyes widen but I don't blink. "There's a reason we said to keep this fucking quiet and you don't even waste one *night* before putting it on your public podcast?"

Mari pulls me off her. Aimee starts to cry. "Nobody really listens to my podcast, but I was excited about this . . . I didn't think anyone would react like this to a cheating scandal. I'm just trying to help."

"Spare me," I groan.

"Gigi," Mari says, voice trying to be kind and patient. "Aimee messed up, but come on, you're scaring her."

"Good." I twist toward Aimee. "I hope you're scared enough to realize what a selfish bitch you—"

"Cut it out," Mari injects.

"Is something going on over there?" Principal Daniels snaps.

Aimee keeps crying like I'm some kind of monster. "I made one mistake! I just want people to like my podcast and it's not like anyone got hurt."

This time, Sean and Luca have to assist Mari in holding me back so I don't tackle her. "Fuck you, Aimee, and double fuck your shitty podcast!"

Mari lets go of my arm to step in front of me, filling my red-tinted vision with her face. She puts a hand on my cheek, voice low and soft.

"Hey, Gigi, it's okay. I know you're stressed, but this isn't Aimee's fault."

I hate that her touch sends my heart in a frenzy. I hate that I'm embarrassed she has to see me like this. I hate that I still care so much about what she thinks. That she makes me soft. Weak.

My muscles loosen.

She smiles. "Why don't you apologize and we'll talk this all—"

"What?" I snap. "I'm not fucking apologizing. Screw that."

"Gigi, you're acting—"

"Acting like what?" I laugh. "Like a bitch?"

"I didn't say that."

"You don't have to. Everyone knows I'm an unstable bitch who just wants to fight everyone. That's what I'm good for, not playing goddamn Scooby-Doo with a bunch of nerds."

"Hey," Luca snaps. "Sean's your best friend."

Sean shrugs. "She's not wrong about the nerd part though."

Benji nods in agreement.

I feel my eyes start to burn. I know I'm being terrible, and they are still supporting me and letting me lash out. Both of them are too good for me. I can't do this.

I'll die before I cry in front of an auditorium of people.

"Whatever, I'm done."

Mari steps toward me, voice low. "Gigi, come on. We're doing this for Mr. Ford."

My lip wobbles but I bite it still. "You do it, then. But keep me and Luca out of it."

I turn and jump off the stage, starting to walk up the aisle.

Principal Daniels marches up to me but I hold out a hand to stop him. "I'm sorry for yelling. I was upset about my brother almost being killed by your freak accident. Maybe I'm a little messed up given we just lost Mr. Ford to another *accident*. But I didn't break anyone's nose, so let's chalk it up to improvement and I'll reflect on my actions."

He sighs. "Can you at least promise me you'll see Mrs. Goode tomorrow?"

"Sure," I say. "Yeah. Promise."

Eyes threatening tears, I speed walk until I'm out of the building. Finally outside and alone, I sit on a patch of grass.

This is what I get for thinking I could be more than what I am. For believing Mr. Ford when he made it seem like I was better than an angry, violent bitch with barely two brain cells to my name. Solve a murder? Please.

I'm good at one thing, and using logic isn't it.

My eyes burn and I can't stop a few tears from welling up. Plus, it's fucking cold and I don't have my jacket.

My phone buzzes in my pocket. I check it.

Four calls from Dad and six messages from Mom. They got notified and are on the way. I type out a quick response to assure them everything's okay. I then open my email and click on the threat from Watch Your Back. I don't care if replying impacts the investigation or our plan to get on Big Willy's good side. I'm done with this.

From: gigiricci25@gmail.com
To: watchyourbackwestbridge@gmail.com
Re:


Listen up, you murderous fuck.

I'm done investigating, so leave me and my family and friends alone.

Also, choke on a dick and die.

Respectfully,

Gianna Ricci


Send.

I drop my phone onto the grass next to me and drop my head into my knees. I've been trying to keep going, to focus on figuring out what happened and not allow myself to feel much of anything at all, but it's hard. I wish I were in my room, where I can layer on blankets and cry into my plushies in peace.

"What happened, MacGregor? You lose a fight?"

God really hates me. Not only does someone have to see me on the brink of an emotional breakdown, but it has to be Cedar Martin. If not for the snark in her voice, I almost wouldn't recognize her. She's not wearing the usual makeup, and her hair is now a pastel purple. She wears a jacket over a navy cropped hoodie, leggings that really hug her thick curves, and step-on-me, white, heeled boots.

"What happened to me?" I ask. "What the hell happened to you? Hot Topic close down or something?"

She rolls her eyes. "No. I realized I didn't feel like myself anymore and wanted to stop it." Her eyebrows lift. "Guess it took the human equivalent of a rabid raccoon threatening me to realize I turned into someone I don't want to be."

Wow. That's almost admirable. Was she abducted by aliens or something, and this is the replacement?

I snort. "Seriously? A raccoon?"

"Feisty assholes that are annoyingly cute?" She looks me up and down. "It fits."

My heart flutters in a weird way. Did Cedar seriously just call me cute?

She sighs. "Maybe I should ask your mom to sign me up for jiu-jitsu. Girls putting me in danger is hot."

I can't help but laugh. "Trust me, it's not cute or sexual when said girl is trying to break your arms or choke you."

"I don't know, that might be my exact kink."

I roll my eyes, but even something about her teasing feels a little different. Maybe I really did miss it. "You're not still mad at me, then?" I ask.

"Didn't say that." Cedar slowly crouches down and joins me in the grass. She eyes me. "My ass is cold and now I'm wet. How the hell are you doing this?"

"It's all a ploy to get pretty girls to tell me I got them wet."

She snorts. The silence that passes after isn't so bad. It's weird. I obviously noticed that Cedar was hot, but the new hair looks great. It's effortless. Especially with her so close to me, enough that I can see her long eyelashes and even a little skin tag she has on her chin. It's ridiculously cute. Like I almost want to kiss it.

Which is a gross thought to have. This is *Cedar*. I don't want to kiss Cedar.

Shit, now I'm thinking about kissing Cedar.

Am I really that romantically repressed that I'll fantasize about the first person who is nice to me, even if she's normally the worst?

"I'm glad," I say, burying my chin in my crossed arms to hide my blush. "I don't know what I'd do without my archnemesis."

"Please, you're not even in my top five enemies, Gigi."

I grip my chest like my heart is throbbing. "I've never been so hurt in my life."

"But seriously, what's wrong with you?"

I can't believe I'm about to confide in Cedar of all people, but maybe it takes someone who can be a bit of a bitch to understand someone like me. She's seeing the worst of me and staying. That's something.

"The person who killed Mr. Ford tried to kill Luca, and I lost my shit on this freshman for not keeping her mouth shut."

Cedar's eyes light up with concern. "What the fuck? Is Luca okay?"

"Yeah, Sean saved him, so he's better than ever."

"Can't wait to hear the romantic play-by-play later." She calms down enough to give me a look. "And you lost your shit? So what?" I roll my eyes, but she continues. "What I'm saying is, it will all work out, happily ever after."

I snort. "You don't seem like the happily-ever-after type."

"I'm filled with surprises." She gets back to her feet and sighs. "I know you like Mari, Gigi."

My face heats. She clearly knew but saying it aloud like that is different. It feels weird, like I don't want to hear it from her. "That obvious, huh?"

She shrugs out of her jacket, dropping it over my shoulders and speaking with a low voice right near my ear. "Why do you think I'm always so annoyed with you?"

What does *that* mean? That she does like Mari too, or . . .

My entire body tingles.

With a smile, she starts to strut away, and with all the power in me, I try not to stare at her ass.

"Cedar?"

She turns around.

"Your hair looks good," I say. "Really good."

She makes a show of flipping it. "It does, doesn't it?"

"Don't fish for more compliments though."

"Wouldn't dream of it." She tucks a few light strands of hair behind her ear in a way that's so cute I can hardly believe this is Cedar at all. "Oh, but, Gigi?"

I blink. "What?"

"I don't give up that easily."

She winks and walks off.

I'm more confused about my feelings, but I'm not gonna lie: I feel a lot better than I did before.

# TWELVE

## What You Get for Trusting a Murderer

**THURSDAY AND FRIDAY** pass all too slowly, and while I hate to admit it, I already miss the Mystery Club. While I'm still talking to Sean and he mentioned that he and Cedar made plans in their shared AP econ class to work on the flash drive at his apartment on Saturday, I don't care.

Not even to be jealous.

Of Cedar, I mean. For stealing my best friend on a weekend. I wouldn't be jealous of Sean for spending time with Cedar. Obviously. It's better than her being alone with Mari. Who isn't really talking to me, which sucks since it's less than a week since I'm supposed to confess to her.

But it doesn't matter. I'm not investigating shit with them. I gave up.

Watch Your Back hasn't said anything to me since. No threats, no creepy phone calls, no attacks on my brother's life.

Mom and Dad are on edge about that anyway. They don't know there's an actual murderer involved, but I think even the idea of Luca getting hurt on accident has their anxiety levels shooting up. Dad's having bigger glasses of wine at dinner and Mom's taking on, like, double the classes. They've been glad the past two days had me coming straight home after school and basically only leaving the house for jiu-jitsu. Aside from planning on not getting brutally murdered so the big penis prick can make it look like an accident, I'm not doing much of anything. It feels like jiu-jitsu is the only thing I have left, and I still feel like I've been off my game and distracted the entire class.

I lean back against the wall, retying my belt over my gi. Of course, Mom's covering this class, so they walk over to me as the buzzer starts the round of rolling.

"It's not like you to sit out a round," Mom says. "Is everything okay? Do you need to talk?"

"My stomach hurts," I lie. It's not exactly hard to believe, since my stomach gives me trouble all the time. There're days I've had to miss training because of my IBS flaring, and even more days that my biggest goal for the class is not shitting my gi pants.

"Sorry, did you bring anything to take? I might have some Pepto in the car."

I shake my head. "I'm fine."

It's the last round anyway. There aren't any late classes on Saturdays, so we'll go home right after we clean the mats. If none of the white belts volunteer, that is.

"Okay . . ." They frown a little as they take two steps away. "I'm here to talk if you need me."

I give a thumbs-up and Mom takes that as an excuse to watch the class. I line up and bow out on autopilot when the round ends, forcing smiles and congratulations when Mom gives out stripes to two people. I feel out of it, like I woke up in a dimension where everything is the same except me.

No one exactly volunteers to clean the mats, so it's Mom and me that get stuck with it. I spray them down while they mop behind me.

"I'm sorry, love," Mom says, cutting through the silence. "You're going through so much and I feel like I should help you and . . . I just don't really know how." They look down at the streaky mats. "You had to see your math teacher's body, for Christ's sake, and we can't even afford to send you to a nice therapist or psychiatrist or psychologist—I'm not even sure what the hell the difference is." They sigh, looking back at me. "It's . . . I know you probably need a parent that has all their shit together and knows the answers and the right thing to say, and I'm sorry I'm not that parent."

My eyes threaten to burn. I don't want Mom to think they aren't good enough. Yeah, maybe they aren't the best at being emotional and open, but it's not like I am either. Maybe sometimes it would be nice to have parents that were stricter or had nicer jobs that would pay for whatever, but at the end of the day, I wouldn't trade Mom or Dad for any of that. Maybe they are a little immature at times for parents, but they're funny and they do everything they can for me and Luca.

"It's okay, Mom. Seriously." I throw on a smile. "Although . . . are you telling me I won't magically have it together once I turn eighteen?"

They laugh. "I'm turning thirty-eight and still waiting to magically have it together." Mom leans on the mop. "I thought that way too. That once I became an adult, I'd be way more mature and always know what to do. Turns out, it's a scam. You don't grow up, not really. You just get older and have to take on more responsibilities. But honestly, I don't feel all that different from my clueless teenage self." They grimace a bit. "Same shit, just more back pain."

Sometimes it's easy to forget how young Mom and Dad are, at least for parents. Like they were both nineteen when the accident that was Luca strutted into this world. I guess once they decided to have the one kid, they didn't want to wait on a second because Mom didn't want to have an only child. Knowing they were fighting MMA as a purple belt at the time, they were probably imagining some kind of Ruotolo brothers situation.

But it seems so wild. I can't even *imagine* having a kid in three years. That would be like if Luca was a father *next year*. He couldn't even be trusted to take care of a houseplant, let alone a literal human baby.

"I don't know, Mom," I say. "I think you're doing pretty great. I don't expect you to always know the answer. I just expect you to be here for me." I spray the last section of the mats. "And to yell at me for trying to heel hook white belts in no gi."

They cross their arms. "You're supposed to be a mat enforcer, you little shit."

Otherwise known as ego crushers, or the high-level girls and small dudes that absolutely wreck any new assholes at the gym until any sense of toughness and superiority they have is choked out of them.

I smile. "Things are hard now, but I don't need some fancy therapist or whatever. I'll be okay."

"You'll tell me if that changes though?"

"You got it."

"And you'll meet with that school counselor at least?"

Ugh. Of course Mrs. Goode would reach out to them. "Sure," I reply.

"I love you, kid," Mom says.

"Yeah, you too, old man," I tease.

But they pull me into a hug, and when I hug them back, I think it says everything I'm not comfortable enough to say.

I unlock the side door of the house first, wishing I could skip over the shower and just be in bed with my plushies, and immediately hear Dad talking to a woman. What the hell? I know he's not cheating on Mom. He is ridiculously in love with them and they can easily kick his ass.

Even still, I can't help but blurt, "What's going on?" and step into the kitchen, Mom right behind me.

Dad is sitting across the table from Mrs. Ford. I'm so shocked, I barely even take in the espresso cups and cookies set on the table.

Both her and Dad turn to me. She's dressed in all black still and her eyes are as puffy as the last time I saw her.

"Gigi!" Dad says, to make up for my potentially rude greeting. "Mrs. Ford stopped by to check on you."

Now I feel like shit. "Sorry, I was just surprised." I internally cringe but try to externally wear a little smile. "Hope you weren't waiting long. I'm sorry I'm gross. I can clean up and change really quick . . ."

"No need. I just was in the area when I called, and your dad said to stop by. I only came a minute or two ago, but I have to head out soon. I'm sorry if this is weird. I just . . . I wanted to thank you for stopping by before and . . . I found something I wanted to give you."

There's a long pause. Mom and Dad both look incredibly awkward. Dad's the one who makes a move first, slowly pushing his chair out and standing. "We'll be right in the other room, doing . . ."

"Things that we need to do," Mom finishes.

It's painful, but the two of them rush off. I sigh, taking the seat that my dad left pulled out. I'm not sure what to say in this situation.

"You want to give me something?" I ask.

Did she find evidence? But I'm not looking into his death anymore, I remind myself. And even if I were, she didn't want us looking into it.

"I was going through his computer and . . . he had started writing you a recommendation letter. He wasn't sure if you were going to apply to colleges, but he wanted you to. Said you were one of his smartest students."

I have to choke back a laugh. "Smartest? Are you sure?"

I don't think I've ever been called smart in my life. Tough, sure. Violent, perhaps. Kind of a bitch or an asshole or probably involved in shady shit? Absolutely.

But smart? Never. Luca's the smart one.

It's like she can read my mind. "Grades aren't always a good measure of intelligence," Mrs. Ford says. "There's a lot more to being smart than what's on your math tests. Maybe he wanted you to work harder on those, but he saw past that." Her lip wobbles. "He always saw the best in people, to the point of being hard on them so they'd see it themselves. Now that he's gone, I . . . well, I guess I wanted to make sure you were starting to see the best in you too."

Shit, now I'm crying. My eyes burn and I brush at them, smearing the tears into my skin like that makes them less visible. I got this. I can still look strong and calm and collected.

Mrs. Ford blinks. "Anyway, I thought you should have it." She slides a printed paper across the table to me. Her arms shake slightly as she stands and gets her purse together. "Seriously, thank you. For everything. It's been tough, but Artie really cared about his students and it really means a lot to see he had students that cared about him too."

I can almost see her shatter with that statement.

"We really did," I say. "Or at least I did. So thank you."

She gives me a quick hug, and while I'm awkward and stiff, I don't shy away from it.

"Have a good night, Gigi," Mrs. Ford says. I give her a final wave and she heads out the door. Alone, I pick up the recommendation letter.

To Whom It May Concern:

I am writing to sincerely recommend the acceptance of one of my brightest students, Gianna Ricci, into (INSERT COLLEGE HERE). While there are times, due to a rigorous extracurricular program and part-time job, her grades have slipped, Gigi has displayed a great perseverance in pushing forward and continuing to improve.

She has made the time and effort to dedicate herself to bringing her GPA from a 2.5 to a 3.1 and only continues to grow. Any institution would be lucky to have such a well-rounded student among them. I have been fortunate to see her growth as an academic, and her ability to be a quick thinker and tackle the toughest problems with a sense of humor makes me proud to be her teacher.

A dedicated and disciplined martial artist and student, Gianna is fearless when it comes to stating her viewpoint but always makes sure it has legitimate backing. Hard-working, diligent, and fair toward her classmates and peers, she would be a strong addition to (MAYBE ASK IF THERE IS A SPECIFIC PROGRAM?) and certainly has a bright future ahead.

I can't wait to see where it takes her.

(NOTE: CHECK ON COMMUNITY SERVICE OR SOME FEEL-GOOD CRAP TO ADD. DOES TEACHING KIDS SELF-DEFENSE COUNT? add to online calendar - priya83)

Sincerely,

Arthur Ford

aford@westbridgecle.edu

I head straight into my room, dropping the letter on my desk and grabbing what I need to shower. Mom and Dad try to say something, but I give quick responses and rush into the bathroom and turn the water on high.

That's when I allow myself to finally cry.

I can't believe I've given up on Mr. Ford when he never gave up on me. Fuck, he was working on a recommendation letter when I hadn't even asked for one.

All through the shower, I go back and forth between deciding to continue investigating and staying out of it. I don't want to put Luca in danger again, but Mrs. Ford deserves to know what happened to her husband.

Mr. Ford deserves that much, wherever the hell he is.

I toss on my fuzzy pajama pants that have cats all over them and a cropped lightweight hoodie. It's still early in the day, but it feels like a stay-in-bed kind of Saturday. I'm barely through towel-drying my hair when my phone rings.

My heart stops for a moment, picks up when I realize that it's Sean calling, and then elevates a little too much because Sean never calls.

"Are you okay?" I answer. "Is Cedar with you still?"

"I don't know and yes," he says. "Can you come over?"

I don't bother changing. Instead, I grab Luca's old bike that hasn't been used in years and pedal as fast as I can to Sean's apartment building. I nearly get hit by a car and almost fall twice, but somehow make it unscathed. Sean's outside with

Cedar. Not far away are Sean's mom and Greg, both of whom look high as shit, but they are talking to the police.

What the hell is going on?

I toss the bike next to the rack like a complete asshole but leave it, because now's not the time to worry about that, and rush over to Sean and Cedar.

"What's going on? Did Greg do something? Are they in trouble?" I grab Sean's arms, lifting them and checking him over for injuries. "Are you in trouble?" I turn to Cedar. "Do I have to fight someone?"

"It's cool, Gigi. I'm okay, I promise." Sean gives his best attempt at a forced smile, which is almost comical in how awkward and still intimidating it looks. He drops it. "Someone broke into our apartment."

*"What?"*

This time Cedar answers. "We almost got into the flash drive and were waiting for it to finish, so we walked to get some milk tea. When we got back, the place was a mess."

"More of a mess than usual," Sean amends.

Jesus Christ. My voice comes out as a squeak. "And the flash drive?"

Sean and Cedar look at each other, faces cringing enough to be their answer. "Gone," Cedar confirms. "They smashed my damn laptop too."

I move both my hands through my hair. This is bad. This is really bad. This is why I wanted to stop with the investigation. Even with them still going, that's a major piece of evidence lost, possibly something that could have told us Big Willy's identity, and the murderous asshole is adding breaking and entering to their list of crimes. Sean and Cedar could have seriously gotten hurt.

Or worse.

Shit shit shit.

"We also got this message," Sean says. He holds out his phone to me and I start to read.

Yep. We're fucked.

From: watchyourbackwestbridge@gmail.com
To: mysterythrillerlitscholars@gmail.com
Subject: Got You

Hello Mystery Club,

I tried to give you a warning. I tried to let you save yourselves.

But I think my efforts were in vain. You already know too much, don't you?

Clever little rats. But not clever enough. Where's your evidence now?

Look over your shoulders. Don't go out alone. I know where to find you, each of you, and all I need is the right moment to strike and you rats will stop squeaking.

Respectfully,

Watch Your Back

# THIRTEEN

## Never Gonna Care about My Bad Reputation

**WHEN I ARRIVE** at school on Monday, I'm immediately called to the principal's office. I didn't even do anything. Is Principal Daniels doing preemptive check-ins, like he's a doctor for troubled teens?

At least I get to miss some of first period.

My silver lining is ripped to shreds when the gods of the universe all conspire against me to put Ethan freaking Mitchell in my path. Everyone else is already in class. Why do I have to run into him of all people?

He's walking toward me, face twisted in that permanently smug expression he wears. It truly is punchable. Everyone knows that person that's so annoying, the sound of their breathing can piss you off. That's Ethan.

"Finally getting expelled for beating someone else up?" he asks as a greeting.

"No, but I can clear my schedule for you," I snap.

He opens his mouth in a shocked expression. "Really? Threatening violence when we just lost a teacher? How could you say something so insensitive?"

I scoff. "Give me a break. Student council organized a

candlelit vigil for your fucking dog last month, but didn't even give a moment of silence for Mr. Ford."

"Are you seriously making light of my *dog* dying?"

So help me bisexual Jesus, I want to smack him. "A *person* died, you miserable shit stain. Any pet dying sucks, but come the hell on, Mr. Ford's dying is obviously way worse." I rub my hand across my eyebrow to try to contain the incoming headache.

"I'm not saying his passing wasn't also sad," Ethan argues. His face is red. "What does it matter anyway? Shouldn't you be running around with the Mystery Club or whatever?"

I clench my fingers into fists. Does he know that I'm back in the investigation? No one should know about that. Hell, they shouldn't even know we're investigating. "What does Mystery Club have to do with anything?"

"You're all making such a huge deal about looking for Big Willy. I heard Aimee's podcast." The damn podcast. I forgot.

"What does it matter to you anyway?" I ask.

Ethan rolls his eyes. "It doesn't. The Mystery Club will be done on Friday, so you can quit it, Nancy Drew."

Friday. The day of Spring Fest. Shit, it's coming up quick, and while there are new members, the club still doesn't have a faculty advisor.

I keep my expression calm and grip my backpack to get some of the tension out. "Why do you even care if we're looking into Big Willy? Almost seems like you have something to hide."

Is it possible that Ethan is Big Willy? I wouldn't put it past him. He's probably smart enough, and I could definitely see him keeping that list of clients as a form of blackmail. His name was on the list, but it would be easy enough for him to add it quickly to make it look like he was only a buyer.

Ethan laughs. "Everyone has something to hide. That's not a *mystery*. It's politics. I'm trying to help by suggesting you stay out of it." Ethan adjusts the sleeves of his suit. "Make sure the room is cleared by the end of the week."

He gives a smile that feels more like the finger, turns on his overpriced heel, and walks off. I have to swallow my anger. I'm already on the way to meet with Principal Daniels, I don't need an actual reason to get in trouble. I keep breathing on a count as I walk the rest of the hallway.

I'm so distracted keeping my heart rate low that I accidentally bump into Emma, who walks out of the office the same moment I approach, but instead of saying anything, she makes a point not to look at me and keeps her head high as she quickly strides away.

Weird. Does she have something against me?

Oh no. Did Kyle tell her what happened in the locker room? Maybe they actually are in a relationship and she's mad that I saw him naked? I try to push away the visuals involving that memory, thankful that it wasn't Kyle I bumped into.

"Morning, Ms. Leslie," I say as I enter the main office.

"Gigi." She shakes her head. "What did you do this time?"

I shrug, plopping down onto one of the seats. "I'm actually not sure."

"No fights?"

"None. Scout's honor."

We're not counting the thing with Aimee. I didn't hit her and if I was going to get in trouble for yelling, it would have happened at that moment. Also not counting the thing with Cedar. That was hardly a fight. And apparently it inspired her to get a cute hair color. If anything, it was a helpful intervention.

I need to stop thinking about Cedar being cute.

Ms. Leslie doesn't seem convinced. "Did you miss gym again?"

"I'm going today." I cross my arms over my chest. "Bad move, I'm sure. I still can't find my uniform. And to make matters worse, we're starting the pickleball unit. What the hell is that? It wants to be tennis and Ping-Pong and isn't as fun as either."

Ms. Leslie's expression falls. Even her glasses droop. "I'm part of a pickleball league."

Of course she is.

"It's also a totally legitimate sport and a great way to get that cardio in, of course." It's not the most convincing response, but I already dug my hole. "The point is I've been better about showing up to class. It's not my fault things have been tough and I've been called to the office more lately."

"You've been missing class when you haven't been called to the office," she says.

It's a fair point.

"It's self-care, me time. I'm sensitive."

"Oh, that's not a word I'd use for you, sweetie."

I widen my eyes and blink twice. "Well, damn, Ms. Leslie. I'm not sure I want to know which words you would use."

She keeps her smile on full wattage. "Language. And speaking of self-care, Mrs. Goode is still available for all students."

Before I can make a promise I won't keep about not swearing or entering trauma teatime with Mrs. Goode, Principal Daniels steps out of his office. He looks like he also picked the wrong time to give up coffee or something, the bags under his eyes are so dark it's almost aesthetic.

"Ms. Ricci, come in." He gestures inside, and I have no choice but to follow him into the familiar office.

Principal Daniels doesn't say anything, just takes a seat at his desk and gives me a stern look. I may as well be back at the doctor's office, when they said *something* is wrong because it isn't normal to pendulum between constipation and diarrhea like a metronome needle, and finally figured it is IBS most likely, and I should just try eating better and keep exercising, even though I only can do one of the two because clean eating is for rich people.

Same kind of stomach-pain-filled, am-I-okay tension.

"I'm sure you suspect why I called you in," Principal Daniels says.

I give a hopeful smile. "You missed me?"

He doesn't find it funny. "We received a tip that you were involved in a recent incident."

"Sean called me over after the break-in already happened, so I won't be much help. He and Cedar told the cops everything though, so not sure why you need me."

Principal Daniels sighs. "We heard about that, but I'm talking about the other incident."

"Oh, the Luca thing? I thought you already decided that was an accident."

"No, not that," he says impatiently. "I'm talking about something *you* did."

Something I did? What the hell did I do?

I lean back in the chair. "Okay then, no, I don't actually know why I'm here."

Principal Daniels gives a big sigh. "This isn't the time for joking, Gianna."

"Apparently it is because I feel like I'm being pranked right now. I didn't do anything."

This sigh is even longer and more drawn-out than the first, and it's accompanied by a forehead rub. He must be seriously stressed. I'm assuming a death and near-death at your school will do that to you. That has nothing to do with me though.

Principal Daniels puts his hands down on the surface of the desk, maroon shirt riding up his arms. He looks directly at me. "It's about the recent fire."

My face heats. How did he find out about that? "It was a complete accident. I seriously didn't mean it."

"You started the fire on accident?"

"I . . . *What?* Started the fire? No, I was . . . I accidentally ran into Kyle Sinclair . . . by the bathrooms at gym."

"What?" Mr. Ford asks. "Why would you sound guilty about that?"

That's a good question.

"We . . . Well, I was running. When I shouldn't have been. And . . . we hit our heads. Hard. I mean, no, nothing was hard. I mean . . ." I close my mouth before my brain short-circuits. "Why would you think I had anything to do with starting the fire?"

"We received a tip—"

"Oh, a *tip*. Even though I have no past behavior that suggests I would do that?"

He almost laughs at that but, aside from a small twitch, remains serious. "You have a history of violence in this school."

"I've gotten into fights; I've never done *arson*."

"It's clear that you have a certain upbringing that allows for behavior like . . ."

I don't allow him to finish that sentence. I stand up so quickly from the seat, it pushes back with a loud screech that might scratch the floor.

"What the fuck are you getting at?" I snap.

"Watch your tone and language, Ms. Ricci." Principal Daniels shakes his head. "I'm simply saying it's clear that your mother being a female fighter influenced you to make bad—"

"My mother is a *fighter*. They fought in the female division, but you damn well know their pronouns now, and words matter." I'm shaking, looking down at him sitting at his smug little desk. "And the reason they allow for my behavior is because they know I don't fight anyone who doesn't deserve it." I could punch him too. Mom has come here enough for him to know not to misgender them. And I hate when people talk like that. Plus, Mom hardly allows for my behavior. They are the first to scold me when I fight off the mats, regardless of my reasoning. "You don't know what goes into fighting, how hard people work, train, the dedication they have. They are elite athletes, not criminals. So with all due respect, Principal Daniels, shut the hell up and leave my mom out of this."

My chest tightens and my skin burns. I clench my hands together.

"I apologize for offending you," Principal Daniels says finally. "But that doesn't change the fact that someone did come forward with information regarding the fire and you weren't in your class when it happened."

"I wasn't in class, no, but Kyle Sinclair was with me. Ask him."

Principal Daniels frowns. "I'll talk to him. You said you were by the bathrooms?"

I squeeze my lips together. "Locker rooms. Outside of them. Yeah."

I don't know if Kyle is going to tell the whole truth, but I'd rather get in trouble for sneaking into the boys' locker

room than for starting a fire that literally destroyed potential evidence of the case I'm back trying to investigate. After
Big Willy went all wild in the you-know-too-much threat
department, our best bet is to just figure out who they are
before someone else gets killed.

But this doesn't even make sense. One person says it
*might* have been me and Principal Daniels has to waste my
time and misgender my mom?

My eyes drop. I don't want to look at him. I'm still pissed.
If he wasn't the principal of the school, I would've thrown
hands already. Does that make me the kind of person he's
saying? Is immediately resorting to fighting bad?

People basically cheered when I choked out Matt Russell, so that certainly didn't pin me as the bad guy. Nobody
gets mad at Spider-Man for beating up shitty people. It's
not like *I* killed Mr. Ford.

That's the person they should be fucking concerned
about.

"This is a serious accusation, but I will talk with Mr.
Sinclair." Principal Daniels's voice drones on, but I hardly
listen. "Gianna? Do we have an understanding?"

Principal Daniels's tone is hard. He seriously thinks I
had something to do with this. My mind scrambles to put
together some options for what he could've said last, but my
subconscious needs to get it together too.

"Yes," I say, because it seems right. My thoughts are else-
where.

It's like he can see right through the response.

"Just because we don't have concrete evidence now doesn't mean we aren't taking this extremely seriously." Principal Daniels lifts his eyebrows to make the point. "But if we find anything, and I mean anything, that points to you as the one who did it, that's the last straw. We're talking about expulsion."

"I understand," I say. "Didn't do it though."

Principal Daniels takes that as a promise I won't step out of line, and I still think he's convinced I had something to do with it.

But what I really understand is that Big Willy is trying to frame me for the fire, and I need to know why.

Looks like the "stress less" suggestion from my doctor on combating my IBS won't be happening anytime soon.

I stomp out of the office and almost immediately run into Mrs. Goode, standing in the middle of the hallway like a sleep-paralysis demon waiting for me.

"Gianna," she greets warmly. "I haven't seen you in my office yet."

"And you probably won't," I confirm.

I'm not in the mood to uncomfortably talk about feelings and shit. I don't have time for that. Not when Big Willy is planning something and the Mystery Club won't even have a closet by the end of the week.

Mrs. Goode hands me a hall pass that's already signed with her name. I notice the date and time were intentionally left blank. "For whenever you might need it," she says.

That's actually kind of cool.

"All right," I say. "Thanks."

I might not have real plans to make a visit to Mrs. Goode, but I have to respect that she basically gave me a get-out-of-detention-free card, especially since I just came from the principal's office.

I'll need it, considering if I don't find out who Big Willy is soon, I might actually be the one to get arrested.

# FOURTEEN

## Keep Your Real Friends Close and Invite Your Cute Enemies Over

**MARI ASSIGNED THE** Mystery Club members different tasks in an attempt to really push the investigation forward. She and Aimee would take the first page of the client list to try to get any info on Big Willy, Sean and Benji would take the second page, and I would get the third with Cedar. Mostly, I think Mari wants me to have time to apologize to Cedar, though she doesn't know about the conversation we had after I stormed out of the theater.

Which is why I'm walking toward Cedar's red Tesla in the senior lot in what might be one of the most awkward moments of my recent memory. Well, if not for the whole locker-room thing with Kyle. We're a little too quiet. It makes it all the easier to hear the loud and angry person from a few cars down.

"I swear, if you tell anyone, I will literally kill you," they snap.

I grab on to Cedar and practically push her down to hide between the two Toyotas closest to us. Nearly a second later, Ethan Mitchell storms by on his phone. His face is twisted with anger. While Cedar has a moment of confusion, his voice is enough to keep her quiet.

Ethan looks around before lowering his voice slightly.

"I don't give a shit. That goes against everything we agreed on." He looks especially pale, but his nose and cheeks flame red. "You're fucking dead if you do, man."

He hangs up the phone and gets into his nearby car. Cedar and I barely breathe until Ethan pulls away.

"What the hell was that?"

First Ethan warns me about investigating Big Willy and now this?

"*That* was Ethan becoming a prime suspect," I say.

"Um . . . are you two good?"

We turn to the voice. It's Jane Neal, holding her keys. To the car that we are both crouched next to, leaning in close to each other. I quickly stand.

"Um, we were just . . ."

Jane gives a knowing look and smiles. She gently tosses her box braids over her shoulder, adjusting her backpack. "Oh, no need to tell me. I got you."

My face is heating. It's not that I'm embarrassed to be caught with Cedar; it's not like I'm doing anything. It's just that one of the coolest seniors was perceiving me at all.

"It really wasn't like . . ."

"It's cool." Jane taps a pin on her dark jean jacket. It's a bisexual pride pin, between a pin of a corgi and one of Jamaica's flag. "I ship it."

Now both me and Cedar are completely red.

"I'll see you both at Spring Fest, right?" she asks.

I nod, and Cedar seems to follow.

"Sweet. Have fun." Jane winks before getting into her Corolla, and both Cedar and I awkwardly head over to her car.

I'm so focused on trying to cool my face, I can barely think of what we witnessed with Ethan.

"Where do you want to go?" Cedar asks.

We thought it would be a good idea to look outside of school property, to give Big Willy less of a reason to murder my brother in his low-budget performance costume. We did not, however, actually think of a destination before walking to her car in the senior lot.

There's no way I'm going to her house to hang out. Her parents are the worst. They know that I've gotten in trouble for fights, and Luca told me Cedar's dad tried to stop her from being friends with him because of my reputation. Not that he likes Luca either, but there's not a convenient excuse that makes him look like less of a Christian extremist asshole.

"Your parents hate me," I start, "so we can go to my place."

"Wow, you move quickly, Gigi. Buy a girl a drink first," Cedar deadpans before starting the car. It's a strange situation, being in her expensive electric car and her making almost flirty comments toward me. "Also, don't feel bad. My parents hate everyone queer. They're cutting me off once I graduate because I'm a lesbian."

I'm not surprised that Mr. and Mrs. Martin are homophobic, but I guess I didn't really consider what it was like for Cedar living with them. I didn't even know for sure that she was gay. I just assumed mostly because she basically told me she likes Mari and because she knows everyone's birth chart.

"I'm sorry," I say. It comes out kind of like a question because I don't know how to deal in this situation.

"It's not your fault." She cracks a smile. "It sucks, but I've been getting my own revenge. I use my dad's credit card to donate directly to queer people who need it online. It's honestly super easy to log into his computer and change up some of his records to account for it."

"Isn't that illegal?" I ask. I can't imagine having the kind of money where you don't have to track spending that closely.

Cedar shrugs. "You aren't recording me. And being a piece of shit father that basically neglects and emotionally abuses their kid is also illegal, so we'll call it even." She shrugs it off, keeping her expression light. "I can hardly even call it hacking, but maybe someday he'll regret enrolling me in all those computer camps. Or using the same password and pin code for literally everything."

While I definitely recycle the same two or three password options and can't make fun of him on that front, Cedar seems so *cool*. Not in the usual way of being slightly over-the-top and unapproachable. I didn't expect this. I guess there's a lot about her that I didn't really expect—or notice.

Do I just not pay attention to people?

"How long have they known?" I ask. "About you?"

"Well, I've been doing the anonymous donations longer, but they only found out I'm a lesbian last week. Which is kind of shocking considering I feel like I haven't even tried to hide it well. But I actually told them the day we broke into Mr. Ford's room and you called me out on my bullshit. I realized I was tired of pretending." Her voice doesn't betray her by showing any emotion. It's almost impressive how everything can be a joke. "And it went super well. Dad threatened to kick me out of the house, but Mom cried and convinced him to let me stay until graduation." She notices me start to open my mouth. "Not because she cares. Because we have family already coming in for graduation and she doesn't want to look bad."

Well, shit.

Cedar continues, not missing a beat. "Since I won't have to keep caring about what they think, I dyed my hair and started wearing the clothes I like and Mom always said I'm not the right shape for." She rolls her eyes. "Her way of saying I'm fat. Which isn't even an insult. She's just a bitch."

That makes a lot of sense as to why her whole vibe and appearance changed recently. Her clothes before had been loose-fits and all black, but today she has on high-waisted jeans and a light green, fitted sweater.

"I like you like this," I find myself saying. "It's hot."

Wait. I'm not supposed to admit she's hot. She'll never let me live that down. I brace myself for the teasing that will only set off my blush that affects my nose way too much compared to the rest of my face.

Instead she simply says, "Thank you. I like me like this too. It's nice to be able to be open about being a lesbian. Being kicked out isn't ideal, but it's almost like this weight lifted off me because they already did that. One of the worst outcomes that could happen already happened and I'm alive. I'll be okay."

That's a positive way of looking at things. If I were in her situation, I'd probably be acting up and making a fool of myself out of anger. "I'm sorry," I say, not sure what else I can tell her.

Cedar sighs, turning the wheel as she pulls out of the school lot. "Seriously, I'm okay. I do wish I had a mom like you and Luca. They're so cool. I'm not completely bitter and jealous, like I'm glad you have them. I wouldn't wish parents who hate you on anyone, especially not the people I like."

My chest flutters a little bit at the "people I like" part. Am I sexually repressed or something? Why am I getting excited like she's confessing her feelings for me, which she *isn't*, and like she isn't Cedar, which she *is*.

"You can probably live with us if you need to," I say. "Luca will be in Chicago, so his room's open."

We'd have to ask Mom and Dad, but I don't think they'd say no given the circumstances. They love Cedar, although I sometimes wondered if it was mostly to annoy me. Maybe they saw all these sides of her that I somehow missed.

Cedar gives a little smile but keeps her eyes locked on the road.

"I have a friend downtown who goes to Cleveland State. I'll probably crash with them once I start taking classes there." There's a beat before she adds, "Maybe I'll hit the Riccis up for the holidays though."

"Our Christmas Eve is the best," I say. "If you like seafood."

"I'm not picky."

"Then you'll be fine."

The fact that I'm hanging out and getting along with Cedar Martin is almost harder to believe than the fact that we're all being threatened by a killer with a bad pun for a name. For some reason, it also seems to have a similar effect in messing up my resting heart rate.

There's not a single red light on the way home, although I live close to the school, so it's a short drive anyway. Cedar parks in front of the house. I'm half surprised she remembers it. While she's been over a lot, even my aunt sometimes gets the address wrong since the one-story boxes on our street all look the same.

There's an awkward moment where we both sort of sit there.

"Want to come in?" I ask, like that wasn't the damn plan to begin with.

I'm pretty sure Mom has a late shift today, and Dad usually works out before he starts his job because nice arms give him better tips, so with Luca at rehearsal, the house should be empty. Although announcing that we'll be alone seems kind of weird. Like I'm trying to hit on her immediately after she came out to me.

"Yeah," Cedar says. "Okay."

It's definitely a weird situation. She's acting like she's new here.

We get out of the car and walk up to the side door. Without really thinking, I enter and stand by the stairs to go down to my room. Cedar shuts and locks the door for me.

"We're going to your room?" she asks.

It's only then that I remember none of Luca's friends have been in my room before. Sean's the only person outside my family who has. But I feel like it's kind of rude to say no now, and who cares if Cedar judges me for it? She's always making fun of me anyway.

"Yeah, I guess," I say, trying to keep cool.

It's not embarrassing. If I keep telling myself that, it won't seem embarrassing.

Although once we make it down the basement stairs and turn the corner past the heater and laundry to get to my bedroom setup, it's like I'm seeing it for the first time. All the dozens of plushies scattered about, the obvious favorites placed carefully on my bed. The posters of random adorable cats as well as a pride flag hanging over light pink walls.

It's so . . . cute.

Even the display of my previous jiu-jitsu belts hardly looks intimidating when the wooden display holding them is covered in cat stickers.

Cedar doesn't seem all that fazed. "Is that a Pusheenicorn plushie?"

It's the most excited I've ever heard her sound. I don't know how to respond to that. It's not like I can lie when he is proudly on my bed next to Amber and Gingersnap.

"Yes," I say. "It is."

"Queer icon," Cedar says. "I love Pusheen."

"Me too."

"Really, I never would have guessed." Cedar steps across the room to point directly at a Pusheen poster. "I'm shocked."

Yeah, I guess it is kind of obvious.

"Can I sit here?" Cedar points to a fluffy pink chair with a stuffed T. rex on it to the right of the bookshelf. I nod. After placing her backpack on the floor, she sinks into the seat, holding the T. rex on her lap.

"I know we're supposed to be questioning some of Big Willy's clients," I start, "but after what we witnessed today, I feel like we should be looking into Ethan, right?"

Still with the T. rex nestled in her arm, she reaches into her backpack and takes out a new laptop. I don't know if it was her parents or insurance, but it does make me feel better that she was able to get it replaced so quickly.

"The thing with Ethan was super weird and we should totally look into it." Cedar happens to spot the recommendation letter from Mr. Ford. "What's that?"

As if I needed a reason to keep the embarrassment going. "Mrs. Ford gave it to me. It's a letter Mr. Ford wrote."

"Can I read it?"

I shrug but then force a smile. "You can see that *some* people appreciate me."

Cedar skims the letter, and I try not to look too embarrassed or reveal that it meant a lot to me.

"I knew he was a man of taste," Cedar says. "But what's with the online calendar note? Is that his password?"

I feel like I skimmed over that part, considering I was a little preoccupied with trying not to cry. Cedar doesn't even wait for an answer. She is already typing away at her laptop.

"What are you doing?" I ask.

"I think all the teachers use Outlook. If this is really his password, we can log into the online version." Her eyes widen. "Holy shit, I'm in." I nearly fall over scrambling to her side to look at the computer. Cedar scrolls past emails until she gets to the Friday before last.

Sent only about an hour before the end of the school day was an email from Watch Your Back.

Cedar clicks it open, but the message is short.

*This is your last warning.*

*Give me the flash drive.*

"Shit," I say. "I mean, we knew they killed him, but this is literally evidence. If we just figure out who Watch Your Back slash Big Willy slash Miss Mystery is, we still have something."

Cedar bites her lip. "I'm really sorry. I should have kept better watch on the flash drive or got it done faster . . ."

"It's not your fault. I don't even know how they knew you'd be at Sean's place with it."

"Maybe they overheard us talking in class and assumed?" Cedar's hazel eyes grow wide enough to match the marbles of the plushie still in her arms. "Ethan Mitchell is in that class."

"So it could really be him."

Cedar smiles. "Are you ready to search for Big Willy online?"

I groan. "Somehow not what I expected to hear the first time I brought a girl home."

I lean over to grab a large pillow plushie so I can really settle in next to the chair. Cedar looks down at me.

"If we make it out of this alive, maybe the next time will go more how you expected."

My nose is red as I reach up to lightly shove her arm. "Can we keep focused on this totally serious investigation we're doing?"

I knew she would resort to teasing at some point.

And something's wrong with me, because while my face is too hot and my heart is too quick, I don't entirely mind.

# FIFTEEN

## All's Fair in Love and Murder

**FROM HIS SOCIAL** media, Ethan doesn't have a clear alibi on the day of Mr. Ford's murder, so he remains the top suspect. Cedar has a friend from the gaming club she's in who is also a member of the student council and confirmed that they don't have any after-school obligations on Friday.

We give Mari and Sean an update and agree to look into Ethan more tomorrow after school, but after getting nowhere messaging some of Big Willy's clients, we decide to take a break for the day.

Cedar stays for dinner and even decides to hang out a while after. I promised Mom to train with them, so while they pull out our cheap puzzle-piece mats since I missed class today, Cedar hangs out with Luca. I thought they'd go into his room so I could avoid the embarrassment of a girl watching my mom kick my ass, but no. They thought it would be fun to hang out in the living room, cozy on the couch with the TV turned on, but with my struggles in full view.

Mom isn't going easy on me in the slightest today. I don't know if they think it's funny to embarrass me in front of

Cedar, but it's not like I have a competition coming up or anything.

"Are you sure you can't stay here tonight?" Luca asks Cedar on the couch. "I mean, seriously. I'll sleep on the couch if you need me to, but my bed is big enough to share."

Cedar eyes her phone before looking back at him. "My dad won't be okay with it."

"I can kick your dad's ass," Mom suggests to Cedar as she easily gets me in side control. "What's the point of all this training if not beating up homophobic men?"

Luca nods. "And you're almost eighteen. Would they even really care?"

"I'm not eighteen yet, and yeah, probably, for appearances or whatever."

I can't add my opinion because Mom's crossface is killer. Their shoulder digs into my cheek, pressing my face against the mat and making it a hell of a lot harder to even attempt to hip escape. I struggle to get back my frames, playing a little dirty as I dig my knuckles into their neck to make them create enough space that I can work to recover my guard.

Mom's no stranger to being uncomfortable or in pain, so they're hardly out of breath. "Still, sweetie. Whenever you need to be here, don't even ask." They look up at Cedar and smile. "My offer's not off the table."

"Don't get me wrong, I'd love to see you beat up my dad," Cedar says. "It would almost be as good as Gigi choking out Matt Russell."

It really was an iconic event, and despite myself, I smile

at Cedar for acknowledging it. Her lips curl in response, eyes meeting mine. It's almost weirdly a moment, but in those few seconds I let my guard down, figuratively and literally, Mom easily passes and slides into mount. I'm back to defending against an arm bar or whatever else she'll smoothly go for.

"Don't encourage her," Mom groans. They look down at me. "If you get in another fight this year, I'm not paying for your jiu-jitsu membership."

"I literally work there sometimes," I argue. "And it's a little late for that anyway. I already know how to fight."

Mom considers that, still pressuring down. "I'll take away all your plushies."

"That's *unfair*."

"Then stop fighting random boys at school."

I think what they really mean is stop getting *caught* fighting random boys at school.

I manage to make enough room for my knee and escape into half guard, but Mom goes fullspeed ahead with their unholy amount of cardio and immediately pushes past my guard, gets a Kimura grip, and takes my back like it's the easiest thing in the world. I try to defend, but they get a bow and arrow choke and I'm tapping before I know it.

I'm out of breath, and not just from the choke, so I sit back on the mat. "Okay, can we break?"

"You wouldn't be tired if you trained more consistently."

I've had enough of this person. "Yes, Mom, I know how it works."

The worst part is, I do really like training. When I'm fighting, I don't have to think about anything else. How I'm not enough, how I'm afraid I don't know who I am, how some murderer might be after the people I care most about. Training is only defending myself, thinking about the next move. Plus, it doesn't normally come with the consequences actual fights do, so that's a bonus.

But things have been a little strange lately. Especially since my grades dropped immensely in eighth grade, and Mom and Dad thought it would be better for me to stop competing. I didn't really mind. It was hard to compete with the teens that were literally homeschooled so they could spend all day at the gym or were able to afford one-on-one lessons with famous coaches.

It would be great to train multiple times a day, but I still have school, and friends, and sometimes even on the days I have time and really want to go, I'll have an IBS flare and can't stray far from the toilet for fear of shitting my gi.

I look over toward Cedar. "I promise, next time you come over, I won't ditch you to grapple my mom."

She laughs. "I don't mind. I have Luca." She hugs his head to her chest.

"Happy to be second choice, I guess," he deadpans before shrugging it off and kissing her cheek.

"I don't think I've seen you come over to hang out with Gigi," Mom says to Cedar. "Since when are you two so close?"

Cedar doesn't miss a beat. "Since she threatened me."

Mom laughs. "Gigi, you can't be so aggressive to the girls you like. What are you, a caveman?"

Cedar's face goes red, and I feel bad Mom's putting her on the spot while misreading the situation.

"It's not like that." I lightly shove Mom, even though that much movement of my arm hurts. "Cedar's helping me with . . . a project."

I don't exactly think now is the time to admit we're looking into the murder despite the threats from the person who did it. Clearly, they were bullshit, as Watch Your Back didn't stop when I tried to. I don't even think I should admit we *know* it was a murder. Mom would freak.

"A project?" Luca raises an eyebrow, looking between the two of us.

"Yeah, you're not the only one with good grades." Cedar flicks him and he tries to bat her away like a cat. "I'm a much better tutor."

"I thought Sean tutored you?" Mom asks me.

I shrug. "I need a lot of help."

"You should've invited him over to train."

"Luca would love that," Cedar says, unable to resist.

His face is bright red.

Mom's expression fills with hope. "Luca, you like Sean? Is he queer? I love Sean, that's perfect, he can still be my son-in-law."

"Oh my god, Mom, stop." Luca's phone drops to the couch cushion as his arms try to cover his deepening blush. The face turning fire-engine red at the slightest embarrassment is something both Ricci siblings unfortunately inherited. "I don't know if he's queer, and even if he is, that doesn't mean he likes me."

"Gigi, don't you know?" Mom puts a hand to their heart. "Sean's the best. He's at least three thousand times better than your last boyfriend. Jeremy? A theater gay can't date another theater gay, y'all are too loud."

Luca rolls his eyes. "You didn't like him because he walked on your mats with shoes."

Mom is completely serious. "I stand by that."

"They were these cheap mats. It's not like he went to your academy and did it."

"It's the principle. He was annoying, and you deserve better," Mom says. "Like Sean. Sean is better."

I mean, Sean won't step on mats with shoes, even if they are these cheap mats that have seen better days. His mom won't let him train at the academy because of the price, but Mom gives him free lessons, so he has an idea of the basics.

"Stop," Luca groans, dragging out the vowel like it's a song.

"Sean's some kind of queer," I say. "If he thinks you're cute and you tag him in cat videos, he's down." I glance at my brother, currently curled up in a ball. "Not to say that he'd find you attractive. I'm obviously the better-looking sibling."

"Maybe in a funhouse mirror," Luca mumbles into his legs. "We all know I'm the prettier one, Gigi, you aren't fooling anyone."

The sad part is I can't really argue; he totally is the prettier one. He's also smarter and can sing. I got the muscles, I guess, but that has yet to really help me out in life.

Unfair.

"Luca's personality aside," Mom starts, "you're telling me there's a chance."

"I hate you all." Luca pulls the blanket over his face before immediately peeking over it. "But I mean, there is a chance, right?"

"Totally," Cedar says. "I mean, he saved your life, right?"

"Right?!" Luca exclaims. "Before anyone else even reacted, he was already there. He put himself in danger for me. And I swear, there was a moment. We had a *moment*."

I don't want to bring up Sean's just-like-rescuing-a-cat comment. "For sure."

"It wouldn't be weird, though?" Luca asks. "Me and Sean?"

"Not if he's into it," I say. As much as I want to cheer on my brother, Sean's also my friend, so if he's not interested, I'll support him. On the bright side, if Luca gets turned down, he gets to leave the entire state in a few months. I, on the other hand, don't get the same luxury.

"Seriously," Cedar says. "Nothing wrong with dating your sibling's friend, you're only like a year apart."

"And long distance can totally work," Mom adds.

Cedar leans onto him. "It's not even that far."

Luca smiles a little. "Unrelated, but I was talking with Gigi, and I think y'all should get a cat."

"From the shelter Sean volunteers at?" Mom asks, eyebrow raised.

He's not even looking at any of us. "That way, there can be at least *one* cute thing in the house without me."

"There're plenty of cute things," Cedar says. "Just look at Gigi's room."

Now *I'm* blushing. She didn't have to bring my plushies into it. Luca's supposed to be the one we're teasing.

"I'm fine with it," Mom says. "You'll be paying for yourself, so all our extra money can go toward the cat."

"Wow," Luca says. "I feel so loved." But he's smiling.

My brother is so easy to read. He's like the worst liar, so I don't really get how he's so good at acting.

Cedar glances down at her phone. "I should probably get going."

Mom makes a face. "Ew, are you sure?"

"Unfortunately." Cedar grabs her backpack and stands. "But the benefit of a big house is that I won't really have to see them."

"Well, let me know if you need anything," Mom says. "I get how shitty it can be. And you're so brave. I'm old, and I'm still too afraid to come out to my parents."

Cedar's eyes look a little glassy. "I think coming out to yourself is just as brave," she says.

Luca pulls her into a hug, which is probably for the best because Mom was ready to give her a hug as well, but they're covered in nearly as much sweat as I am. "I'm glad you're able to feel like yourself now. As Shakespeare said in

*Hamlet*, 'to thine own self be true,' because that is arguably Shakespeare's gayest play."

"Save the theater kid shit, Luca," I grumble. "No one cares about *Hamlet*."

He looks offended, but when Cedar sniffles, he gets over himself so he can pull her in tighter. "Sorry, I'm sorry. Actors, we're the worst."

"No, I'm sorry," Cedar says. "For being terrible, for not being myself, for being scared." It's like a little piece of her broke off, and the words rush out along with her emotions. It's almost strange. Another new side of Cedar Martin.

One that sort of makes me want to hug her too.

Mom stands from the mat and puts a hand on her shoulder, their touch gentle.

"Nothing wrong with being scared," Mom says. "I'm scared all the time." They laugh, a smile showing off the little space between their front teeth they never got fixed. "And honestly, I've always liked that you had a little attitude. I don't trust people who are constantly nice. Makes me feel like they have something to hide." Mom thinks for a moment before meeting eyes with Luca. "Except Sean. He's just a good guy."

They're not wrong. My whole family can start his fan club.

"Thanks, Mx. Ricci," Cedar says from Luca's shoulder.

"If you really must go, Gigi can walk you out." Mom gives me a smile. "Since she invited you over."

It's not a suggestion. It's a Midwest-Polite order.

I get up as Cedar peels herself from my still-blushing

175

brother and walk her over to the front door. I know Mom and Luca are one hundred percent both the people to listen in, so I step outside with her and shut the door behind us.

The cool air slams against my sweaty clothes, and it is refreshing and terrible at the same time. But it's not like I'm going to be out here for long, so I might as well deal with it.

"I can walk you to your car," I say.

It's dark by now and hard to make out her features.

"I think I'll be safe down the driveway." Cedar looks in the direction of the street. "It's a long ten to fifteen feet, but I've trained for it."

"Well, you never know. There could be killers out there."

It's not funny anymore. It's like the night grows silent. The air so still I almost don't feel it.

Cedar breaks the tension. "It's okay. You can admit you want to spend more time with me."

"Just because I don't *dislike* you doesn't mean I want to spend time with you."

"It's a start, though, isn't it?"

We walk down the driveway. And it really is short, but we're moving slowly, taking slow steps, like her words secretly caught me.

"What do you like about Mari?" Cedar asks abruptly.

It's so out of the blue it stops me in my tracks. Halfway down the driveway, standing outside in my spats, unable to function.

Why would she ask that now?

"I guess . . . she saw me when no one else did."

There's a long pause, all sound swallowed into the night.

"Huh," Cedar says finally. She's not looking at me. "But if you're so focused on one person, how do you know who else is looking?"

I don't know what to say to that, so I don't say anything. Instead, it's like we both fall back into motion at the same time, stepping toward her car. My stomach sinks with the weight of a terrible feeling because something doesn't look right. When we get closer, I can see it: the window is broken, cracks spiderwebbing through half the glass that remains attached to the driver-side door.

"Shit," Cedar murmurs.

"Did you have something in the car?" I ask.

I don't know what else they'd be looking for. They already got the flash drive.

She shakes her head. My foot crunches over glass as I step up to the door and look inside. There's something on the seat. The glow of the streetlight isn't quite enough to see well, so I turn on the flashlight of my phone and shine it inside of the car. There's no one inside.

But there is something.

Pictures. Of my house. Of Sean, Cedar, and I outside his apartment. Of Mari, Sean, Benji, and Aimee in the Mystery Club room. Of Aimee and me during the fire drill, the client list between us.

And over the scattered pictures, in a red the color of blood, words are drawn out to spell a pretty clear message.

*Who's Next?*

# SIXTEEN

## The Murderous Essayist

**CEDAR ENDED UP** staying a lot later than intended, since we had to report the break-in to the police. Her dad took forever to arrive and was nearly impossible to calm down, so the already-delayed questioning from both the cops (annoying) and my mom (terrifying) had been stretched into hours. I'm lacking in sleep, having a bad day with my almost-as-irritable-as-I-am bowels, and pissed off that this Watch Your Back/Big Willy bitch not only followed us home but continued on their B&E spree with Cedar's car.

So when I see Ethan post to his Instagram story that he's in the student council room before class starts, I conveniently forget that Mari had me promise not to confront him without actual evidence.

"Gianna Ricci," Ethan says. "Didn't peg you as the type to show up early."

"I have to pick a good spot to skip class," I say. "If I don't come early, the stoners get all the nice views, and then where am I supposed to complete my Satanic rituals?"

"You don't strike me as a Satanist," Ethan says, still writing. "Dropout, maybe."

"Unfortunately for both of us, I've got nothing better to do than be here."

Ethan's sense of humor must be all used up because he doesn't crack a smile, just looks up at me with a stern glare. "If you have a petition or something, you can always come to our regularly scheduled meetings."

I step up to the desk and give him my best smile. "Not necessary. This won't be long, and I only need to speak with you."

His face scrunches like he can't imagine why I would want to talk to him.

"Don't get your panties in a twist, Ethan. I'm not asking you to Spring Festival." I toss my backpack onto the floor as I fall into the seat in front of him. "I just want to talk for a moment about Mr. Ford."

"Why would I want to talk about Mr. Ford?"

"Oh, I don't know," I say. I make a show of trying to think about it. "Maybe because he knew that you're a goddamn cheater."

Technically, I don't know how much Mr. Ford knew, but if he had a flash drive of evidence that Ethan was willing to kill for, it's probably safe to say that he knew enough.

Ethan's eyes narrow. "What are you trying to do here?"

"I'm trying to work with you, Ethan. Come to an agreement." I lean back in the chair with my spine straight like good posture will give the impression I know exactly what I am trying to do here. "Look. You're no fan of the Mystery Club. You were unaccounted for when Mr. Ford died. And I have evidence that Mr. Ford knew you were cheating."

I don't, but I'm desperate. And if he is too, maybe he'll fall for my bluff. Besides, in the extremely unlikely situation he isn't Big Willy, he still was on the list of clients, so he did cheat in some way.

His body is tense, but I can tell he's trying to remain calm. I got him. "What are you getting at?"

"Someone is threatening me, Ethan. The people I care about too, and I would sure like to know who it is." I give a theatrical sigh that would make Luca proud. "Unfortunately, it really has been looking like it might be you."

"It's not."

"Then talk."

He won't look at me. "I don't have to tell you anything."

I stand from the chair and step behind him to put a hand on his shoulder. It would be comforting, maybe, except before he can react, I drop into position for a rear naked choke, twisting him in his seat. I don't apply pressure, but my elbow is locked on the center of his neck, my face practically against his so I can keep my voice low.

"You *don't* have to tell me anything. Just like I *don't* have to give you a chance, Ethan. This is me being nice and I really don't think you want to see me angry."

He's completely stiff. His foot kicks out and he tries to stomp my toes.

"Fun tip," I whisper. "Don't focus on feet when there's already arms around your neck. You gotta address the biggest problem first." Now his lower body freezes up. I can feel his heart pounding. "My biggest problem is this murderer trying to fuck with me and my family. You're saying it's not you, but what you aren't saying is a single reason as to why I should believe you."

Mom would kill me if I get in trouble for choking out someone again. But desperate times call for desperate measures and the big thing is that I'm only *threatening* to choke him . . . and just can't let myself get caught.

"Murderer?" His voice squeaks. He tries to pull on my choking arm, but it's already locked in and he's not even that strong anyway. "What are you talking about?"

"Here's what I think," I continue. "Mr. Ford found out you've been behind a lot of cheating. Since that's a bad look for Mr. Squeaky Clean Student Body President, you decided to take it out on Mr. Ford. Put yourself back in the clear to save whatever scholarship is allowing you to study political science or some shit."

I tighten my grip just enough. I keep my breathing calm, emotions under check, to not let my anger get the best of me and choke him unconscious off the bat.

"Fine!" His strained voice escapes in a bark. "Mr. Ford emailed me to meet with him because he found out I've been buying from Big Willy!"

I'm so surprised, my hold almost loosens. Does that mean he really isn't Big Willy? Just a client?

"But I didn't kill him!" Ethan quickly continues. "I didn't even end up meeting with him. I swear. I just . . . I was going to meet with him, but I couldn't exactly do that when he *died*. And now you're telling me he was *killed*?"

It's hard to see his face from this angle, but his voice is strained and scared.

"Why should I believe you?" I ask. "That's motive."

"I wasn't even at school the afternoon he died. I was so worried about Mr. Ford turning me in, I went to my dad's firm to talk to him about my options. There's footage of me on the security cameras. When I heard Mr. Ford died, I saved it. Just in case. I couldn't have had anything to do with it because I was literally downtown."

He seems sincere enough. People probably tend to be when in danger of being choked. I'm not saying he is by any means a good person, but it doesn't seem like he's Big Willy. Besides, it's believable that he would run to his dad at the first sign of trouble.

"Can you show me the footage?" I ask.

"I'll show you, send it to you, whatever." He sniffs. "Just don't hurt me."

I relax my arms, pulling away from him, and the change in his breath is noticeable. "You're such a little bitch, Ethan, calm down and let me see it."

He pulls it up on his phone. I guess it was smart of him to save it. The footage is time-stamped, even though I can't hear whatever he's saying to Mr. Mitchell. There definitely seems to be crying and yelling on Ethan's part. Ew.

He couldn't have killed Mr. Ford.

"I heard you threatening someone," I say. "In the senior lot yesterday. What was that about?"

"That was Big Willy. I know he still has evidence of me cheating, so I was threatening him not to tell anyone. Someone said there was a list of clients going around."

Shit. Is Aimee still unable to keep her mouth shut?

"You have Big Willy's number?" I ask.

"It's a burner and he used a voice changer, so I have no idea who it is. I don't even know if it's a he, that's just what the edited voice sounded like. I threatened him into giving me a number because I didn't want emailed evidence. Of course, he still ended up sending me the essays through email. Asshole."

"Give me that number," I snap.

He scribbles it down and I snatch the note before turning away.

"You won't tell on me?" he asks. "Right?"

Tell on him? What is he? Ten?

I just shrug. I don't really give a shit about anyone cheating, but I can let him sweat.

"How do I know it's not really you who murdered Mr. Ford?" Ethan says. "You clearly could have choked him easily."

Damn, I didn't know the rumors were that bad. Are people saying that? They probably wouldn't find me so intimidating if they saw my ridiculous plushie collection.

"I liked Mr. Ford. I don't fight people I like unless we're sparring on the mats."

He swallows. "But the rumors are true, then?"

I snort. "I don't think you should be concerned over whether or not I almost killed someone. Not when there's someone in this school who has."

Ethan doesn't respond, just gulps with his scared and scrawny meerkat expression.

"Forward me any conversations you have with Big Willy," I say. "If it's a call, record it."

He nods, knowing it isn't a suggestion.

I gather my things and start to head toward the door before remembering his assholery with trying to kick Mari and Sean out of their club closet.

"The Mystery Club is going to figure out who this murderer is. So if you try to shut us down before that happens, I'm going to show you firsthand how I fight people I don't like. Understand?"

Ethan shoots up. "It's not me! It's coming from the principal; you need a faculty advisor to be a club and get an assigned room."

"Figure it out."

He lets out a huge sigh. "I can give you until Friday. They're all distracted by Spring Fest. But that's the best I can do. Seriously."

At least that gives us the rest of the week to try to convince another teacher to sign on. If one of us isn't murdered before that even happens. I shouldn't be thinking like this. With that kind of stress, I'll really be skipping class to spend the period in the bathroom, cradling my flushable wipes.

"Fine," I say. "I better see those Big Willy updates. And if you tell anyone about any of this, I will literally break your knees."

I don't bother to check his expression before walking out the door.

At the Mystery Club meeting, everyone's mind is on Big Willy and yes, I do know how that sounds. At least the murderer has a sense of humor, I guess. Something tells me Mr. Ford appreciated that part. Shockingly, Aimee is late, leaving the four of us to go through the client list, trying to get any intel on Big Willy.

I'm waiting on a response from one senior who admitted they used him a few times when I see Sean and Mari grinning at Mari's phone. There is no way they'd be smiling over this unless it was a lead they'd immediately share.

"Hey," I snap. "A little focus?"

"Sorry," Mari says quickly. "It's just, the next *Purrfect Meowder* book was announced. *You're Done Fur.* It looks amazing."

"So cool," Benji says, just because he's nice enough to lie.

I seriously can't with them.

But even I have to admit Mari looks adorable when all excited over her weird cat mysteries.

"We just need ten minutes to take a picture for the Cleveland Meowderheads," Sean says quickly. "Then we will be right back and totally focused."

I almost forgot they are literally part of a fan group. Which is saying something, since I painted on Sean's whiskers when they did a cosplay of the vet-assistant detective and her cat, Purrlock Holmes.

I wish I were joking.

I sigh. "No worries, take your fandom pictures."

They practically skip out of the room. I'm barely able to read the response (which seems to be going nowhere and reads more like a glowing testimonial) when Aimee comes rushing in.

"I'm sorry I'm late," she says quickly, "but one of my friends said she just got an essay back from Big Willy and will give it to us if we want . . . We can question her for intel!"

Well. It's better than nothing.

Which is why Benji and I follow Aimee to the other side of the school, where we head into the home ec room for Cooking Club. Of all the places to interrogate people, it's a pretty good one. Especially because they're making puppy chow. The human, delicious snack kind.

Peanut butter, chocolate, and powdered sugar over Chex is a god-tier combination.

"Hi, Aimee!" One of the girls in the club immediately bounds over. For some reason, her high-energy bubbliness isn't as annoying as Aimee's. "What's up?"

"Vicky!" They hug like they didn't see each other in class earlier. "I wanted to ask you about the Big Willy thing. Is Nicky around?"

A boy who has the exact shade of auburn hair and brown eyes that Vicky does walks over to us, holding a large bowl of puppy chow. "Always," he says.

"Wait . . ." I can't help the need for clarification. "Are you two siblings? And your names are Vicky and Nicky?"

Nicky gives a few solemn nods. "Twins. Our parents thought it would be cute, and it saves them the time of having to remember too many letters."

As someone who has been called Child Number Two multiple times by my mom when they were upset and couldn't get the name out fast enough, that makes a lot of sense. Plus, it is kind of cute, although that might be more because both Vicky and Nicky are good-looking, and beautiful people are my weakness.

"Here, sit down," Vicky says, gesturing to the stools at her station. "Have some puppy chow."

Nicky puts the bowl right in front of Benji and me, and I'm not saying I now have a crush on the Icky twins but I'm not *not* saying it.

"Oh, right," Aimee says, ignoring the snacks but having her journal at the ready. "These are some of my friends from Mystery Club, Benji and Gigi."

"Friends" is generous. I'm not that much of a dick to correct her though.

"Oh, we know," Nicky says. "Everyone knows Gianna Ricci."

I'm almost flattered.

Vicky's eyes are bright. "Did you really hit Ethan Mitchell with a lead pipe?"

Jesus.

"Gigi wouldn't even need a pipe," Benji says, but he's ignored.

"Where'd you get the pipe?" Nicky asks.

I don't even have the energy to argue. Instead I drop a handful of puppy chow in my mouth. "You don't have a pipe guy?"

"My dad's a plumber. Does that count?"

"Sure, Nicky, that counts."

Vicky laughs as she opens another bag of Chex. "He seems like a creep; you should have hit him harder."

I can't say she's wrong, but maybe I do have to hit Ethan with a lead pipe if he's telling people I threatened him. As long as he kept Mr. Ford out of the gossip, I can let it slide at least.

"What about Big Willy?" I ask, trying to keep on topic. "One of you has an essay?"

"Oh, we both do. I love Big Willy," Vicky says.

"Big Willy literally saved my life," Nicky adds.

I don't think they hear the words that they're saying, or my mind is more in the gutter than everyone else's. I swallow the laughter that tries to bubble up and maintain a somewhat serious expression.

"Can you show us the essay you mentioned to Aimee?" I ask.

Vicky uses her hand that isn't still coated in powdered sugar to pull up the essay on her phone and then hands it over to me. I read through it, but there isn't anything in particular that really stands out to me. It's on *Romeo and Juliet* and seems good but doesn't specifically point to anyone.

"We had a Shakespeare assignment and Big Willy killed it," she says. "Not surprisingly, I mean, they use the guy in their logo."

"Mr. Mora was literally obsessed with mine," Nicky says, pulling it up on his phone. "I've gotten As on my other essays, but he wrote comments on how good and unique this one was. So whoever Big Willy is, they are amazing."

Or a murderer. But you know.

Nicky slides his phone across the counter, and I look down at the essay.

My heart stops at the title.

"To Be or Not to Be Yourself: The Queer Implications of Shakespeare's *Hamlet*."

No. No way.

My hands are shaking. "I'm sorry. I have to go to the bathroom. It's an emergency."

All four of them start to say they're sorry or mutter in confusion, but I'm already out of the room before I can hear any of it. I'm not even sure if anyone comes after me because I keep running down the hall and toward the main doors. I feel bad about leaving the Mystery Club, but I can't be with anyone else right now.

I wanted to figure out who Big Willy was, yes, but I sure as hell didn't want it to look like this.

My chest is tight and my palms sweat. I guess it makes sense as to why I've been a target. I'm basically the connection.

Because Big Willy, the murderer, is my fucking brother.

# SEVENTEEN
## Luca Ricci Is Definitely Screwed

**LUCA IS LUCKY** that both Mom and Dad have late shifts today because I feel like I'll blow up on him the second he walks through the door. How could I not? It's bad enough he'd keep this whole thing from me, but to think that he might have murdered someone? I mean, that's wild. My brother is a princess. He literally played one onstage last year as the titular Cinderella.

To think he killed Mr. Ford?

Of course, I didn't think he'd be selling essays and test answers using a code name that's a bad dick joke either. Not sure how well I really know him at this point.

I know I should've immediately told the rest of the Mystery Club—it's super shady of me not to—but I want to talk to Luca first. If I'm wrong and the whole gay *Hamlet* thing is a coincidence, I don't need his best friend and his crush to have lost their faith in him.

It's bad enough I lost mine.

If Luca really is Big Willy, then I'll tell them. I'll have to. And I'm not sure what we'll do at that point. Turn him in, even though that sounds so off. Like a song in a minor key. My brother is a murderer who murdered my favorite teacher.

It doesn't fit.

Still if he did it, he did it. And he's dead to me. Because I'll kill him myself.

Unless it was an accident? But no, then he could've called for help immediately. I still don't believe Mr. Ford died hanging a damn cat poster. Even if he did, that means Luca left Mr. Ford to die alone and that's inexcusable. I don't care if we share queer graphic novel recommendations, a bathroom, and most of our DNA.

I've practically been pacing the kitchen since getting home, after lying to Sean and Mari about why I left by blaming my IBS. Not a total lie, as I've had a few trips to the bathroom since then and Imodium to follow.

I should've raced into that rehearsal and made him talk to me. But it's like I'm hoping I'm somehow wrong and don't want to confront him with an audience.

I'm still not even sure what this means. Luca has been the one leaving threats and sending those emails? That's certainly possible, and he seems like he'd be crafty enough to pull the move with Cedar's car window, and maybe he got pictures of himself from others. It would be a smart move to make himself look like a target and push aside possible suspicion. But how the hell did he manage to call me on the catwalk and nearly kill himself while performing onstage?

I guess he could have paid someone off or somehow timed the light to fall at that exact moment, but Luca is serious about his acting. I can't see him intentionally sabotaging his own rehearsal time.

I don't know what to believe.

Only that I feel like I need to poop or throw up or burn both ends with a combo of the two, and how long is it going to be before he gets home?

I squeeze Pusheenicorn to my chest. I need someone to help get me through the conversation that is bound to happen and a soft plushie is always the answer.

My phone buzzes. Oh no. It's probably Luca. Does he know I know somehow? Is he going to try to kill me too? I frown to myself. No way. He knows I can kick his ass. I've done it before.

If Luca can't even take a five-foot-one girl, how the hell did he kill a grown-ass adult?

I glance at my phone, but the message isn't from Luca. It's from Cedar. My chest lightens and I smile despite myself.

Weird.

**Cedar:** Everything good?

No. Absolutely not.

**Gigi:** Yeah, why?

I hope I don't sound too much like a bitch. But I sort of have a lot going on. Who am I kidding? I usually sound like a bitch, and Cedar would be the last person to judge me for it. I don't think I can confide in her on this though. She might try to kill Luca herself with the whole car window and laptop thing. As if reading my mind somehow, her response comes in.

**Cedar:** dad finally untwisted his panties and got my window fixed. Not sure I'll get to keep car after graduation anyway. I'm technically grounded since I wasn't supposed to be at your house, but can I come over tomorrow?

If my brother's not in jail, I don't see why not.

**Gigi:** yeah. Need help sneaking out?

**Cedar:** I'll let you know

Despite everything being terrible and my persistent question of whether I need to run to the toilet again, Cedar's interjection makes me feel better. It's a distraction from the fact that my own brother may have threatened to kill me and his closest friends.

Except now I'm right back in it.

Wait. I'm wasting a golden opportunity here. How can I be a member of Mystery Club if I didn't even think of investigating his room while he's still out? That's like my thing when it comes to trying to solve mysteries—I'm not good at coming up with smart ideas, but I can sneak and break into places.

I'm not sure how much time I have left, but this is my best chance.

I take Pusheenicorn with me. I can't face this alone.

Luckily, we don't have locks on the bedroom doors because Mom and Dad aren't those kinds of parents. Hell, I don't even have a bedroom door; my only privacy is that I'm around the corner from the laundry, so you can't see directly into my room from the top of the basement stairs.

I walk into Luca's room, light on my toes even though no one is around.

His room is impossibly neat. I don't know how anyone can be so put together that they don't even have a chair that always holds unfolded laundry. He has his desk organized, his bed made, and posters of all the shows he's ever been in taped above his bed. He must be an android. Or something worse.

I never thought about it before, but this is like a murderer's level of organization. No dust on his bookshelves, no scattered papers on his desk, not even a sock on the floor. I don't think it's possible to be this clean and not have caused someone's death.

"Focus," I mutter to myself. I don't have a lot of time, and I'll have to be careful to make sure I put everything back in place.

The most obvious spot to check is his desk. Based on the rest of his room, I can't imagine Luca hiding something where it doesn't belong.

I pull open the first drawer.

Nothing but college brochures, acceptance packets, and the few rejection letters he doesn't like to admit to. It's crazy that someone with a great ACT score, an above 4.0 GPA, and a powerful singing voice could still get rejected from colleges. The hell are they looking for? Do you also have to save kittens like Sean? Figure out time travel? Conduct groundbreaking research on a specific kind of sea turtle?

Or maybe it's just a money thing.

Either way, I'm screwed. That's for sure.

This drawer is clean. I slide open the next one. I don't really know what I'm expecting to find. Like I doubt he would have a giant printed Big Willy logo with a *shh don't tell* reminder. I flip past random assignments and notes he kept. There's also a picture of the two of us and Sean at Edgewater Beach, which I would tease him for endlessly in any other situation because of course the one photo he keeps is of shirtless Sean. But there's nothing there to connect him to Big Willy.

I kneel, trying to feel around the bottom of the drawer for some secret compartment like they have in the movies.

Which is when I see a book in a makeshift cubby under the desk's surface.

That's not suspicious as hell.

I slide it out; it has a tight fit and would be difficult to notice if I wasn't specifically searching for something strange. It's a planner.

I open it to two weeks ago.

Luca has normal things written down, like rehearsals and reminders. But in his neat handwriting, there are also various initials and projects. Last Monday has *BN–Stats Test Unit 15*. Tuesday has *FG–Animal Farm Response* and Wednesday is *NS–Hamlet Essay*.

Friday—*flash drive*

Well, there's that.

"Fuck," I tell Pusheenicorn.

Luca is Big Willy. And he met with Mr. Ford the day he died.

"What are you doing?"

The planner falls from my hands to plop on the ground as I look up at my brother. Luca steps into the room, halfway between me and the door, rehearsal bag still hanging from his hands. He doesn't look mad, more like shocked and afraid. Which is a good sign, but he also might be a murderer, so I can't take any chances.

I've never been one for really thinking before acting.

Instead of starting a conversation, I rush forward into a double-leg takedown and knock him to the floor. I slide into knee-on-belly, lifting my foot so all my weight is on my knee as I pull him up by the collar of his shirt.

"You're Big Willy, aren't you?"

Luca's eyes are wide; he coughs from the pressure. "Gigi, what the hell?"

My voice is raised and for some reason my eyes are tearing up. I'm so mad. "Did you send the emails? The threats? Break into Sean's apartment? Did you kill Mr. Ford because he was looking into you?" I pull the collar tighter until he grunts. "Answer me or I'll break your nose, Luca. I don't give a shit."

"Not the face. That's my money maker."

"Jesus Christ, Luca, this is serious!"

"No, I didn't kill Mr. Ford. What the hell are you on?" He squirms from under my knee, trying to push against it, but I keep my pressure.

He probably regrets not training with Mom and me now.

I lean down, pulling on his collar tighter. "But you are Big Willy?"

He grimaces. "Can you get off me so I can explain everything? I promise."

"You might be a *murderer*, Luca."

"I can't believe you would think I'm a fucking murderer! Really, Gigi? Me? I can't even defend myself from my little sister! And even if I could kill a man, which is questionable, why would I kill the only teacher who actually liked you?" He sighs as I loosen up. "I'm Big Willy, okay? But I didn't kill anyone! Or send any threats. Just let me explain."

Now he's almost tearing up, which makes me feel like an asshole. But he did admit to being Big Willy, not that he could hide it at this point. Is it possible he had nothing to do with the murder? The threats?

"I can prove it," Luca adds.

"Fine." I get off him. "But if you try anything, you know I can easily snap your joints."

Luca rubs his stomach. "Yeah, I know. That's why I wouldn't be a murderer—you and Mom would both kill me. And I know you can." He pulls out his phone and opens to the Big Willy email.

From: watchyourbackwestbridge@gmail.com
To: bigwillywestbridge@gmail.com
Subject: say anything, and you're next

if you give up any information about clients or projects you've worked on, you'll be the next body your sister finds
you've been warned enough

I hate the relief that washes over me. Maybe Luca was profiting off helping people cheat, but that's a business. I can live with that. I can't live with him killing people over it. But maybe he isn't lying.

I glance at him cautiously. "You could've sent this to yourself?"

Luca rolls his eyes. "Right. Just like I nearly dropped a stage light on myself." He pouts and crosses his arms. "Do you really think I could've killed Mr. Ford with my bare hands? I liked him! Plus, I can't even do a chin-up. That's easier than a pull-up. But I'm going to go around killing adult men with zero weapons?"

"Okay, but what's the deal with the flash drive? Your crime diary has it right there. You met with Mr. Ford on Friday."

Luca says, "So . . . Mr. Ford found out it was me. I agreed to turn myself in and made a flash drive with all the essays I wrote and emails from students that bought from me. He must've made a copy though because the one you found wasn't the same one I gave him."

I guess it makes sense that Mr. Ford asked him for a flash drive.

"So what happened to the other one?" I ask.

"When I met him, it was between classes and he was in the math office. He probably left it there."

Which means that flash drive went up in flames.

"So Watch Your Back destroyed your flash drive and stole the copy. Why are they still after us then?"

"Because Big Willy still has all the evidence, and your little freshman friend apparently told everyone that I was helping the Mystery Club." He looks scared, but I can't blame him. That light did almost fall on him, and if the killer didn't know Luca was Big Willy before, they do after stealing the flash drive.

"First of all, she's not my friend," I defend. "Second, why were you helping us?"

"I feel guilty," Luca admits. "I was supposed to turn myself in, but after what happened to Mr. Ford, I figured I could just . . . get away with it. I know it's bad, but people needed it. And it was a way to get money for school. So I wanted to find the killer with you all without totally giving myself away."

"Yeah but you should have told me. I don't give a shit that you sell essays. I just want to know who killed Mr. Ford."

He bites his lip. He's so easy to read, I can see the regret playing over his face. "I thought if you knew more, you'd be in more danger." He swallows. "And I was scared you'd hate me."

I sigh. "I already hate you."

He shoves me. "I'm too emotional for your teasing right now."

"Sorry," I add. "You know I love you, bitch."

"I love you too, asshole." He sniffles.

Still, this is a lot to take in. Plus, I've been so focused on the idea that Big Willy was the one behind everything. Now that I know who he is and that he's not the culprit, I feel a little lost.

"But if Big Willy wasn't the one to kill Mr. Ford, who was?" I ask.

"What I've been trying to help you all realize this whole time." He moves to his computer and opens the document that is a clean version of the list of names he'd left in the locker. "One of my clients."

# EIGHTEEN

## A Taste of Heartbreak

**MARI DIDN'T TAKE** the news of Luca being Big Willy well. On the bright side, she's so pissed at him that she doesn't even think to be mad at me for not going to her and Sean first. Not that she'd really hold it against me. Immediately after class, she went to catch him during the break before rehearsal to possibly end his existence, or at the very least, chew him out for details.

I got Sean and Mari to agree to keep this update between the three of us. None of us want to get Luca in trouble, and while I would trust Benji more than Aimee, it's safer not to tell either of them. It's better the killer thinks Luca hasn't told us anything and that we're still in the dark, fully believing Big Willy is the culprit. So we told Benji and Aimee that Big Willy met with a client the Friday of Mr. Ford's death (without actually mentioning Mr. Ford), and if we find out who the client is, we find Big Willy.

It also is a convenient way for them to look for alibis for the murder without knowing we're looking into it.

In the Mystery Club closet/room, we tackle the list again, but this time checking for clear reasons someone couldn't have been free on that Friday. Mari is helping Aimee and Benji comb through one half of the list at the table, while Sean and I are seated on the floor, backs against the walls, with the other half.

"Can't be Amanda or Jamie," I say, showing the video they posted outside the Science Center, Lake Erie shimmering in the background. I cross both their names off the list as I look over at Sean. "How come we never go to the lake? Sometimes I forget we live so close."

"I haven't even been downtown since I saw a Browns game when I was fourteen," Sean says. "We went to Edgewater Beach last summer though."

Oh yeah. Luca printed the picture. I shouldn't tell Sean that.

I try to study his expression. Or would he be into it?

"Well, we should go to the lake more," I say.

"What the hell would we do there? We basically only went for the picture last time."

"I don't know." It looks nice though. "Whatever people do in lakes. Swim?"

Sean gives me a look. "You don't know how to swim."

"I can float. Mostly. That's all you really need to do anyway."

"The bacteria levels are going to be way too high, I'm sure," he counters.

"So we become X-Men or whatever." I continue before Sean can explain that's not how people become X-Men. "Besides, Luca would be down to go back. Especially if he knows you'll be there."

I look up at him quickly. Is that the lighting or did Sean blush a little bit?

"Can we focus on the murder stuff?" he whispers.

I sigh. I guess I'll save my Lawn investigation for later—I already decided that's the superior ship name for my best friend and brother.

I search for Olivia Davis. "Wait, didn't Olivia move to Mentor?"

Sean nods. "Yeah, right in January, must have sucked."

It's soon confirmed on my phone, so I cross her off the list too.

Benji speaks up from the table. "I can't find an alibi on Kyle Sinclair."

Am I the only person who didn't use Big Willy's services? No wonder Luca rarely helped me with homework. He was too busy doing everyone else's.

"I don't think Kyle did it," I say.

The three of them at the table look toward me.

"Met with Big Willy, I mean," I amend quickly.

"Why not?" Mari asks.

"Well, they also had to start that fire, right? I know for a fact that Kyle couldn't have started the fire, because I ran into him when I broke into the boys' locker room." The words are out of my mouth before I can think them through.

"You broke into the boys' locker room?" Aimee asks, her jaw dropping.

"Wait, did you see Kyle Sinclair changing?" Sean asks.

"What? No." My blush probably betrays me, even though it's technically not a lie because he wasn't changing. He was already extremely naked when I ran into him. "The point is, he couldn't have started the fire."

"What does the client who met with Big Willy have to do with the fire?" Benji asks.

Sean, Mari, and I all share a look. Damn, this is confusing. I almost want to risk it and tell them everything just to make it easier on ourselves.

"Apparently, they met twice," Sean says quickly.

Mari holds the pen she's using up to her lips. "Right. That they did. So. We should also be cross-checking who was MIA during the fire alarm and focus on the people who have no alibis for either event. Since Gigi was watching Kyle change, we can note his alibi for that."

"Whoa, hold up. I was not *watching him change*. I ran into him. Briefly."

"So you didn't see him naked?" Sean asks.

"What does it matter if he was naked?" I snap. "Can we focus?"

"Gigi definitely saw him naked," Sean confirms with the rest of the club.

"Oh my god, I hate you. Next on the list."

Since a lot of people are going out and posting on Friday afternoon, we actually manage to narrow it down quite a bit. There are some that could've been scheduled posts, but we're able to confirm their time and location during the murder by asking other witnesses.

"What if we highlight the people who have Mr. Ford as a teacher this year?" Sean suggests softly when we get through the final person. "Otherwise, they probably wouldn't know that he was even looking into it and would have no reason to confront him."

Mari had already asked Cedar to get ahold of Mr. Ford's class schedule, so I pull that up on my phone and we search for names until we get some matches.

When it comes to people who bought from Big Willy, have no known alibi for both the murder and the fire, and had Mr. Ford as a teacher, there's only eight.

I hardly pay attention to most of the names on the final list because there's one that certainly stands out.

Matt Russell.

He's known for being the literal worst, maybe second to being known for getting choked by me. I wouldn't put it past him to be shitty enough to kill someone over risking losing his college acceptance, especially since he was scouted for football.

"Definitely worth looking into," I whisper to Sean, pointing to Matt's name.

Sean sneaks a nod.

"Oh, I almost forgot!" Benji rushes over to us with a laptop and I nearly smack my head on the wall as I jump, trying to hide the rosters open on my phone. "I have to head out soon, but I have photos from the tournament over the weekend! Some professional photographer came and had to give them to us on a flash drive, but they look great."

He already has the flash drive in and the photos loaded and I have to admit, he looks great with that gold medal around his neck.

"Did you win by points or submission?" I ask, looking through the pictures.

"Points the first fight, submission the second by rear naked choke, and submission the third with a triangle arm bar," Benji says proudly.

"Hell yeah." I fist-bump him.

Benji blushes. "Do you ever miss competing?"

I shrug. "I just couldn't balance it with everything else, so it didn't make sense to do it anymore." Mom and Dad made me promise that if I wanted to keep competing, I'd have to keep my grades up and not get into any fights. It doesn't take an amateur detective to deduct why that didn't work out.

It's fine. It's not like I'm some prodigy or something.

Even a natural talent can only get you so far if you don't have the time or money to be on the mats every day. And I'm not *that* much of a natural talent.

I love my friends, but goddamn if being around all these impressive people with their skills and good grades doesn't make me feel like an average-at-best failure.

I can't tell Benji that though.

"I think it's for the best, seriously." I toss on a winning smile. "And jiu-jitsu helps me in ways even better than medals."

"What's that?" Benji asks.

Kicking Matt Russell's ass for a second time until he gives me a good reason to believe he didn't commit murder.

"Friendship," I say, putting a hand on his shoulder. "Obviously."

When I agreed to help Cedar sneak out from her evil parents grounding her for basically no reason, I didn't really consider the fact that I can't drive. I'm one of the younger kids in my class with a late August birthday, so I haven't been sixteen *that* long. Regardless, with Dad, Mom, and Luca all sharing one car, there's literally no time for me to practice enough to pass the test. I get the gist of it, but I'm laughably bad at the whole maneuverability bit with cones. So I had to take a bus that got close enough to her rich-ass neighborhood in Westbridge *Village* and walk over so she can sneak out and call an Uber back to my place. Since her dad isn't the type to check every charge on his card, it doesn't seem like a bad idea and is faster than waiting for a bus back.

It did give me time to DM Matt Russell to try to get him to meet up with me tomorrow, but so far he's ignoring my messages.

Incriminating? Maybe not. He hates me.

He still probably did it though. Piece of shit.

**Cedar:** can you distract my mom? Trying to sneak out the window

Cedar's neighborhood is literally in the kind of area Mom and I would drive by to bitch about the houses, and I feel incredibly out of place. I take a deep breath before walking over to the Martins' address. Cedar's house is huge, with a neatly trimmed lawn and a fountain up front.

Who the hell has a fountain? In front of their house?

Rich people always want to make their shit look like an art museum.

**Gigi:** you owe me

**Cedar:** I know

I don't know how I'm going to distract Mrs. Martin, but I don't think about it too much before walking up the stairs to their front door. It has a brass knocker thing, but I can't bring myself to use that, so I knock with my fist.

No answer.

I don't really know what I'm supposed to do here.

I knock again.

Footsteps sound from the other side of the door, and it is opened by an older Cedar with Botox and a pinched face. Her eyes trace down me, and I can feel the judgment. It sort of makes me want to dress in all black and act like a dick to everyone too.

"Yes?" Mrs. Martin asks.

She doesn't even recognize me. It's clear enough on her face. After calling Luca and I white trash degenerates while we were in hearing distance on Cedar's birthday last year, you'd think she would. Although I did have a black eye then.

"I'm from Westbridge High . . ." I start. "Doing fundraising for the Spring Festival this Friday. If you're interested."

She looks around the porch, but it's just me.

"Aren't you supposed to have something to sell?"

A fair point.

"We're actually gathering pledges for a donation program at the Spring Festival," I say. "Interested community members will get more information there." I'm pulling the words out of my ass, but I have to think of something when she looks ready to shut the door in my face. "They are looking to rename the auditorium after a donor, and there will be a plaque with the names of everyone who donates, as well as a banquet to honor and celebrate the esteemed donors."

That's shit rich people like, right?

It seems to intrigue Mrs. Martin. "Oh, really? And this donation would benefit . . . ?"

"The arts," I say quickly. "The arts programs, all of them. But mostly theater because it is restoring the auditorium." I feel like I need to sell this more. "The equipment is old. A student almost died when a light broke and fell on them, so it would really mean a lot."

She fakes a pity smile.

"Well, I suppose you can put us down as maybes, if there will be more information on Friday."

"Absolutely," I say. My eyes dart over to the side of the house, where Cedar is watching me with an amused smile. I'm sure this house is big enough that Cedar could get away without being heard. I force my eyes back to Mrs. Martin, trying to hide the annoyance. "Perfect, thanks, have a good one! Go Wildcats!"

Before she can respond, I'm walking away, and thankfully, the door closes without any additional remarks.

I keep my pace up as Cedar joins me.

"That was quality entertainment," she starts. "Ten out of ten. Are you sure you aren't an actor too?"

I roll my eyes because I don't even want to deal with the fact that she totally did this on purpose. "You didn't even need me," I mutter.

"Maybe not." She twirls one strand of lavender hair around her finger. "But I get to spend some extra time with you."

We walk down the street to wait for the Uber.

"Any leads on the murder mystery, detective?" Cedar asks.

"Please, I'm way more like the sidekick." My palms are sweaty, and I wipe them on my pants. "But yeah. Figured out who Big Willy is, for one thing."

"Wow." Cedar tilts her head to the side. "Who's Big Willy?"

"Someone we should've realized earlier given he's smart and would be the little shit to make a Shakespeare dick joke and write an essay on Hamlet being gay."

Cedar almost trips on the sidewalk. "Luca killed Mr. Ford? No fucking way."

"He didn't. He is Big Willy though. We're pretty sure a client of his is the murderer, since he's been getting threats too."

"That bitch. I can't believe he didn't say anything all this time."

Her and me both.

The Uber arrives and we're pretty much silent the entire

ride to my house. Not that Greg in his silver Prius has any connection to Westbridge or Mr. Ford, but it's still not worth the risk. It's not a far drive, so soon enough the car drops us off in front of my house. When we step inside, Luca is home—rehearsal must have ended early, or he pretended to be sick because he's freaked out about everything. He and Mom are getting dinner started, which seems like stuffed peppers.

"Hi, Cedar," Mom says. "Please tell me you're staying for dinner; we always make too much."

"I'd love to," Cedar says.

I think she's happy for the excuse not to go home, and I don't really blame her.

"All right," I say. "We'll be in my room."

"Will you now?" Luca says, completely suggestively.

I flip him off. "Don't be a huge dick, or should I say a bi—"

"Love you both, have fun, bye!" he quickly interrupts.

Cedar follows me down to my room, and it doesn't feel as weird this time. Almost natural, like she's been over a few times instead of just once recently.

"Want to watch something?" I ask.

"Sure, or we can chill, whatever." Cedar shrugs. "I'm not picky."

I grab my laptop and plop on my bed. She takes a seat on the chair. I glance over. Last time, we moved upstairs to chill, but I'd rather not let Mom butt in with their comments and read into the situation. "You're gonna have to come here. I don't have a TV."

"Oh," Cedar says, suddenly a little stiff. "Yeah, right, of course."

She sits next to me, and it's weird. We're close, separated by a few inches, but the distance seems so much more noticeable.

"What are you in the mood for?"

"Maybe something light," Cedar says. "Given all the threats and murder."

"Fair."

We decide on an old, straight romantic comedy that looks a little ridiculous. It starts playing, but it's hard to focus on the movie, like I can't get over the idea that Cedar Martin is sitting next to me.

"Can I hold him?" Cedar points to Gingersnap, right behind her on my bed.

I nod. "That's Gingersnap."

She doesn't seem to think it's weird that I clearly have names for all of them. She leans over, shirt lifting right above her hips as she gently takes Gingersnap and places the dragon right next to her so she can pet his head.

"I like dragons," she says, looking up at me with a smile. "I would one hundred percent have a dragon as a pet."

She's really close. Her eyelashes are long. And her lips somehow look fuller with light colors.

"I don't like high fantasy, but I agree that dragons are awesome."

"I feel like being high is the best way to watch fantasy."

I gently shove her and she pushes me back.

And somehow, we end up a little bit closer.

I try to focus back in on the movie, even though I seem to have clocked out completely for the first ten minutes of it. The heroine has a business job that she's great at, so she'll probably give it up for a sexy, rugged, small-town guy and a newfound passion for glassblowing or some shit.

The characters speak, but my senses are tuned in to the girl sitting next to me.

On my bed.

As if she can read my thoughts, Cedar looks over to me. There's a long pause in the dim lighting, and I'm stricken with how beautiful she looks.

I don't mean to, but I think about what it would be like to kiss her. Her lips look soft, and it's like my body aches with some need to feel that pressure, the way she might taste. My lips tingle.

"Mari told me you saw Kyle Sinclair's penis?"

That is probably the last thing I want to hear and think about right now.

My face heats. What the hell was I thinking anyway?

"Oh my god, no. Not like that. I accidentally ran into him. It's not like we were hooking up or anything."

"That's good," she says. "You're not into him?"

I laugh. "Please. He's hot, but in a favorite book character kind of way, not someone I'd want to date."

"Who would you want to date?"

Why does she have to look sexy with slightly parted lips

when she asks that? This is CEDAR. WHAT THE HELL, BRAIN?

I shrug. "I don't know. You know I like Mari, but . . . I mean, there's no way she would like me like that. I know that. No one would."

Cedar's eyebrows pinch, a little line forming in the center of her forehead. "What does that mean?"

I rub my face. Does she really need me to spell it out? "I'm kind of an asshole. I get angry easily. I'm more of a little shit than serious. I'm the kind of person who will punch first and ask questions later. I know what I am, and I know what I'm not. I'm not like *that*," I say, pointing at the screen where the leading lady is crying while wearing her heart on her sleeve. "Emotional in front of everyone. Delicate and kind and cute. The kind of person someone falls in love with."

The silence shatters earlier than I expect.

"Well, that's a pretty fucking ridiculous thing to say considering I've been basically in love with you for years now."

It's hard to tell if Cedar or me is more surprised. My jaw goes slack, while hers clenches. My heart pounds in my chest. It's like I didn't hear the words correctly.

Cedar likes me? Not Mari?

"Really?" It's all I can say.

"Yeah." She doesn't look at me. "It's been painfully clear to everyone else."

Am I really that oblivious?

"I'm sorry," I say, even though that's wrong.

Cedar laughs. "Not exactly what someone wants to hear after a confession."

"What do you even like about me?" Immediately after the words come out of my mouth, I wish I could take back the question. But she's ready with the answer.

"I like that you are always yourself, no matter what other people think. That you don't have to hide your personality, even the sides of it some people don't like. But I like all of it. I like that you can be kind of mean but always funny. I like that you are quick to fight, that you are loyal and fierce and stand up for people who can't stand up for themselves." Cedar's tearing up now, and my entire torso is tight. She locks her eyes on mine. No escape. "I like that you shine, everywhere you go, even when you think you're blending in. I like the way you lift your shoulders when trying to look tough, making yourself bigger." She continues through her smile. "I like the emotion you try to hide, the fact that you aren't always happy and can admit that sometimes things are just shit. I don't like you despite your faults, Gigi. I like you with them, all of them, because they are real and beautiful and make up who you are." Cedar goes silent for a moment, wiping her eyes. "And that's the person I fell in love with."

I don't know what to say. It should be perfect. It should be everything I've ever wanted. It is in some ways.

But I can't be like that. I can't tell her how I'm feeling, how she makes me feel. I can't admit those weaknesses because whether it takes a day, or week, or a few months,

215

she'll use that against me. It's like giving up my back for someone to take it and sink in the choke.

It'll only end in me getting hurt. I can't let that happen.

"I . . ." Words race through my head but my chest hurts at the thought of saying them. "I'm planning on confessing to Mari and . . ." I don't know exactly where I'm going with this and immediately as I say the words, I want to take them back.

But it's too late.

In front of me, Cedar breaks.

Maybe a part of me does with her.

"I'm not Mari," she says. "I'm the one that's here though."

I should answer. I don't. The words jumble in my mind, and none of them come out. I'm scared. Of her feelings. Of mine. Of falling deep into something only to face something like what I'm feeling now but so, so much worse.

But she's right.

She is the one that's here.

And then, she's not.

# NINETEEN

## Paella, Platonic Confessions, and the Missing Member of Mystery Club

**I CAN'T BELIEVE** I ruined everything between me and Cedar and it's not even five p.m. It's strange how quickly things can change. Part of me wants to wallow under the covers in a cocoon of all my plushies for the rest of the night, but Mari sends a text to the Mystery Club group chat and the subsequent flood of texts causes my phone to buzz violently off the bed, not used to so much action, before I finally get the motivation to pick it up.

**Mari:** can you all come over for dinner? I want to talk strategy

**Ace Pokémon Trainer:** I'm free? what time?

**Mari:** we eat at 6 but come sooner

**Annoying Aimee:** I can't :( have to help peace studies club since spring fest is fri

**Annoying Aimee:** message me everything!

**Benji BJJ:** I'll be right over!

**Benji BJJ:** I'll bring brownies!

**Benji BJJ:** *heart emojis*

Something tells me Mari's talking strategy is to convince me not to immediately and violently confront a potential killer like I did with Ethan Mitchell. Which means I probably won't be able to get away with skipping.

The distraction might actually be nice. Especially if I get to see Mr. and Mrs. de Anda. They'll probably make me feel not so much like the worst person on the planet. Plus, if I don't go, I'm doomed for an awkward dinner with Mom and Luca asking too many questions.

**Gigi:** heading over

**Gigi:** *happy cat GIF*

**Ace Pokémon Trainer:** *cat heart eye emoji*

At least I didn't immediately change into pajamas like I wanted to. I head back upstairs, where both Luca and Mom look at me like we all just found out I'm dying. I don't know what Cedar said as she left, but regardless, I'm sure it didn't look good.

"Did you two hear any of what happened?" I ask.

"No," Luca says quickly. His lips tighten into a line. "Well, maybe some of it. I mean, we weren't listening, but you don't have a door."

I want to disappear. Maybe I should buy a one-way ticket to Southern California and try to get a job cleaning the mats or managing the front desk at whatever jiu-jitsu academy will have me. I could even change my name. Get a different totally harmless hobby like bird-watching. Dye my hair purple.

No, purple is too close to lavender, which is making me think of Cedar and how we almost kissed and how she confessed to me and how she probably hates me now.

Fuck.

"I don't want to talk about it," I say. "Can someone give me a ride to Mari's?"

"I can," Luca says.

His kindness might be because he feels bad for me or because I have newly found blackmail material I could hold over him while in a particularly bitchy mood, but either way I'm taking it.

The entire car ride over, he gives me his big-cute-kitten eyes, like that will prompt me to spill everything about what happened with Cedar, but I wasn't lying when I said I don't want to talk about it.

It's honestly better if she hates me. Even if that hurts now, it will save me from much more pain in the future. Confessing to Mari is one thing. It's a quick rejection, and then I'll get over it. Whatever's happening between Cedar and I, or whatever was happening, isn't like that. It could get serious, and that makes everything worse. That's dangerous.

I shouldn't think about it. If I distract myself, show that it doesn't matter and that I don't care, everything will be fine.

When Luca pulls to a stop in front of Mari's house, he opens his mouth to say something. The little breath intake is dramatic enough to make me think it's something like a mini Gigi intervention, which I can't deal with right now. Maybe he can talk to me about my screwed-up personal issues *after* I solve this murder.

"Thanks, I'll see you later," I quickly say, and hop out of the car and shut the door before he can argue. I think I'm halfway to Mari's front door when he even registers that I already left and gives an uncertain wave.

I brush past the flowers on either side of the de Anda's porch and knock on the red door. They have a doorbell off to the side, but I know it hasn't been working since I was like eight, and Mr. de Anda never replaced it because he's not a fan of the sound. For some reason, it feels like it's been too long since I've been here, even though I practically grew up in this house. I guess I had less of a reason to come here after Luca no longer had to drag me along because I was old enough for my parents to at least pretend they trusted me to watch the house alone.

Mari opens the door and lets me in. "Glad you could make it."

"I figured you wanted to actually talk before I lose my temper and try to fight Matt."

Her resulting smile is guilty. "I mean, that's definitely a part of it."

I knew it.

"Hola, Gigi," Mrs. de Anda says from the kitchen. "¿Cómo estás?"

"Bien," I say, stepping over to give her a hug. She pulls me in and after the last hour I've had, it makes me feel a lot better. As I reluctantly break it, I notice the paella mix boxes on the counter. My stomach practically growls in response. Mrs. de Anda swore us to secrecy, but she always makes paella from the box, adding her own additional seafood.

I know Cleveland, Ohio, isn't exactly the paella capital of anything, but even the times I've tried it at a restaurant haven't been as good as Vigo Paella Valenciana. Especially not the way Mrs. de Anda makes it.

Mrs. de Anda asks me something else, but I can't quite grab on to all the words. She lowers the volume of her music like that's the issue. My brain lags enough in English, let alone with a language I'm struggling to learn in only my half-assed classes at school and Duolingo.

"Lo siento, no entiendo," I manage.

Mari leans against the counter. "You don't have to make Gigi speak Spanish." She grins at me. "She's terrible at it."

I blush. "I'm not that bad. If you don't include all the vosotros conjugations, since Señora Alvarez isn't going to bother with that, I can probably almost understand as much as you."

Mari crosses her arms. "Okay, give me a sentence. Dime algo."

Because I am the way I am, I face Mari with full confidence before saying, "Mari, tu mamá es muy guapa."

She rolls her eyes but smiles and Mrs. de Anda laughs out loud.

"You're right, Gigi, tu español es perfecto," she says.

"Sean and Benji should be here soon." Mari grabs two cans of pop from the fridge and passes me the ginger ale, because she knows I'm like the one person that likes it even when I'm not on an airplane or sick. "We can wait for them in my room while the food's still cooking."

My ridiculous chest has the audacity to tighten with nerves. I was already alone with a girl in a bedroom today and handled it terribly. Maybe I should ask if we could just wait out here?

No, I don't want to be weird.

"Sure," I say. "Cool."

After offering help to Mrs. de Anda and getting waved off, I follow Mari into her room. I'm kind of glad I have the ginger ale, as popping open the tab and sipping from the can gives me something to do with my hands.

Mari closes the door, cutting off the drifting melody of what I recognize as Jarabe de Palo, an old favorite of Mari's parents. I take the desk chair. Her brown eyes are studying me, far too serious for the plaid pajama pants and the *Purr-fect Meowder* sweater she's wearing.

Why does this feel like another Gigi intervention?

"So . . . I thought you were hanging out with Cedar today, but when I asked her if you both wanted to come over, she did not respond well." Mari raises an eyebrow. "Something happen?"

I'm clutching the can with both hands. Did Mari even have anything she needed to talk about with the rest of the Mystery Club, or was this just an excuse to get me over because she's Cedar's best friend?

"Nothing happened," I snap.

222

Mari holds up her hands. "You don't have to tell me anything," she says quickly. "I know it's hard because I'm friends with both of you, but that sincerely means I want the best for you *and* Cedar and won't share anything I'm told. It's fine if you don't want to talk about it, but I want you to know that I'm here, and I'm a great listener."

I slouch in the seat. Maybe Mari has a point. As long as she's not just trying to gather information to report back to Cedar, it might not be bad to get some things off my chest. On the other hand, isn't it weird to talk about it with Mari? Considering she's basically the reason I screwed everything up with Cedar?

She looks so open and understanding though. I already feel terrible. I guess talking about it with Mari doesn't make me that much worse.

"Cedar told me she liked me . . . and I didn't have the best reaction," I admit. My face heats, almost like she can somehow tell from that what my reaction was. "Okay, it was a terrible reaction."

Mari frowns. "Do you not like her?"

"No, of course I like her. I like her a lot." The words fall right out of me, almost shocking me. I didn't mean to say that. "I mean, that's not the problem. The problem is I'm—" I cut off. I can't tell Mari my confession plans for Friday. Not like *this*. "I'm not the kind of person who does relationships and serious things like that."

"That's fine." Mari tilts her head and gives a soft smile.

"There's nothing wrong with that. But you should be honest that you aren't interested in dating or let her know what your boundaries are."

I look down at the Canada Dry can, like it can somehow help me. "It's not that I'm not *interested*. It's that . . . I can't risk it. I'm not a serious person. I like making jokes and gliding through life not really giving a shit. When Cedar and I would just tease each other, when we didn't *like* each other like that, it was easier. It was fun because it was safe. But seeing her so serious and feeling . . ." I pause. How was it that I felt hearing Cedar's confession? Excited. Scared. Confused. Elated and also pretty damn certain she couldn't possibly mean me, but also like a veil was lifted or some shit because *of course* she does? It's almost hard to remember because now I just feel guilty and like someone punched and squeezed all my internal organs without having to break the skin. I shake my head. "One of us will just end up hurting the other. I can't let myself get hurt like that." My voice drops a little. "And I don't want to hurt her. Not any more than I did today."

There's a long moment that passes between us. I hate to admit it, but I do feel a little better for saying that all aloud.

"Sometimes I wonder if you've had a crush on me so long because you figured nothing would ever come of it, that it was safe," Mari admits. "I think maybe I'm right."

I gape at her. "You *know*? That I like you?"

"Gigi, love, everyone knows. It's cute."

Is today actually the worst day of my life?

Okay, second-worst day. My embarrassment can't com-pare to what happened to Mr. Ford.

"I'm sorry if I sound full of myself," Mari says. "You can always stop this conversation if you want. It just seems like the reason you want to run away now isn't because Cedar and you suddenly went from teasing to liking each other. It's that you both *already* liked each other, and she took that terrifying first step of making it clear."

I don't really know what to say to that. It's easy to pre-tend like going back to before Cedar's confession would make everything normal between us, but maybe it wasn't that different. Maybe Mari's right, and because I knew that there was something between us, I've been running away the whole time.

I'm still a little hung up on the fact that Mari has known I've had a crush on her. Why wouldn't she say anything?

"Can I tell you something personal?" Mari asks, cutting through the silence and saving me from my own thoughts.

I nod. "Of course. Apparently, I am very accidentally open with personal things, so I can't judge."

Besides, while I didn't know my crush was so obvious, we do know a lot about each other. Mari was at our house when she got her first period and Mom had to explain pads and tampons through the bathroom door. Mr. de Anda helped me first learn to ride a bike, and Mrs. de Anda would bribe me with crema catalana or arroz con leche to make sure I'd take my fiber or MiraLAX when the summer constipation hit. I don't think we could really be impersonal if we tried.

Mari takes a breath. "I'm actually aromantic and asexual. So you might be getting more of an objective perspective when it comes to dating advice, since I only really feel platonic love. The reason I ignored your potential feelings this whole time was that I didn't really have the words to explain it. But now that I do, I'm glad I can share this with you." Her smile is small, almost hesitant. "That being said, I'll always platonically love you and be around to give you dating advice."

For some reason, my eyes prick a little. It's not that I'm disappointed. Sure, I'm a little surprised, but I'm *happy* Mari told me. It's almost like a little bit of the distance between us disappeared. "Thanks for letting me in on that." I wipe my thumb across the corner of my eye. "I swear, I'm not upset. I'm just secretly emotional because I'm proud and excited for you to find those words. I'll always platonically love you and will graciously accept your dating advice."

Shit. I'm really tearing up. But before I can try to stop it, Mari moves across her bed to pull me into a hug. "Nothing secret about the fact that you're emotional either. But you don't have to pretend not to cry with me. We are pro-crying in this house."

I snort and lean into her. "Is this okay?" I ask against her hair.

"Gigi, if you suddenly treat me like some aro-ace stereotype who doesn't like physical contact, I will hit you. You know I fucking love hugs."

I pull away, only enough so we can look at each other while still keeping our arms in place. My face heats with embarrassment and the thought of saying something that upset her kills me. "I'm sorry, I just meant, like, consent-wise, but I can . . ."

She laughs. "I'm teasing. I'll let you know if you actually make me uncomfortable."

I lean back into her. Her hand rubs my back, which feels incredibly comforting.

"That being said," Mari continues. "I do think you owe Cedar an explanation. Don't you think she was just as scared of getting hurt when she told you how she felt? She was brave in taking a chance. I'm not saying you have to date her, but you should at least respect that enough to give her a real response."

My chest tightens. I was so preoccupied with my own avoidance of things getting serious and potentially one of us getting hurt that I didn't really stop and think about what I did to Cedar in the moment.

Damn. I'm such a selfish bitch.

And Mari's right. The least I can do is give Cedar an actual response.

"How did you get to be so smart and mature?" I complain. "We're only a year apart."

"I read a lot more than you do," Mari says like that's the discrepancy. I don't think cat-themed cozy murder mysteries will make me much smarter.

At least knowing what I did wrong and how to take the first step in making it better is relieving in some ways. Even though it will be terrifying, I feel more motivated. And a lot better.

"You know," I start, "I was going to confess my feelings for you at Spring Fest."

Even though the plan I had for so long is spoiled now, I don't feel bad. I really didn't think anything would happen between Mari and I romantically. But in a weird, unexpected way, I got what I wanted.

To be open with her and not feel like I have to hide.

In that way, this botched, unexpected, and premature confession was perfect.

"That's really cute." Mari lifts an eyebrow. "Although you might not have to scrap that plan entirely. It still would be a perfect spot for a confession slash apology."

My heart flutters with nerves. "You think she'd be okay with that?"

"I think the Gigi Ricci I know would be brave enough to find out," Mari responds.

I don't even get much of a chance to sit in my mix of feeling flattered and nervous and warm. There's a knock on the bedroom door, which immediately opens to reveal Sean.

He looks like he just saw a ghost.

"Sean, what's wrong?"

"When I was biking over here, I got this message," he passes his phone to Mari and me.

My stomach drops into my gut as I look at the message.

From: watchyourbackwestbridge@gmail.com
To: mysterythrillerlitscholars@gmail.com
Subject:

I warned you bitches
this is on all of you.

"Fuck," I say. "What did they do?"

Mari's eyes are wide. "Where's Benji? Shouldn't he have been here by now?"

She's right. Mari and Benji both live in Westbridge Village. He's only a few streets over, so even if he walked or biked, he should have been the first to arrive.

No. No no no no no.

I immediately dial his number. The rings are excruciating, but the line finally picks up.

"Benji?" I ask. "Benji? Where are you?"

"Gigi," the voice on the other end sobs. It's not Benji. I instantly recognize it as Lyndsey, one of Benji's moms. "We're at the hospital."

# TWENTY

## Anyone Who Harms Benji Denver Must Die

**BY THE TIME** we get to the hospital in rush-hour traffic, my heart is ready to explode. We gather enough information to know that Benji is okay, but he was attacked while walking to Mari's house. Based on the email Sean received, it's clear that Watch Your Back did this. Which means I have just another reason to pop every fucking joint in their body until they're walking backwards.

Luckily, visiting hours aren't over when we arrive, even though they won't let all of us in the room at once. Out of the Mystery Club, I get to see him first. I'm not a fan of hospitals. While I'm not Luca levels of squeamish, there's something unsettling and creepy about them. Like it reminds me of how we're alive and existing for a limited window, which is not something I really like to think about but is something that's been on my mind more often than usual with everything that's going on.

I stopped at the hospital gift shop and used my emergency cash for a cat plushie holding a little balloon that says "Stay Pawsitive!" It's the kind of ridiculous thing that might get Benji to smile. Mari and Sean approved.

When I walk into his room, it feels way less fun.

The top left of his head is covered in bandages.

"Shit, Benji," I say. "I got you a cat."

Somehow, he's all smiles, like he didn't have to get some number of stitches in his face. "That's hilarious."

I head over to where he's sitting and pass him the plushie. Unable to help myself, I pull him into a hug. My arms are still shaking from the nerves coming over, but he doesn't seem to notice as I press the uninjured side of his body to my chest. "I'm so glad you're okay." I let him go as he winces from pain trying to hug back. I immediately pull away. "What happened?" I ask.

A small smile plays on his lips. "I already talked to the police, but I've been waiting for the questioning by my fellow Mystery Club members."

I rub my eyes. "Come on, this is serious."

I can't even look into both his eyes, the left one is mostly covered by a mess of bandages. It's like he can see me staring at it.

"Don't worry, my eye wasn't damaged," he starts. "I was walking over to meet you all when I felt like I was being followed. I started to call you but then someone attacked me from behind. They basically tackled me onto the sidewalk, which is nothing like getting taken down on the mats because the sidewalk *hurts*. They held a knife over me and started saying something, but honestly, I was too freaked out to even hear what they were saying. They searched my backpack and took my flash drive of photos. I managed to get my feet to their hips and kick them back, but they sliced at my face. Blood started to get in my eye, so I just did kind of a technical stand up and ran the fuck away until I was able to call for help."

I squeeze my hands into fists. I can't believe they would just assault Benji in the middle of the street. "They took your flash drive?"

He nods.

Shit. If they saw him with it during the school day, they must have thought it was a copy of Luca's evidence. They really attacked him over his fucking jiu-jitsu competition photos. A rage builds in me to the point where I'm trembling.

"Did you see who did it?" I ask.

Benji shakes his head. "They had a mask on and loose clothes. I think the voice was deep, but it almost sounded like they were trying to deepen it on purpose?" He looks down at his hands, rubbing his fingers together. "I should've fought back. I mean, they didn't seem much stronger than me. I could have stopped them and we'd have solved it, but I let them get away."

I shake my head. "No, fuck that, you did what you train to do, Benji. You got away. You don't bring a gi to a knife fight." He gives a little chuckle at that, and I sit at the edge of the bed next to him. "What's important is that you're okay. Sometimes, the bravest thing to do is *not* fight. You did great."

For someone who has been sunny and holding himself

together the whole time, this is what seems to get him. His right eye starts to water and his lip trembles. "I was really scared."

"Of course," I say. "When I found out you got hurt, I was too."

I reach my arm out, inviting him to lean on me. Benji gives me a look.

"I know I'm younger than you, but I'm not a little kid, Gigi."

I bite back the response to argue that he basically is. Benji might be a freshman, but he's still a guy. Even if I have seen Mom training him since he was like four, we're only two or three years apart. Of course I'd embarrass him by treating him like he's still in middle school.

He looks away as his cheeks redden. He sticks his arm out. "You can lean on me, though."

A laugh escapes me, but I do, making sure I'm not resting my full weight on him. It's comforting, to be able to feel his breathing. He's okay. He's alive.

I kind of get what Mari means about platonic cuddling being the best.

"Shit," I say as my eyes start to burn. "I didn't want to cry."

"I'm pretty sure your friend getting stabbed in the face is a good reason to cry," Benji says.

"Is it still considered being stabbed if the knife grazed you?"

"My eye may be okay, but they said it will leave a scar. So

I'll say stabbed if I want to." He turns his head down to me to stick out his tongue.

It's hard to laugh at that though, so more tears leak out instead. "I'm so sorry, Benji."

He shouldn't have been targeted at all.

"It's fine," Benji says. "If anything, maybe it will be like cauliflower ear and the other guys will be afraid of me at the next competition I can do."

I sniff back some leaking snot. "And the girls will love it. You'll be the hottest sophomore at Westbridge this fall."

"My moms will be so proud."

I swipe my eyes, but it doesn't seem to be doing any good. "Still, this is so fucked up, Benji. You only joined the Mystery Club because of me, and now this person is after you because I wanted to find out what happened to Mr. Ford. Why are you being so nice to me when it's my fault this happened to you?"

Tears are really falling now, and I can't even imagine how I look. Part of me is glad I'm leaning on his shoulder, like that might make it harder for him to see how pathetic I am. I wouldn't blame him for shoving me off onto the floor and never wanting to see me again. Sure, he's putting on a brave face now and handling it incredibly well, but he still went through a traumatic event that had to hurt like a bitch.

"Shut up, it's not your fault," Benji says, his voice sounding firmer than I've ever heard it. "I joined the Mystery Club because I wanted to. It started because I admire you, but I've been having fun. I like Mari, Sean, and Aimee. I like being with all of you. Yeah, getting hurt sucked, but it's still worth it, and no matter what, I'm not going to regret joining Mystery Club." He bites his lip. "But what does this have to do with Mr. Ford?"

I tell him everything. Or at least, the abridged version of it. I think it's clear that Benji isn't involved at this point. A part of him seems a little disappointed at being left out, but ultimately, he's understanding, considering. It doesn't change his stance on being glad he joined Mystery Club despite everything. While I can be kind of oblivious about a lot of things, it's not lost on me that I've been running away from the possibility of getting emotionally hurt, while Benji got literally stabbed in the face for his friends and doesn't regret it.

He's right. Getting hurt sucks. But what if not taking a chance for fear of future rejection is way worse? What if I'm letting something good pass me by just because I don't want to look weak?

That's way weaker. Especially when she seems like something really *really* good.

"I'm a dumbass," I say. Then I bite my lip. "Shit, no, that's ableist. What's a better word for it? I'm . . . I've been walking around with my head so far up my own ass, it's probably the reason for my occasional constipation."

I'm trying to be better about inclusive language, especially since I've learned more about ableism since my IBS diagnosis. I still slip up at times, but while my style of talking will rarely be polite, I'm clever enough to be an ass-hole without the use of problematic language.

"Um, why do you say that?" Benji asks.

My face heats up. "I haven't exactly been taking my own advice. It's a lot easier to tell you that being vulnerable doesn't make you weak than to really believe it myself. But I'm going to try."

"Good," Benji says. "I don't want to have to resign as president of the Gigi Ricci fan club because you've disap-pointed me."

Great, another thing to worry about. Even if I know it's mostly a joke. I think. I'm pretty sure if I did have a fan club, it would be less popular than the Mystery Club, and that asshat Ethan Mitchell would've already gotten it shut down.

"I'll make it my life's mission not to disappoint you," I say.

Benji twists so he can face me, and I lift my head to meet his gaze.

"In that case," he says, "promise me something."

"What?"

"Don't stop the investigation because of this."

I can't help but stare at him, only able to blink a few times as I struggle to come up with the right words. "Seri-ously?"

He nods. "Do you know why I've always looked up to you?" I slowly shake my head, but he continues like he wasn't needing an answer. "You're small, but you're tough, so even when the odds are against you, you problem-solve the shit out of it and never stop fighting. I've seen you struggle against some of the bigger people, getting pressured for entire rounds, only to keep working on your weaknesses and keep trying again until you were kicking *their* asses. You're my hero because you don't give up, and you stand up for people who are getting pushed to the point where they might want to, so they can have the motivation to keep going. You see things through, Gigi. So I need you to see this through because I'm not in the mood to find a new hero, and it will be a lot harder for me to see anything through since I'm currently down one eye."

I snort even though my eyes are burning from all the tears and wiping my sleeve across them hardly helps. I can't really complain. Benji has literal stitches in his head and could have suffered so much worse had he not gotten away in time. I can deal with some crying discomfort.

"All right, I promise." I hold out my pinky. "I'll see this through."

He wraps his pinky around mine and it's done.

I'll find out who hurt the amazing soul that is Benjamin Denver.

And I'll make them regret what they did to him.

# TWENTY-ONE
## Mistakes May Have Been Made

**CLASSES GO BY** in a haze the next day, with my emotions still a frustrating mix from everything that happened. Benji's at home and seems to be doing well, considering. The rest of the Mystery Club agreed to look into our split-up suspect list instead of having our traditional meeting in the club room that we might not be able to keep past tomorrow.

I check my phone for the hundredth time today, but my multiple messages to Cedar asking to talk have been left on read. I don't blame her for ignoring me or completely avoiding me throughout the day, but it's setting off my nerves. Mari and Luca have assured me that she's not in danger and they're in contact, so it's obvious she just doesn't want to talk to me.

Did I fuck up so bad that it's already too late?

I lean against the wall outside, waiting for Mom to come pick me up. To distract myself, I tap through Instagram stories, only to see a shitty meme that's supposed to be a gotcha moment toward nonbinary people (but fails on both accounts of logic and humor) posted by one of the moms from my academy. I immediately unfollow her, but can't shake away the general feeling of wanting to punch some-one in the face. At least it will give me motivation to train harder and get even better so I can kick the asses of people like her, even if they have more experience than I do.

It's not exactly the best mood to see Matt Russell in, especially when I promised Sean and Mari I wouldn't let my emotions get the best of me. That's a possibility for some emotions, but anger seems to be one I struggle with hiding.

"Hey, fuckface," I call out. "We have to talk."

Matt stops walking and snaps his head in my direction. He's average height (although it's hard to judge since every-one feels tall to me) and stocky, with blond hair cut close to his scalp. It's easy to not be fazed by his glare but difficult to ignore his beard growing in splotchy over his pale skin. He should really shave it.

"I already got your messages," Matt says. "And the answer is no."

He tries to walk away, but I rush forward and grab his arm. While it might be a little too schoolyard bully, I switch my grip to his collar and pull his head down toward me.

"I think the answer is yes, actually. And the next ques-tion is where the fuck were you yesterday evening?"

He struggles to lift his head and push my hand away because jiu-jitsu grips are no joke and I'm pretty sure my fingers adapted to this exact positioning. "Get off me," he growls.

"Not until you answer."

His glare deepens. "It's none of your business."

"It is if you're threatening and attacking my friends."

It would be so easy to punch the smirk off his face. To feel his nose crunch under my knuckles. If he did that to Benji, he deserves so much worse. So much anger rushes through me at once, my eyes threaten to tear, so I level my breathing and try to keep calm.

*You promised not to fight. You promised not to fight.*

"You're an idiot," he sneers. "Think you're so cool because you get felt up by guys at a gym and make jokes about shitting your pants before people can make fun of you for it? You're just a white trash whore."

I want to kill him. My grip tightens on his shirt and it would be so, so satisfying to bust his chin with an uppercut.

"You're an ableist piece of shit," I say, "and a cheater, so I don't really care what your opinion of me is, Russell."

He snorts. "What do you mean by that?"

"I know you bought from Big Willy. Multiple times. Colleges won't like the looks of that."

Matt steps closer to me, looking down to meet my eyes. He blinks a lot but keeps his shoulders spread apart, taking up more space. My muscles tense. I already have a lower center of gravity. I can take him down before he is able to react. I know I can.

"It's a good thing no one will tell them," Matt says.

Is he trying to intimidate me?

"How far were you willing to go to make sure of it?" I ask.

He frowns. "I don't have to tell you anything."

He's right. Matt's not going to confess himself. Not without actual evidence. If I try to physically threaten him, I'll be carted off to Mrs. Goode, if not immediately kicked out of Westbridge.

I let go of his shirt.

Matt smirks, standing up tall and adjusting his neckline. "If someone went a little too far wanting to shut up Big Willy, maybe look into the person who started the fire." He turns his head so quickly, his blond hair falls over his crinkled eyes. "I wonder who that could be."

There's something in that tone that makes me think he knows Principal Daniels suspects me.

Which means it has to be him.

I keep my voice low, practically spitting the words out as my entire body shakes. "I will find out who did it, and when it's you? I'm going to make you wish you never woke up from the last time I choked your bitch ass out."

"Fuck you," he snarls.

I give him my biggest smile and bat my lashes. "Get real, Russell. Not even a white trash whore like me would agree to that."

Before I know it, I'm back home in bed and have nothing to show for the day in terms of the investigation. While a part of me still feels like I won the confrontation with Matt, I didn't exactly get anything that incriminates him in the murder of Mr. Ford, attempted assault of Luca, or the actual assault of Benji. Sure, he made it seem like he knew I was being blamed for the fire to get a rise out of me, but that's hardly solid evidence. I can't even prove he said it.

Shit. I really should have been recording or something. Maybe I do need to read more of those cat murder books. I lean back into my pillow. Getting nowhere is annoying the hell out of me. I need some concrete evidence and fast.

Luca has proof that Matt used Big Willy, but where the hell can I find evidence he killed Mr. Ford? There was nothing in Mr. Ford's room, and anything that *might* have been in the math office is now ashes. It's not like I can break into wherever the hell Matt lives. Breaking into areas of the school is one thing. I'm not about to try my hand at home invasion.

It's frustrating though, that for each additional piece we get that seems to bring us closer to solving the case, we get thrown two steps back. It's like spending a whole six- or eight-minute round trapped under a bigger person's side control, only the buzzer signaling the end of the round refuses to ring.

I glance at my phone again. Still no response from Cedar.

I'm the worst. Why can't I seem to do any single thing right? It's like, if I'm not training on the mats, I'm completely useless. I might as well add "jiu-jitsu blue belt" and "porrada everyday" to all my bios even though I've found it kind of cringey because what the hell else do I have going for me?

I pull Amber in tight to my chest.

"Can I come in?" Mom asks, even though they already

stepped into my room. I still nod, wiping away any stray tears. Mom fully walks inside before they take a seat at the edge of my bed. "Are you all right? Stomach okay?"

They probably noticed that I've been running up to the bathroom every twenty minutes. There's a lot of stress right now, which never helps on the diarrhea front. At least I remembered to put some paper down in the water first to avoid stains.

"I've been having soft-serve shits all day and it's super uncomfortable, so no." If there's any person who is okay with TMI, it's Mom. I sigh. "That's not even my biggest concern right now, but we do have to restock on wipes soon."

The last thing I need is to develop another rash tomorrow. It's bad enough that I'm going to be seventeen years old in August and have had to ask my mom to put Cortizone-10 between my ass cheeks in the past, I'm not dealing with that on top of everything else.

"Are we going to talk about what happened yesterday?"

I suppose my internal tangent on butt rashes masked the moment of silence. I glance over at my mom. "What happened yesterday?"

They roll their eyes. "With Cedar."

I forgot for a blissful moment that Mom and Luca heard far too much of it. No, I don't want to talk about it. I'd rather stay in bed until Matt the murderer is caught and I turn eighteen and can move to Alaska to catch salmon or something where no one will ever have to see me again.

Mom reaches over to scratch my back. I would push

them off, but it feels nice. "Come on," they say. "I will take your side—you're my kid. But I want to make sure you're okay."

"Anyone who says they are okay in this day and age is probably a liar."

"Understandable," Mom says. "I wouldn't be okay either if I ruined a confession like that."

I flop my face into my pillow. "Stop."

"I wish I could," Mom says. "I'm still secondhand embarrassed. It was horrible."

I want my bed to swallow me whole. It isn't too late to start a new life somewhere else. I'm pretty sure there's a whole island dedicated to cats off Greece or something. I can go there. Sean might even come with me, and we can get platonically married and take care of fifty cats overlooking the Mediterranean. That wouldn't be bad. And Mom, Dad, Mari, and Luca can visit if they promise to never mention Cedar Martin or anything from my past life in Cleveland, Ohio, ever again.

"Great," I say.

"Hey, maybe this weekend we can go to West Side Market and get those good gyros," Mom says, resuming the back scratches.

They know I love the West Side Market. We haven't been in forever; it's not like we go to the West Side that often. Even though you'd think Westbridge wouldn't be east of the river, nothing has been making sense in this town, so it's fitting. With the work schedules of Dad and them, it's hard to do much of anything, especially with their training on top of it. Who has time to go past the river?

Though I really relate to the Cuyahoga River—so polluted I'm literally water that caught on fire multiple times. I'm the Cuyahoga River of people.

"And fancy popcorn and coconut bars," I say into Amber's fur.

"And fancy popcorn and coconut bars."

That sounds nice. If I even make it as far as this weekend considering how much I've been pissing off a murderer.

"I really fucked up, didn't I?" I ask.

Mom isn't against swearing, as long as the swearing is not *at* them.

"I can't tell you, kid," Mom says.

I mean, that's not the answer I'm looking for.

"Helpful talk." I let out a big sigh and roll onto my back. "I don't know what to do."

"If you apologize to Cedar and she doesn't accept it, that's her right. If she does, amazing. I know it sounds like adult talk, but you're young. What seem like huge deals now are things you probably won't even remember in two years. Hell, I barely remember yesterday."

I don't laugh.

"What I know," Mom continues as they take Amber off my face to meet my eyes, "is that while you make mistakes because you're human—and a teenage one, at that—you're extremely loveable, and no matter what happens, you will find happiness, because you're the kind of person who spreads it." They smile, tapping my knee. "Even in a bitchy, roundabout way."

I snort. It's making me teary-eyed though. Between Mom, Benji, and Cedar saying all these nice things about me, I'm almost expecting Matt Russell to kill me soon. Like the universe is giving me some hype before I die a virgin.

"How do I know I won't regret it, though?" I ask.

"You don't," Mom says. "And you might."

I turn to my side to better look at them. "Wow, Mom, you're so good at pep talks."

"Let me finish." They flick me. "You might regret it. But that's okay. You can regret one moment, two weeks, four years, but what makes it worth it is who you are and who you will become. When you remember that, regret isn't such a bad word. It just means you grew as a person."

That sounds nice, and I guess it makes me feel better in some ways, but I still have no idea what to do about my current situation. And again, I might have a teenage murderer wanting me dead, so I don't know if I even have to worry about getting to a point where I regret any of this.

It's almost reassuring.

"I can't tell you what to do," Mom says. "Cedar's new look is very cute though."

"That's kind of implying you are telling me what to do."

Mom holds up their hands. "I would've cut off my right tit for a guy to say something that nice to me as a teenager."

I roll my eyes. "You wear binders all the time, Mom, you'd cut off your right tit for less."

Mom shrugs. "But I stan who I stan."

"Ew, Mom. No."

They give a light smack to my leg and get up to their feet. "I know you'll be okay. And on the bright side, Cedar's graduating in like a month, so it won't be that hard to avoid her."

I'm about to make a comment about their lack of faith, but the doorbell rings.

"Girl Scouts don't go door to door anymore, do they?" Mom asks.

"It's probably Jesus people."

"Can you get it?" Mom asks. "I have to do laundry. Scream if they're weirdos and I'll come knock them out."

"Fine."

It's better they do laundry now and not at like eight tonight, while I'm trying to watch a show. The dryer is absurdly loud, and since I don't have a real door, it's basically right next to me.

Mom heads over to put the clothes in—they already brought the basket down—so I begrudgingly head up the stairs and hope my emotions aren't too visible. I'm pretty sure anyone wanting to talk about Jesus isn't going to want to hear about my sapphic love life troubles.

I don't even know why I need to answer the door. They'll leave eventually, I'm sure.

We should really hang a pride flag out front or something to ward them away. Unless that would only encourage them more?

I reach the front door, and open it, keeping the screen door locked.

But there's no one there. I glance down at the steps. There's a piece of paper.

I open the door and step outside to grab it. The writing is angry and harsh.

*TOMORROW YOU'RE DONE*

I don't even know if the threat is for me or Luca at this point, but my heart pounds in my chest. I'm hardly thinking—it's just like alarms going off in my head.

So when I spot the person dressed in black with a ski mask pulled over their head hiding behind a bush across the street, I don't head back inside to call for help like I probably should. Instead, anger flaring, I run.

# TWENTY-TWO

## Who Follows Their Own Advice?

**THE PERSON LOCKS** eyes with me and sets off running once I start after them. They're fast, and I'm not exactly a sprinter, but I push myself. I can't tell how tall they are, but they're certainly bigger than me, not that it's some huge accomplishment. I run up the driveway of the Browns across the street and spot the culprit trying to climb over their fence.

Hopefully Ms. Brown will understand me trespassing in her backyard and possibly starting a fight. She and her husband seem very young and cool. I mean, they have a closed-in catio in the back of their house. That's goals.

The person has one leg over the fence when I catch up to them, but they aren't very balanced and seem a little stunned. I don't know how they didn't get away fast enough after leaving the threat, but I can't worry about that now.

I shouldn't engage. Hell, I was the one who told Benji he was smart for running away, and he *was*, but the image of him with that bandage on his forehead and all the shit Matt said to me has me forgetting my own sound advice.

I reach up and grab on to the bottom of the suspicious

person's shirt. If I have anything going for me, it's my grips. I pull back with all my weight and they tumble down onto the grass. Not letting them get to their feet, I scramble into a side control and use all my weight as pressure, driving my shoulder onto their masked chin with everything I have so their cheek is against the dirt and I can slide into mount.

I have to apologize to Mom later for teasing that jiu-jitsu doesn't work off the mats.

"Who the fuck are you?" I snap. It's got to be Matt.

I reach for their mask, but they use both hands to keep it in place. They start to move under me and since they have strength on their side, I don't want to give them a chance. I elbow them in the face, but with a grunt, they toss me off.

I tumble into the grass, swallowing the hit against the dirt. I thought Benji said he was as strong, if not stronger, than the person who attacked him. Did they suddenly bulk up overnight? While they might still be pretty average in height and fairly thick in build, this person is bigger, and a lot stronger, than either me or Benji.

They're getting to their feet, and I don't have the power to knock them out. But I don't want to let them get away, so I try a bit of a Hail Mary. Charging forward, I jump their back and lock my hands in a seat belt. They wobble, and I adjust so I have them in a rear naked choke.

If this is Matt Russell, and it likely is, he must be freaking embarrassed to get caught here again. Good.

The masked person's hands go up to defend their throat, but I have it locked. My right arm is tight around their neck, and my left hand pushes on the back of their head with my own chin tight.

But they do the one thing I was hoping they wouldn't.

The person jumps down onto their back, crushing me under their weight. With the wind knocked out of me, I make the mistake of releasing my hold and they scramble to their feet as they cough and rub their throat.

I groan and roll to my side. I'm used to pressure on me but not a fucking WWE slam into the dirt. Shit.

The person looms over me, and my adrenaline and anger is quickly replaced with fear. What if they have the knife? They could kill me just like they did Mr. Ford. Stab me like they did to Benji.

I gave them the perfect chance.

My eyes sting as I wait for them. Why did I rush into this?

Will I see anything when I die? Will it just be nothing? My heart ices over and panic rushes up my throat.

I have to defend. I have to fight back.

I clench my teeth and slowly get back to my feet. My stomach aches from where I landed with their full weight on me, but it doesn't matter. It can't.

I rush toward them to go for a double leg and nail them back onto the ground. With both their hands, they shove against me and sweep me. Their mask twisted, so I can barely see their eyes, only small glimpses of the white skin on their face, as they pin me down.

This is it. I brace for whatever comes next.

"Shit," they mutter in a deep voice I don't quite recognize. "Sorry."

And then they get up and sprint back up the driveway and away from me.

What the hell?

I blink, getting up to a sitting position. Did the killer seriously let me go? The same killer that has been threatening to hurt me?

There's no way Matt Russell would ever apologize to me. But if it wasn't him . . . who was it? Does that mean he's *not* the killer?

A black cat and a gray cat stare at me from the catio, and both of them seem just as confused at the turn of events.

"Sorry you two had to see that," I murmur, getting up to my feet. I head up the driveway back to my street, but there's no sign of the masked person. I sigh, trying to get my breathing back to normal and cross the street. I left the door unlocked and everything. I'm a freaking clown.

I step back through the door, where Mom is biting into a chocolate bar. "Where the hell were you?" they ask. "I was gonna share some of this Spring Fest chocolate I got earlier. I'm so glad they came again because I have been craving something sweet . . . Wait . . . are you okay?"

"I think we should call the cops," I say.

I explain everything—or at least a selective version of today's events that focus on the fact someone threatened us and I tried to attack them—and Mom quickly calls the cops before spending a good ten minutes yelling at me for running after the person.

We wait for someone to arrive by eating some of the chocolate.

Mom looks at me, finally done with their rant. "You sure you're okay?"

"I'm great, I'm fine, just lovely." Because I'm clearly not.

"Uh-huh." Our awkward silence doesn't have to stretch on too long.

The black-and-white car pulls up our driveway. Not that it really matters. Whoever it was, they are long gone by now.

My phone buzzes, and I figure it's either Mari or Sean responding to the update text I sent and also to nag me for my actions. I don't really blame them. But it's not a number I recognize. I answer it anyway.

"Gigi?" the voice says.

"Mrs. Ford?"

My heart almost stops. Did something happen to her? Was this just a distraction and that's why the person didn't try to hurt me?

"I'm sorry for calling out of the blue like this. I tried your parents but didn't get a response, and since you left your number on the card . . ." She sucks in a breath. "I wanted you at least to hear it from me before it ends up everywhere."

She must have called Mom while they were on the phone with the emergency line. I don't mind that she reached out directly, but what could be so important that she wants me to hear it first?

"No worries at all," I say. "What is it?"

"The independent autopsy came back. Artie didn't die from an accidental fall." Her voice cracks as she croaks out the rest. "He was suffocated."

While I knew it wasn't an accident the entire time, having actual proof hits a little differently. Suffocated. That certainly doesn't happen from an accidental fall.

Mr. Ford was murdered. And now everyone else, including the cops and all of Westbridge High, will know it too.

# TWENTY-THREE

## Out of the Frying Pan and Still Freaking Talking about the Fire

**THE ATTEMPTED ASSAULT** case sort of disappears immediately after it happened. Apparently, there's not much that can be done when it's only me saying someone left a basic threat outside the door and no one else saw the alleged masked intruder. I didn't think it through exactly, but it also didn't look good that *I* attacked them first, and the officer warned me they might be back if someone presses assault charges against me. Even Mom couldn't argue much in my defense, as they didn't see any of it.

The Browns don't have cameras on their property, and their cats can't exactly defend me.

Regardless, all of that seems to disappear with the released results of the autopsy. MURDER IN THE MATH ROOM and HIGH SCHOOL HOMICIDE are splashed across every local news station, with the police promising to reopen the investigation.

It should be a good thing, but I can't help but feel worried over how Watch Your Back has been silent. Especially since they threatened that something would happen today.

It's possible the news of Mr. Ford's autopsy scared them and they decided to cut down on the creepy criminal activity. Something tells me that's not the case, but maybe that's just the pessimist in me.

Despite the news being everywhere and Westbridge being a hot topic, school still happens. It feels a little different than normal, with bodies tense as everyone gossips and whispers in the halls. There doesn't seem to be a student who isn't freaked out or on edge. I have first period history, and I'm almost to the classroom, but Kyle Sinclair and Emma Galligan are blocking my way to the door. I don't think I've talked to Kyle since seeing him naked, and I never want to interact with Uptight Emma, so I can't really imagine a worse pair to have to run into.

Icing on the crap cake is that they seem to be in the middle of a heated whisper argument. Kyle's eyes are tinged in red as his mouth moves quickly and Emma's expression is furious as she jabs her pointer finger into his chest. I'm not exactly a lip reader, but it does seem like she's threatening him.

Guess even the Peace Studies Club president has violent days.

Are they actually dating? It's the day of Spring Fest, so maybe it's only high tension with last minute things working out? Luca's been in enough theater shows for me to know how stressful opening nights can be, and I imagine planning a huge festival would cause the same amount of anxiety. Emma storms off the same moment I awkwardly approach.

"Everything okay?" I ask.

Kyle jumps, startled by my voice, before he twists around to face me. His pretty face is painted in some weird combination of spooked and embarrassed.

"Um, yeah, for sure," he says. "I just messed up one of the Spring Festival tasks, so Emma wants to kill me." A blush grows across his cheeks. "Sorry. I mean, she's really mad."

"Rough," I say.

I wait for him to step out of my way, but he doesn't make any move to do it. Instead, he scratches the back of his neck.

"Are you, uh . . . Will you be at Spring Fest?" he asks.

"Wouldn't miss it," I say.

His smile recovers full force. "I'll see you there, then."

"Yeah, for sure."

Kyle nods, then starts to head off to his class next door, so I can finally step into the history room he and Emma had been blocking. I make it right as the bell rings, not that missing a few minutes would really matter. I doubt anyone will be paying attention between the murder news and Spring Fest. Mr. Franklin already has some video from the History Channel queued up on the screen, so no one is trying today.

"Oh, Gianna?" Mr. Franklin looks up at me before I turn the third row to my desk. "You've been summoned."

He holds out a pink slip. Again?

"After class?" I ask.

He shakes his head. "Right away." He gives the screen a glance. "Honestly, you won't miss much. Skim chapter sixteen before Monday."

My stomach sinks as I hold the slip. It's from Principal Daniels. Now that Mr. Ford's death is an actual murder investigation, are the cops back to talk to me? I should have a clear alibi since I was in detention right up until finding Mr. Ford, but if Principal Daniels told the police that I'm his somehow-suspect for the fire, they might still think I'm involved.

Dammit.

I force a smile and walk right back out into the hallway. I need to go. It's going to look way worse if I don't, and it might be nothing.

Doesn't stop my stomach from feeling sick though.

Did I take my fiber this morning?

It feels like I can't focus on anything lately.

Ms. Leslie eyes me as I step into the main office. I try to read her face to get some clue of how bad this is, but she must have been kept in the dark. Either that, or she has an extremely good poker face because I'm getting nothing.

"You look nice, Ms. Leslie," I say. "Must be all the pickle-ball."

She waves me off. "Flattery won't prevent you from getting detention."

So she does know something. Detention seems like a light punishment for potential murder involvement. Maybe this is about the fight yesterday? Even though it didn't happen on school property and *I* was the victim this time. Technically.

"What did I do now?"

"You're asking me?" Ms. Leslie removes her glasses so she can wipe them with the hem of her floral shirt. "Maybe you need a planner to keep track of your rule-breaking, Ms. Ricci. I don't get the details."

Okay, maybe she doesn't know anything.

I don't even get to take a seat. At the sound of my voice, Principal Daniels opens the door to his office. "Gianna Ricci," he barks. "Step inside."

He looks how I feel when my digestive distress pendulums to constipation.

This can't be good.

Although a part of me wants to walk on out and avoid the headache, I follow instructions and step into the office. What the fuck?

I was expecting a lot of things, but I was not expecting Mari and Sean to be already seated across from Principal Daniels. They look completely out of place. I don't think either of them have been in trouble in their lives. What the hell is this about?

"I appreciate you taking me out of class for a Mystery Club meetup, but today was a video day, so really not necessary," I start. "Perhaps we can chat another time? I'll bring the Dunkin'."

Principal Daniels is not amused.

"I don't think you understand the gravity of the situation," he says. "Take a seat."

My skin crawls, but I take the empty seat next to Sean. I glance at both him and Mari, but their panicked expressions share that they also have no clue what this is about.

"Principal Daniels," Mari begins. "I think we're all just a little confused about why we've been called here."

Is this because of what happened to Benji? If that were the case, I'd rather go directly to Mrs. Goode and talk about my childhood or whatever.

Principal Daniels opens one of his desk drawers, lifting out a cracked iPhone and some printed photos. I don't know who prints photos anymore, seems like a waste of money. Between Mr. Ford and his flash drives and this, I wasn't wrong in telling Cedar's mom that the school needs donations for new lights and technology.

Principal Daniels closes the drawer and puts the photos down in front of us. "There were items found in a school dumpster that Ms. Ricci might recognize."

I look at the photos. The first is a Giant Eagle plastic bag in a dumpster, but it's hard to make out all that's inside. The second is a close-up of the items taken out. A lighter, lighter fluid, a photo of Mr. and Mrs. Ford, and a West-bridge High gym uniform, singed from a fire.

The name RICCI is still clearly scrawled across the front of the shirt.

My heart stops.

"Um . . . Gigi, what is this?" Mari asks, words soft, high, and blending together.

"I don't know," I say.

Principal Daniels doesn't seem to believe that. He rubs

his face with one hand. "That photo is from Mr. Ford's desk. Setting the fire is one thing, but why did you take that?"

I swallow. Someone didn't just start a rumor—they're trying to frame me for the fire. And I don't know how I'm supposed to defend myself.

"I *wouldn't*. Don't you think the reason the photo and my uniform are there is because someone is trying to make it look like I burned down the office? Come on, Principal Daniels, I know I'm no honors student, but I'm not that clueless."

"Gianna."

"Besides, I couldn't have started the fire," I protest. "I was with Kyle Sinclair."

Principal Daniels' lips are tight. "Kyle did say that, yes. Except we had another concerned student mention that Kyle might be covering for you due to . . . personal feelings."

This is ridiculous. They think Kyle is covering for me because he has a crush on me or something? Kyle Sinclair? I'm grateful he admitted that we were together, but who the hell said he lied about that?

"Who was this concerned student?" I snap.

"I'm not at liberty to disclose—"

"Did you ever think that *this* person might be involved? And *that's* why they're trying to make you think it was me?" I throw my hands up. "My gym uniform was stolen! Ask Coach Phil."

He sighs. "Gianna. I'm finding it difficult to believe that someone stole your *gym uniform* just to frame you for a fire that happened during your gym class period, at the moment when your attendance and location were unaccounted for. Sometimes, the easiest explanation is the correct one."

"I'm sorry," Mari says quickly. "I don't think Gigi had anything to do with the fire, but why are Sean and I here as well?"

That's a very good point. Even if I *did* randomly commit arson, isn't that something I'd be called to the office for alone?

"It's all one big issue. We were also forwarded this post, not long after his case was changed to a homicide."

It's another printed sheet of paper, but this time, with contact info blacked out.

If Mr. Ford was murdered, is anyone looking into the Mystery Club? It seems obvious that they did it to create an actual mystery and give themselves credit. I mean, the fact that Mr. Ford was found with a poster of a CAT PUN? Literally the two main Mystery Club people are obsessed with a murder mystery series that is all about cat puns (evidence below). Seems odd. Plus, they are the ones to come across the body?
Of course. Just as they wanted the mystery to go.
Not to mention, they all of a sudden get Gianna Ricci of all people involved? She's like a literal violent freak who would totally kill people. She's hurt like, what, three students now and seems to have zero guilt over it?
I don't know what the Mystery Club did to make her their literal bitch, but this is all way too coincidental. They are behind it, and everyone in that fake club should be arrested.

"You can't be serious," I say. "You think *we* killed Mr. Ford?"

"I'm not saying anything," Principal Daniels says slowly. "I'm just saying this is all evidence that can't go overlooked."

"Evidence?" I snap. "This is bullshit."

Principal Daniels removes the top sheet to reveal pictures of Sean and Mari in *Purrfect Meowder* cosplay along with information on the cat-pun-filled books. "So this isn't actually you two?"

They both look embarrassed, Mari blushing and Sean's pale face fully pink.

"I mean, it's us, yeah, but we'd never kill anyone," Sean protests. "Also, we're not even the Mystery Club. We're the Mystery and Thriller Literary Scholars. It's more like a book club, really."

"Besides, Mr. Ford signed on to be our advisor," Mari adds. "We turned in the form to student council and everything. Why would we hurt him? That doesn't even make sense logically."

"We have a letter from him claiming that he was no longer interested in being the club advisor as he didn't feel comfortable with it," Principal Daniels says. "It was found during an initial search of the crime scene, although it wasn't considered a crime scene then."

What the hell is going on? There's no way Mr. Ford wrote that. Even if he did have second thoughts about being advisor, he wouldn't have changed his mind between lunch and the end of the day. If he did for some wild reason, he would've told Mari and Sean. Whatever letter they are talking about had to have been planted.

Just like the cat poster.

My stomach drops. Those little details. Leading the Mystery Club to the crime scene. Is this what Watch Your Back has been planning all along?

"We are turning over everything to the police," Principal Daniels says finally. "I'm sure they will be in touch for questioning. In the meantime, I'm afraid I have to give you all a three-day suspension, to be safe. I'm sure your teachers will allow you to complete your work at home until this is all sorted."

I don't know what to say, and I doubt Mari and Sean do either. They're probably spiraling even hearing the word *suspension*. I don't think either of them have even had to stay after class if it wasn't for praise. Is this planted evidence enough for the police to seriously consider us suspects?

"I'll be contacting your parents now, but the suspension is effective immediately," Principal Daniels says. "You can all wait in the office."

I barely even catch those words. I'm too distracted by everything he's just said.

"Okay," Mari squeaks.

Principal Daniels nods. "You're excused."

Dad was at the gym when Principal Daniels called, so he sent me a flurry of WTF texts before saying he'd take a quick shower and then come to pick me up. I didn't respond, hoping that would give him more time to calm down.

Maybe he and Mom will believe me when I say we're being framed for this? At the very least, they'll probably believe Sean and Mari are being framed.

But I don't know if I can explain that to them without revealing everything about Luca. I don't know. Maybe it's time to come clean about everything.

"I can't believe it," Mari says from next to me.

"I know," Sean mutters from my other side. "Kyle Sinclair has a crush on Gigi?"

I shove his arm. "Are you seriously making jokes right now?" I snap. "Watch Your Back is trying to frame the three of us for murder!"

Sean runs his hand through his hair. "I know, I just . . . I don't know how to deal, and if I don't make jokes, I think I'll have a panic attack and throw up."

I guess that's fair.

"Does this mean they think we attacked Benji too?" Mari asks. "Or do they think he and Aimee are in on it?" She sighs. "This is so fucked."

"It's like book five," Sean sighs. "*Feline Framed*. Everyone thought Miranda Morgan was the killer too."

I want to snap at him for even bringing up that damn series when it partially got us into this mess, but there's not much that will change now.

"What did she do?" I ask. "To prove she was innocent?"

"Exactly what we have to do," Mari says quickly. "Find the real killer."

"What?" I ask. "Today?"

She nods, keeping her voice low. "You got something better to do? Because last I checked, we're all suspended. If Watch Your Back is planning on framing us, they must have something else. Something big."

Holy shit. "Big Willy. If they reveal him, it gives us even more of a motive. Covering for my brother and your best friend."

Mari nods. "And if they are going to reveal that, where would they do it?"

"Spring Fest," Sean says immediately.

"Exactly. Which means we have . . ." She checks her phone. "Approximately ten hours to find the real killer."

Great. Like it wasn't bad enough before.

"So what do we do?" I ask.

For the first time all morning, Mari looks determined and puts on an actual smile. "What the Mystery and Thriller Literary Scholars were unintentionally training to do," she responds. "Solve a goddamn mystery."

# TWENTY-FOUR

## Everybody Hates Aimee

**WE ALL HAVE** to wait in the office for our parents to come pick us up, but Mari decided that we should make use of the time still here. While we were given permission to quickly get work from our teachers, we can't exactly run around the school trying to investigate. There's not enough time anyway with our parents already on the way. It's smarter to focus on what, or who, is right in front of us.

Which mean our target is Ms. Leslie.

Sean is the last to arrive back in the office with all his things. He doesn't immediately come to join me and Mari, but instead stops at the front desk. Since Sean is the one who matched Ms. Leslie with her cat (because he apparently is the Westbridge faculty stray cat dealer), he's the one that takes the initial lead in getting her guard down.

"Ms. Leslie," Sean says. "How are you?"

She smiles. "Wonderful, dear, how are you?"

"How's Mr. Meow Meow?" Sean says in a totally serious tone.

Ms. Leslie grins. "Oh, he's excellent. I'm so happy you introduced us at the shelter. He's a sweetie."

"I knew you'd be purr-fect together." Sean gives one of his smiles that comes across a little aggressive but is endearing in the moment. Ms. Leslie is delighted. She must not have heard about the whole murder-accusation thing.

"I stopped by Mr. Mora's class to get our assignment," Sean says, handing me a printed short story. There's a Post-it Note on the top that reads *check online for the rest of your assignments, try not to miss more class :) —Mr. Mora*

He probably wouldn't have added that smiley face if he'd heard the rumors that we killed a teacher. Or maybe he would to stay on our good side. I'm not sure, as this is my first time being falsely accused of murder.

Mari also stopped by some of her classes. I didn't bother. I'm not going to pretend like I'll get any work done today. Maybe I'll shoot off some messages on Monday, if I'm not brutally murdered or wrongfully arrested by then, that is.

"None of my teachers could believe I've been suspended," Mari mutters, neatly writing assignments into her planner. "What a joke."

"Is she coming?" I ask, voice low.

As difficult as it is to see her, Mari texted Cedar to join us in our *Hail Mary, check the main office before we're banished from the school* investigation attempt. She's our distraction. Which makes sense, since I know firsthand how good she is at taking up space in someone's thoughts.

Mari nods quickly.

"She also said that apparently everyone saw that post, and since we got called into the office, there's hardly anyone

268

who doesn't think we all murdered Mr. Ford to give ourselves a mystery."

I can't believe this. And now if people already believe we did it because of a freaking cat poster, they definitely won't consider otherwise if Luca's identity as Big Willy is revealed.

Watch Your Back really had this planned from the beginning. We are fucked.

It's at that exact moment that Cedar rushes into the office. Her eyes are watering, tears already streaking down her face.

It sort of makes my chest hurt, even though I know it's fake. She's not even looking in my direction, but it's like the air of the room changed with her presence. Like even if I didn't see her right in front of me, I'd know she was there.

Cedar's lip quivers. "Ms. Leslie, I need help."

"What is it, honey?"

Cedar darts her eyes over at Mari, Sean, and me before looking back at Ms. Leslie. "Can we talk in private?"

She's practically shaking. I know that Mari convinced her to do all this, but I'm still nervous, like something happened that we don't know about. Not that I can really talk about wanting to comfort her.

Ms. Leslie gives her a warm look. "Don't worry, dear, we can talk." She stands up from her desk, looking at the rest of us. "I'll be just a minute. Don't do anything while I'm gone."

"I don't know what Cedar's excuse is, but we probably

don't have that much time," Mari starts once they leave. "I'll keep watch and you two check the computer."

Sean and I race over behind the desk, trying to keep our steps as light as possible. "We're looking for Mr. Ford's rosters?"

"We want to double-check with the start of the year, since Cedar could only find his classes for this semester," Sean responds.

Ms. Leslie's desk is organized in a cluttered way, the kind of system that Ms. Leslie would know, but no one else. There is a picture of her holding who I assume is Mr. Meow Meow—a chonky black cat with white paws.

"I want a cat so bad," I mutter. I glance at Sean. "Please convince Mom to let me get a replacement Luca. They were into the idea, but for real."

"I probably can," Sean says. "They love me."

"Mom or Luca?" I ask, even though I know who he's talking about.

The tips of Sean's ears redden. "Maybe we should focus?"

"Do you know how to find rosters?" I ask, keeping my voice low, which isn't easy for me since I come from a family that's gay and Italian. But Principal Daniels's office door is closed and we can't afford to miss this chance.

Sean shrugs.

"Just search for it or something!" Mari whisper-yells from her spot by the window.

Sean checks a few places quickly before finally coming up with the class rosters for Mr. Ford this year. He starts taking pictures with his phone, while I quickly scan the names.

"Wait . . . what the fuck?" I breathe.

"What?" both he and Mari ask.

I point to the screen, at the roster for a Math 2 class that was made in the fall. Right in the middle of the list is Aimee Rhodes.

"Aimee has been acting like she didn't even know who Mr. Ford was," I say. "She straight-up told me she didn't have a class with him."

I can't believe this. Sure, she hadn't known we were looking into Mr. Ford's murder, but wouldn't she have at least mentioned when he died that she had him last semester?

Sean bites his lip. "Maybe she transferred out?"

I shake my head. "But why wouldn't she mention that?"

"I don't know," Sean starts. "It might not be anything."

"They're coming back," Mari calls quickly, interrupting us.

"Abort," I say. "Abort, abort." I shove Sean away from the desk.

He closes out of everything, and the two of us quietly race back to our original positions. I'm plopping down on the seat with my things just as the door opens and Cedar walks in with Ms. Leslie, who thankfully doesn't seem to notice anything out of place.

I'm still focused on Aimee and how strange it feels that she didn't say anything about having Mr. Ford as a teacher. I mean, she would've mentioned it on her podcast probably. She talked about everything else there.

I search her name and podcast on Google, but nothing comes up. I don't have any luck with Instagram either.

There're a lot of Aimees with podcasts, but none of them are her.

Finally, I text Benji. While I don't want to really bother him, he's the only person I know that listened to Aimee's podcast.

He responds quickly and sends over a link and I open it.

"That little bitch," I mutter.

"What is it?" Mari asks.

"Aimee's fucking podcast." I turn my phone so both Mari and Sean can see the screen.

*Miss Mystery: A True Crime Podcast*

Their eyes go wide. "Holy shit," Mari breathes out.

Before we can say anything else, Principal Daniels steps out of his office and looks at us. "Shouldn't your parents be here by now?"

As if he summoned my dad himself, a text comes in saying that Dad's outside.

I stand up, shoving my backpack on, only to hear my phone ring. Except my phone is on silent. I glance at the screen, literally confused because everyone else I know has an iPhone and wouldn't have my Android ring. I know because none of them ever have chargers for me.

That's when I notice Principal Daniels pick up his cell and swipe the call away.

He has an Android.

But the phone in his desk was an iPhone. Sure, it had a cracked screen, but why would he have two different phones . . . ?

"No fucking way," I say.

Principal Daniels glares at me.

"Sorry, sorry." I hold up my own phone. "Dad's trying to leave without me. Better go . . . you know . . . be suspended. Thanks again for that. Not sarcastically." I laugh. "See you, Sean. Mari. Ms. Leslie. Send my regards to Mr. Meow Meow." I clasp my hands together, smile too big, and exit the office before anyone can form a response to that mess.

They'll know something is wrong, but I'll follow up with Sean and Mari later. It's bad enough that Aimee was likely the one to send the Mystery Club to the crime scene.

But I'm pretty sure the phone in Principal Daniels's office was the one that Mari left in the haunted classroom.

Which means, despite blaming us, he knows exactly who killed Mr. Ford.

# TWENTY-FIVE

## It's Okay to Ask for Help

**DAD WASN'T EXACTLY** thrilled that I've been suspended from school. But in questionable parenting choices, he still stops to get an espresso for him and an herbal tea for me (because I especially don't need my intestines to detonate today) before taking me home for my lecture.

Once we arrive, he sits across from me at the kitchen table, sipping his espresso.

"You want to explain to me why you've been suspended for arson?" Dad asks.

It took him long enough to ask. He's being calm considering. I guess they didn't mention the possible connection to murder? It's possible Principal Daniels is just letting the police handle that. I don't think Dad would believe I played a part in killing Mr. Ford, but I can't say the same about setting fire to a school office.

"I didn't do it," I say.

He raises an eyebrow in a way that's almost comedic. "Precisely what an arsonist would say."

"What would someone being framed for arson say?"

His eyebrows now furrow. It's like my dad's expressions

are entirely formed from his brows alone. He doesn't even talk with his hands as much as the rest of us do.

I need to focus.

"Probably that they'd been framed for arson," Dad says.

"Well, I've been framed for arson."

He puts his coffee down. "Hmm. And why is someone framing you for arson?"

That's certainly the question of the hour. But if I'm going to explain that, I'd have to explain that the same person is also framing the entire Mystery Club for murder. And, oh, it might be our new freshman member, but probably not just her, since there's a good chance she's somehow working with the principal?

I glance down at my phone. Still no response from Sean or Mari even though I sent them an SOS text.

"Nope, no phone, give it here." Dad holds out his hand. "We're talking."

I reluctantly pass it over, even though that causes a strange bit of anxiety to spike.

"You were saying?" he prompts in a way that implies he doesn't care that I wasn't.

"I'm being framed because the person who started the fire is the person who killed Mr. Ford."

His eyes widen. "But you didn't kill Mr. Ford."

"Obviously not, Dad. I wouldn't kill Mr. Ford."

"I don't think you needed that specification, and that worries me. Putting that aside for a moment, why would the killer start a fire?"

I didn't expect a full interrogation here. I thought bartenders were supposed to let people open up to them naturally. "To destroy evidence."

"So why blame you?"

"Well, they aren't just blaming me. They are blaming the whole Mystery Club and now everyone is convinced Sean and Mari hatched some plan to save their club by working with me to murder my favorite teacher, I guess."

This is a lot for Dad to take in. His eyebrows are all over the place. But I can catch a level of understanding when his gaze slightly narrows.

"Wait . . . Has the Mystery Club been trying to investigate this? Even when it was still considered an accident?"

I'm not a bad liar. I'm usually a great liar or can at least hide behind my sense of humor well enough, but there's something about Mom and Dad. Both of them can see right through me.

"We're not *not* investigating it," I admit.

This is even more for Dad to take in, and I think it borders on too much because, without a word, he stands up and goes over to the cabinet to pull out a bottle of Kahlua. He tops off his espresso with a shot and sits back down.

"I'm sorry, but I need something a little stronger because what you are telling me is that you, my teenage daughter, and your teenage friends, are being framed by a real-life actual murderer that has it out for you? Does that mean the incident with the stage light and what happened yesterday is also because of this killer?" He doesn't even give me the chance to answer because my forehead is tense. Damn active-eyebrow genes. "You told me it was basically a book club!"

I can't even judge him for drinking a little at this point. Dad isn't exactly a traditional parent to begin with, and it's not like he's ever been drunk in front of me. Besides, even if he were stricter or acted more like other dads, I'm not sure that would be all that more helpful in this particular situation.

"It *is* a book club!" I defend, cringing a little. "A mystery book club that wanted to solve this mystery. But they wanted to solve it for Mr. Ford, not because they wanted to save the club."

Dad rubs his face. "We have to go to the police. Do you know who did it?"

"Well, I might possibly know who did it, but it's not adding up."

Aimee is definitely involved, but Principal Daniels also might be? I didn't think the person I attacked yesterday was my middle-aged school principal, but he's not a super tall guy, so the height could have been a match.

That might explain why he didn't want to hurt me, but does that mean it was Aimee who stabbed Benji?

I'm just not sure. It feels like I have all these little pieces but they aren't fitting together.

Dad downs the rest of his coffee.

"Okay, so catching up here . . ." He leans back in his chair. "You decided to look into the death of your math teacher, thinking it may have been a homicide, and now that it was revealed to actually be a homicide, the real killer is blaming you for the fire they started to destroy evidence because they want the Mystery Club to take the fall for the death?"

I nod. "That's pretty much it, yeah." I bite my lip. "Well, the Mystery Club and also potentially Luca."

"What does Luca have to do with this?"

I'm not sure I can get into the details, as they aren't totally mine to share. I don't want to snitch on my brother for cheating when there are bigger issues at hand. "He's also been helping with the investigation," I say, which isn't a lie.

"Jesus Goddamn Christ," Dad says.

"Pretty sure that's blasphemy."

"Pretty sure you're atheist." Dad throws up his hands. "What am I supposed to say to this, Gigi? You're in trouble. This is grounds for being in trouble. I'm talking about no new plushie orders. No little after-school murder club hangouts. No training unless you are specifically working to help your mom."

I wince. Sure, I saw this coming, but shouldn't my noble reasoning count for something?

"I can't miss Spring Fest. It's required."

It's not, but I've now realized it is the perfect time to get that phone from Principal Daniels's office. Besides, Dad's not usually the parent that *parents* as much. He'll definitely be more lax than Mom, so I have to use that to my advantage.

Dad frowns. "Only because your mom and I will be

there, fine. But you can't go off on your own, and if it takes longer than one minute to respond to a text, you're coming home." He crosses his arms. "And that's still a no on new plushies."

Vicious. "Go easy on me. I might get expelled for something I didn't do. And a murderer is after me."

Dad shakes his head. "And you still didn't even tell Cedar you like her."

I roll my eyes, but the grumbling in my stomach returns. "I'm going to try to do it tonight at Spring Fest."

"You might get expelled because you're framed for arson, you have an actual murderer after you, and you're telling the girl you like that you like her tonight? In a public location in front of your whole school?"

I put a hand over my belly button like that can calm the pinch. "I'm not telling her in front of everyone, but yeah."

Dad holds out the bottle of Kahlua to me.

I eye it and look back at him. "I don't think that's model parenting, Dad."

"Oh, I'm sorry for making a joke, Gigi." He puts a hand to his chest. "Let me reread the chapter on Your Child Investigating Murders in *What to Expect When You're Expecting*. I think I skipped over that one."

Annoying eyebrows and sarcasm. That's what this man gave me.

There's a loud knock on the door. Both Dad and I nearly fall off our chairs, and I'm one more loud noise away from ruining this pair of underwear altogether.

"Who is that?" he asks. "The murderer?"

"How should I know?" I whisper-yell back. "You answer it!"

"Sure, send the one with no formal fight training." Despite the mutter, Dad stands because he still is a dad and investigating loud noises is a dad job. I don't make the rules. He grabs a kitchen knife on the way there.

Like he knows how to use that for anything but cutting lemons and limes.

My heart pounds in my chest.

Is it possible that it's Aimee? Or whoever she is working with? Dad tightens his grip around the handle of the knife and quickly opens the door. My breath hitches.

"Um . . . Mr. Ricci? You good?" Mari asks.

All the tension in me breaks when I see Sean and Mari standing on the other side of the screen door. Dad has that same expression of relief, but it's soon replaced with embarrassment as his gaze moves to the knife.

"Yes. I was . . . getting ready to make lunch."

"It's not even eleven," Sean says.

"Ha, always messed up with my work schedule." Dad opens the door. "But speaking of which, aren't you supposed to be in school?"

"Dad, we went over this," I say. "We've all been suspended."

Despite knowing the entire Mystery Club is being framed, it's like my dad doesn't really compute that Sean and Mari could have been suspended. Like he really thought that was just a Gigi punishment.

"Okay, but shouldn't you be at home?"

"Mom and Greg are high on something and probably won't be any help," Sean says. "Plus, my place was broken into, so I don't really think it is safe to be there."

Dad opens his mouth. "I'm sorry, of course you are welcome here. But, Mari?"

Mari shrugs. "Sean needed a ride and I told my parents it was an emergency. They're probably going to be calling any minute now."

"Okay." He looks between the three of us with his best stern, fatherly glare. "I'll wait for the call and then we're going to the police."

"We can't," I say. "Not yet."

"Oh, I'm sorry, prior engagement?" He rolls his eyes. "No, we're going."

"But we don't have enough evidence yet."

"It's not your job to get evidence." Dad grabs his car keys. "It's your job to get good grades and not die, both of which seem to be pretty difficult for you, might I add."

"Unnecessary, but I can't argue that."

"We can tell the police whatever you know, and they can go and figure out how to get the evidence together. I don't care. The point is, you three are staying out of it."

I get it, the situation is scary.

But if Principal Daniels is trying to cover this up, there's no way police are going to believe us with some loose proof of motive alone. If anything, they'll probably be questioning us for the murder.

We need the phone.

At that moment, the call from Mr. de Anda comes through. "We're not done talking about this. So all of you, stay here. I'm going to talk this over with Mari's parents, and whatever we decide, we're doing. No arguments."

I open my mouth to protest, but he holds a finger out.

"No arguments," he repeats.

Dad walks into the other room to take the call. He probably doesn't want us to hear that he'll likely go along with whatever the de Andas want, considering they are older and way more together than either of my parents. I wouldn't change Mom and Dad for the world, but I would be a little concerned if Luca and I didn't also have Mrs. and Mr. de Anda at times to look out for us . . . especially in times of a murder investigation and deciding when to go to the police.

I wait to hear him answer before I turn to Sean and Mari. I might as well get right into it. The clock is ticking.

"Principal Daniels has your old iPhone," I say. "From the crime scene."

"With the EVP recording?" Mari asks.

I nod. "I don't know if he listened to it or not, but we have to get the phone from his desk."

Neither Mari nor Sean can hide their excitement at the development.

"How are we supposed to get into Principal Daniels's office?" Sean asks. "We can't be at school today."

"Spring Fest," Mari says. "We'll break in during Spring Fest."

I almost get a rush of pride that she came up with the same idea that I did.

"Exactly. But what if he deleted the recording?" I ask. "Is there a way of recovering it?"

"I'm not sure." For a second, I think Mari is dejected, but it's probably just a result of her admitting she doesn't know something. Because her brown eyes are still bright. "Who else would the Mystery Club go to for tech help?"

Well, I did tell my dad I'd talk to her at Spring Fest. It's not like we really got the chance to interact this morning. Mari is just giving me the opportunity.

"Okay, great, yeah," I say. "But when do I kill Aimee?"

Mari sighs. "It's weird that she sent us to the room, but that doesn't mean she murdered him."

"Well, it certainly makes her involved."

"Why don't we focus on the phone first, then we can worry about confronting Aimee?" Sean suggests. "We know she'll be there since she's part of the Peace Studies Club."

Both of them look at me.

"Fine," I say. "Phone first, then Aimee."

While I'm excited things are moving and we'll get the chance to find Mr. Ford's killer and clear our names, I'm also feeling a level of anxious I'm not used to. My chest is tight and my gut is filled with a strange sense of dread.

Either way, if everything goes well, there will be two confessions tonight.

And I'm not sure which one is more terrifying.

# TWENTY-SIX

## Iiiiiiiiit's TIME for the Main Event

**IT WAS DIFFICULT** to really prep before Spring Fest, since Mari's parents and Mom met us at the police station. Of course the de Andas, a bit more responsible than Dad, convinced him that we couldn't put it off. Despite us voluntarily going in, it really felt like a questioning. It wasted enough of the day that we had to be dropped off right at Spring Fest, with promises to keep our locations shared, be in constant contact, and not look into the murder.

I'll keep two of those promises at least.

We meet outside of the high school, minutes before Spring Fest is slated to start. There're already crowds of people starting to form, waiting in front of the balloon arch that acts as a makeshift entrance. All around most of the parking lots and fields, tents and booths are already set up, with rides of questionable safety in the distance. It's easy to make out the Peace Studies Club, all decked out in green and white, Westbridge colors, and directing people in line.

And in front of all the hectic excitement, Cedar.

She's striking, and it's like my eyes don't want to look away. Her lavender hair is in a messy bun with enough strands falling to her shoulders to draw attention to her form-fitting jumpsuit. Her makeup is bold and looks great.

While waiting at the police station gave me plenty of time to prepare for how awkward this would be, it still is awful enough to take me by surprise.

I sort of have a plan on how to explain myself to Cedar, but it doesn't exactly seem like the right time, and I don't want to do it in front of Mari and Sean.

"Thanks for helping, Cedar," Mari says. "I really owe you one."

Cedar shrugs. "Not like I had any other Spring Fest plans."

I want to reach out to her. I want to take back everything. I want so much, but I'm still afraid to say it.

We're at the side of the building that's pretty much opposite all the fields and parking lots where the festival is set up, so while it's relatively quiet in the background, even here, the air is buzzing with preparation for the event.

"Ready?" Cedar asks.

She has the door propped open, since she stayed after school to wait for the rest of us. We all slip inside, and she slowly closes the door behind us. Mari and Sean start ahead in the direction of the principal's office, and walking as a whole group might be a little more suspicious, so I take slow steps to stay behind.

It also might be for a less club-oriented reason.

"Hey," I say to Cedar, who's keeping pace beside me.

That's a terrible way to start. Not that now's the right time to say anything.

"Hi."

I don't know why I feel so awkward. Okay, I know why. I just wish I didn't.

"Can we talk?"

She looks right at my eyes without stopping. "Your timing is really something."

I know this isn't the right time or the right place. But I need to know there's some chance of her listening to me. Wanting to hear me out. There's this strange distance between us that's even more noticeable than the feeling when we were barely touching.

"I'm sorry," I say. "I was such a bitch to you, and I need to apologize . . ." My brain can't catch up with my fast-beating heart.

"We can talk later," Cedar says. "We have to solve a murder first, right?"

"Right," I say. "I know. I just wanted to see if you would, but . . . yes, let's talk later. Me and you. Us. Um . . . I promise I'll explain myself, okay?"

That doesn't make sense. Is Cat Island still an option? I shouldn't have said anything yet.

But Cedar looks back at me and gives a small smile. "Okay."

My stomach doesn't hurt so much anymore, and my chest is that little bit lighter.

I'm not feeling one hundred percent. We're still about to break into the principal's office for a recording of a possible murder and we're not allowed to be here at all.

286

The hallway around the main office is empty. Really none of the Spring Festival is inside, unless it rains, but the weather is shockingly dry and relatively warm today. Everyone must already be outside to greet all the guests and run whatever they're supposed to. Besides, the doors automatically lock, so it's not like people can just walk in.

Not without someone on the inside at least.

We slip into the main office. Not even Ms. Leslie is in here.

"Door's locked," Sean says, trying the knob to Principal Daniels's office.

"Did the Mystery Club seriously not plan for that?" Cedar asks. She rolls her eyes, pulls a bobby pin from her bun, and kneels down in front of the door. Within a few minutes, she turns the knob, and it opens.

The rest of us all stare at her.

"You can pick locks?" Mari asks.

"I'm an only child with parents that hate me," Cedar says. "I have a lot of free time. When I got older, I moved on to firewalls to hide my gay online life, but everyone starts somewhere, and I started with physical locks."

Mari crosses her arms. "I can't believe you never officially joined the club."

"I don't like reading, so."

Mari can't really argue against that. Instead, we step into the office. I shouldn't feel guilty, because we're doing this for the right reasons, but it's like the air is different when you're breaking the rules in a new way.

I have a bad feeling. Not sure if that ends in us being caught.

"Where was the phone?" Mari asks.

I point to the drawer where it should be located. Cedar slides it open and thankfully the phone is there.

"It's dead," she says. "Do you have the charger?"

Mari already has the charger pulled out and plugs it into the wall. Once the phone is on, Cedar goes through the files.

"It looks like the recordings were all deleted, but I should be able to recover them," Cedar says.

"What's going on here?"

I had been so focused on all the excitement in finding the phone, I didn't even realize the door opened behind me and Sean, which now reveals a very pissed-off Principal Daniels. The four of us look at him, a mostly Mystery-Club group of deer in headlights.

Well, shit.

"We know what's on this phone," I say, "and we already have the backup to send to the police."

Technically, we don't have the file yet or know if it even managed to record any of what happened, but I don't think I should be admitting that since Principal Daniels might be hiding something or involved in what really happened.

Instead of moving to attack or busting into the expected evil-villain monologue, Principal Daniels blinks. "Wait . . . what? Three of you are not even supposed to be on school grounds. Did you all break into my office to charge your phone?"

What?

For someone potentially covering up a colleague's murder, he's a little slow on the uptake here.

"No, it's the phone from your desk," I say.

His face is all confusion. "The one found in the Peace Studies Club room? A student left it. We've been waiting for someone to claim it."

"The one that . . . you *what*?"

My mind fully processes what he's saying. The phone that was in Mr. Ford's room when he was murdered was found in the Peace Studies Club room? And we're learning this immediately after we find out that Aimee is likely Miss Mystery?

Oh, hell no. It's all Aimee Fucking Rhodes.

That's probably why she joined the Mystery Club in the first place.

I'm going to kill her.

"Principal Daniels," Mari starts, "I apologize and can take full responsibility for entering your office without permission, but we have reason to believe this phone has evidence of who actually killed Mr. Ford, and if we don't get it soon, we're afraid that person will hurt someone else."

Principal Daniels rubs his eyebrows, probably weighing the options of how bad it would look for a guest to get murdered at Spring Fest, should the killer strike again.

"Okay, okay," he says. "I'll stay here with you and we'll

call the police. Anything on that phone, we'll turn over to them."

My phone buzzes loudly in my pocket. Sean's phone makes a chiming noise at the same time. Mari's screen lights up. It seems like everyone got a notification at once.

I pull out the phone and my heart practically stops. It's from Watch Your Back, only this time it seems to have been sent to the entire school. Oh no. Are they seriously planning to do something at Spring Fest?

There's the letter Mr. Ford wrote to Principal Daniels about the cheating scandal attached, with the subject line speaking for itself.

**Westbridge High's Own Big Willy Helped Mystery Club Kill Teacher**

But it's the body of the email that's so much worse.

*And in just ten minutes, you'll all know who it is :)*

My stomach lurches and I feel like throwing up. We figured it would happen, but I didn't expect it to happen so soon in the night.

"What's going on?" Principal Daniels asks.

"They're threatening Luca," I say. "The murderer's threatening Luca." Tears start forming at the bottom of my eyes. It's not even acting, like he or Mari could pull off. "Principal Daniels, Mari and Cedar can explain everything, but please let Sean and me check that Luca's okay. He's just outside at the festival."

I think he's aged about two years from this interaction

alone. "Fine," he says, "but do not leave the school grounds and stay at the festival. Keep Mari and Cedar updated on your location, and we'll send police to you."

I take back every bad thing I've said about him.

Mari and Cedar start to work to explain everything, and Sean and I rush from the office.

"You go to Luca," I tell him. "I have to check on something else."

While his expression gives a *Seriously?* vibe, Sean only nods and runs off. He's not one to argue back when times are urgent, even if maybe he should.

I pull out my phone and call Aimee. I'm almost surprised when she picks up.

"Where the fuck are you?" I ask. "I know you're Miss Mystery."

Her voice comes out small and high, almost like a sob. "Peace Studies room," she says. "I'll explain everything."

With Spring Fest already started, the Peace Studies room is all but empty. Aimee isn't here yet, although I guess I was closer since I was already inside the school building. There are scraps of decorations strewn across the floor, as well as folders and some bags that were left behind.

It would be silly of me not to make use of this opportunity, wouldn't it?

I start with a random bag, but it's not Aimee's and there's nothing incriminating inside. Same with the next one. I open a random gym bag that has a crumpled test on the front with a B– in blue pen and a little note. I check the name on the top.

Kyle Sinclair.

Damn, I thought he was a nerd like my friends and brother. It's a great grade, don't get me wrong, but I thought he was part of the Effortless As club. I'm not here to check people's grades though. But a word on the teacher's note catches my eye and I can't help but read it.

*Nice work, studying with your sister paid off!*

Kyle has a sister? As far as I, or pretty much everyone else, seems to know, Kyle's an only child. There's not another Sinclair at the school, and his parents literally show up to his football games all the time. Wouldn't it be more known if he had a sister that went to Westbridge and was still close enough to help him study?

I don't get the time to really think about the question, because at that exact moment, hands grab me from behind and cover my nose and mouth.

# TWENTY-SEVEN

## When the Pieces Finally Fit

**IT MAY SOUND** weird out of context, but I'm not exactly a stranger to being choked or even to people randomly coming up behind me and attempting a choke, so I immediately tuck my chin and pull on the arm that's attacking me. Once I'm freed enough to breathe, I twist my hips to slam my elbow into the solar plexus of whoever was behind me.

I turn around to see Kyle Sinclair slightly bent over, but he quickly catches his breath.

My eyes go wide. "Sorry, Kyle, you scared the shit out of me." My face heats when I realize that I'm in front of his open bag with the test dropped onto the floor. "I know this looks bad, but you can't just go grabbing people like some kind of creep."

"I'm sorry, Gigi," Kyle says. He reaches into his pocket as his blue eyes look glassy in the classroom lighting.

"You don't have to be that sorry," I start. "I'm okay. Really. But have you seen Aimee?"

It's only after the line of words rush out that I realize the thing he pulled out of his pocket was a butterfly knife and he's now pointing it at me.

293

"I'm really sorry," Kyle repeats, eyes watering, "but I'm going to need you to come with me."

While I still definitely have questions, it's immediately clear that Kyle is the person who attacked me, even if he wasn't the one who stabbed Benji. Now that we're standing so close, I can even make out the concealer covering the bruising around his nose where I hit him. Since he almost got the better of me last time and he currently has a knife, there's not much I can do physically to try to disarm him and not get hurt in the process. Even if I manage to get away (and probably get stabbed in the process), would I be able to outrun him? He had the chance to kill me before, and it seems like he doesn't want to hurt me now, which means I don't need to give him a reason to use that blade.

I'm better off trying to stay on his good side and hopefully getting out of this without ending up in the hospital. Or dead.

My hands rise up carefully. "Okay, Kyle. I'll come with you, so let's stay calm, all right?"

He nods. Still keeping the knife out, he walks around me and stands at my back. My heart pounds in my chest. My body wants to use the muscle memory of years and years of drilling takedowns and judo trips, but the knife really puts a damper on that.

"Is it okay if I touch you?" Kyle asks. He must be able to read the expression on my face because he gives an apologetic smile. "I mean, I know none of this is okay, but I don't think either of us have a choice, so I'm going to have to touch you and let me know if it's too uncomfortable."

I don't know if it's possible to feel comfortable in this situation. I wasn't expecting for someone clearly involved in a murder to ask for consent while threatening me. Is Kyle the one who killed Mr. Ford? Why isn't he acting more . . . like a murderer, then?

I know murderers don't always act like murderers, but I figured the switch would flip after he revealed himself by threatening me with a knife. Unless he'll just keep politely asking me if he can stab me to death.

"Okay," I say. "Thanks for the heads-up."

While I really want to cuss him out and fight, that's not going to help me with solving the mystery or surviving this shit. I breathe in and out slowly. I can be calm. I can be collected. I can totally pretend like I'm not angry and freaking the fuck out because the first dick I've seen is ready to reluctantly flay me like a fish.

The point is, this is fucked up.

Kyle reaches under my shirt, holding the blade close to my skin but careful not to draw blood. Lucky for him, my clothing isn't tight, so to anyone looking, it would probably just seem like he's walking with his arm around me.

"Try to act normal," he says, "and you'll be fine."

"People aren't going to think it's weird that we're walking like we've just had sex?"

I feel his side against me, his arm on my waist, and I'm practically pushed up into his armpit. It would probably be cute if not for the fact that he's one flick of the wrist away from giving me an appendectomy.

Kyle's cheeks flush pink, but he shrugs. "I'd rather them think that than the truth." He starts moving toward the door, and I have no choice but to follow. "Besides, I don't think people would find that weird. I mean, you're attractive."

Oh good. At least the person who might be trying to kill me thinks I'm hot.

"I appreciate that, Kyle, although I don't really think now is the time."

"You're right, sorry."

Part of me was hoping that he would lead me out the front door, past the main office, where Mari and Cedar are talking still with Principal Daniels. They would know that something wasn't right, and even if Kyle has a weapon, there would be witnesses and four of us versus one of him.

Unfortunately, he either planned for the risk of someone being in the office or simply lucked out, since he avoids that side of the school altogether and heads toward the back doors that lead to the senior parking lot.

I really try to keep my breathing calm and convince myself that everything is fine. The flat metal of the knife is cool on my skin as it touches with every other step. It would be all too easy for it to slip right into my skin.

Fear seizes my throat. No, keep calm. Keep calm. I'll get out of this.

"Where are we going?" I ask.

"Not far," Kyle says.

"Is Aimee there?"

He doesn't answer. So much for getting clarification in the meantime.

Is it possible that Aimee is Kyle's sister? It would make sense for the two of them to be working together if that were the case. They were even partnered up when it came to selling chocolates door-to-door.

But is she so smart she's able to help Kyle in classes when she's an underclassman? Also, I know not all siblings obviously share genes like Luca and me, but they really look nothing alike. On top of that, I'm pretty sure Aimee moved to Westbridge for high school, but Kyle has been in Luca's class since they were in kindergarten.

Maybe they are stepsiblings? But would you really be close enough to a sibling you only met a year or two ago to commit murder with them?

I guess people have killed for less.

We manage to make it to the door without anyone passing by, which is just my luck. Immediately as we go outside, the thumping music and buzz of activity over at Spring Fest fills the air. The tents have filled with people, rides twisting and twirling and flashing with lights.

We're a little too far away for people to be around, especially since this lot is already full. If I tried to scream or get away, I'd get stabbed before anyone could help. Even if Kyle doesn't necessarily *want* to hurt me, I won't take my chances when a knee-jerk reaction might disembowel me.

My bowels might be a hot mess, but I like them where they are.

Kyle leads me away from the fields, lights, and crowd, toward the small wooded area at the back of the school. It's not exactly a full forest or anything, like if you walk for five or ten minutes, you'll be in someone's backyard, but it's distanced enough from the excitement and covered enough by trees that it isn't a place you want to be led by knifepoint.

Am I going to get killed? At my high school?

While people are eating kettle corn right on the other side of the building?

I don't know whether to laugh, cry, or shit my pants.

I need some kind of plan. My phone is still in my pocket—Kyle didn't grab that. Maybe once we get in the trees, I'll have a better chance of escaping and I can call for help. Plus, my location sharing should still be on. If I go along with Kyle long enough, maybe someone will notice that it's weird I'm walking out toward the trees and come to help me?

That's about as good of a plan as I can get.

At least it's not totally dark outside. Although I'm not sure if that works against me in any escape attempts.

Kyle leads me into the trees, where a nervous-looking Aimee waits with Emma.

Emma, who shares the same features as Kyle. Who was arguing about something with him. Who had walked out of Principal Daniels's office right before he first questioned me about the fire.

Holy shit.

"Nice of you to finally join us," Emma says.

While Kyle keeps the knife pointed at me, she yanks my hands behind my back. Something cuts into my wrists. Based on the sharp, plastic feel and the fact that I can no longer move them apart, it's clear that she used zip ties. Which is way more messed up than rope. Now there's no way of reaching my phone, and even running away will be difficult.

Emma grabs on to my shirt and pushes me down. With no way of using my arms to frame up, my ass slams on the ground and tucking my chin is the only thing that keeps my head from whacking the tree trunk behind me.

"I have to say, I'm kind of surprised you even got this far," Emma continues. "I figured the Mystery Club was worthless, but you've been quite the thorn in our side. Maybe it's intuition? After all, you were the only one who didn't trust our cute little Aimee from the start, even after she was dumb enough to send an email from her podcast account."

"Nobody listens to my podcast!" Aimee defends.

I glance over at her, hoping the hate in my eyes outweighs the fear and discomfort of falling on snapped twigs and being threatened at knifepoint.

"I'm sorry, Gigi," Aimee adds, "she made me do this, I never wanted to get involved—"

"Shut the fuck up, Aimee," Emma says. "She doesn't care. Gigi doesn't like you anyway. Save it." Aimee clams up with a little cry. Emma rolls her eyes before sharing a look with me. "You're not wrong. She's so annoying. But rodents like her make for good moles, don't they?"

My brain struggles to process everything that's happening. It's like my senses are in overdrive. I'm already terrified but trying to stick to the plan of keeping calm and stalling since I'm down two limbs, Kyle has a knife, and now the president of the Peace Studies Club went full-on villain mode.

"So let me get this straight," I start. "You and Kyle are actually siblings and worked together to kill Mr. Ford because Mr. Ford was going to expose Big Willy, who Kyle used to cheat . . . and then you made Aimee get involved with Mystery Club, who you are trying to frame?"

"Half siblings," Emma corrects. "Our dad's a piece of shit who apparently couldn't figure out condoms twice within the same year."

"Okay, *half siblings*," I amend.

Like that really makes a difference.

"See, if it were just Kyle, it wouldn't have been much of an issue," Emma continues. "He at least has football to fall back on. Issue was, Mr. Ford was looking into *me*. Apparently, he's good friends with Mr. Mora, who was joking that my essays in class weren't unique or creative and didn't match the assignment at all. Asshole."

"Why do anything?" I ask. "Mr. Ford only thought you might've bought an essay."

Emma's face twisted. "Do you know what would happen if I'd been caught? My acceptance to Brown would be revoked. And I'd be a public fraud. It would've been fine if Mr. Ford was just playing detective like you losers but no,

300

your fucking *brother* had to give him evidence that he wrote my scholarship essay."

Oh *shit*. The scholarship that got her on local news and nearly viral?

"So you killed Mr. Ford because *you* decided to cheat on a scholarship competition?"

If anything, Luca should have asked for a cut when he saw the posted essay was the same one he wrote. Whatever he got paid to write the essay can't possibly compare with the tens of thousands she was awarded for winning.

"You don't understand," Emma says. "I *need* that money. If I lose the scholarship, I lose everything I have left. I refuse to stay with Kyle and our fuckboy father, who chose to *ignore* me for *years* until my mom died and he didn't have a choice. Then to make it worse, he gambles and drinks all his fucking fortune away, right before it could help either of his kids." She tries to collect herself, lowering her voice. "I hate that man, Gigi. I hate him enough to get rid of anyone who stands in my way."

Am I supposed to feel bad for her?

"That sucks, sure, but why not just kill your shitty dad if you're so ready to just murder everyone?"

"I'm not eighteen yet," Emma answers. "I'd have no guardian then."

Wait . . . had she considered it?

"You weren't on the list of Big Willy's clients," I say, still trying to make sense of everything.

Emma points at Kyle. "He put in the requests for me.

301

But the essay is basically an exact match to my winning one. Even if Luca didn't reveal himself as Big Willy, if Mr. Ford put that info out, everyone would think I stole the essay from Kyle. I'd still lose everything, and even worse, my brother becomes the victim."

"I told you, I could explain—" Kyle starts.

"That we bought the essay?" Emma snaps. "Again, same problem. Doesn't help."

I can't believe this.

"You seriously killed Mr. Ford over your fucking college acceptance?" I snap.

"I mean, technically he wasn't supposed to die." Emma frowns. "My brother fucked that one up, didn't you, Kyle?"

I twist toward Kyle, as best as I can with my arms stiff behind me. While he still has the knife out, he's shaking.

"It was an accident!" He looks at me. "I was just trying to threaten him a little but when I pushed him, he fell and hit his head on the desk. I seriously didn't mean to."

My throat dries. It was an accident?

"Why didn't you call for help right away?" I ask. "He didn't die from falling."

"I called Emma," he says softly.

Is he saying that Emma was the one who killed Mr. Ford? That she was the one who suffocated him? Anger burning in me, I try to loosen my wrists, but that only seems to dig the zip ties farther into my skin.

My glare turns to her as I look for some sign of whether that's the truth.

"How would it look if the school's golden boy assaulted a teacher? And then I have to be the sister of a criminal? That doesn't exactly look good for Peace Studies Club," Emma says.

"I think *murder* looks a little worse."

"Everyone would know why we threatened him then. I gave Mr. Ford a chance, I sincerely did, but there was no way he'd keep quiet. Kyle fucked up and I had to clean up the mess. If anything, I've been keeping the peace at Westbridge. Everything is still as it should be, with me getting away from my fucked-up father, no more nosy teachers who weren't good enough in their fields to actually do anything with their lives, and violent losers like you and your nerd friends taking the fall for it."

There's something wrong with her. This ridiculous fucking bitch.

"Why are you even admitting all of this?" I ask.

Emma laughs, light and casual. "What does it matter what you know? It's not like you can tell anyone." Emma waltzes over to Kyle to snatch the knife from him. Keeping it ready in her hand, she crouches in front of me. "After all, I have no intention of letting you out of here alive."

# TWENTY-EIGHT

## Gigi vs. the Westbridge High Murder Club

**I'M SO SCREWED.**

My hands are freaking stuck behind my back, my wrists are hurting like hell, and a scary rich girl who has literally lost her mind is threatening me with a knife. Back when it was just Kyle and Aimee, I maybe had a chance of playing nice and finding a chance to escape. All hope of that was lost when Emma forced my hands behind my back.

It doesn't matter how much I go along with her now. She wants to see me dead.

Aimee steps forward. "Hold on, Emma. That's not what we agreed on. You said the Mystery Club would take the blame; you didn't say you'd *kill* her. That's way too far."

I don't know if I can really thank her for that, considering she was totally fine with framing my friends and I for murder. I guess it's nice that she thinks killing me is going too far, but I don't really feel appreciative now.

Emma gives her a sweet smile. "Aimee. It's cute you are acting like you're a part of this and that your opinion matters." Emma steps toward her, almost like she wants to pull the whimpering younger girl into a hug. Instead, she strikes Aimee's head with the handle of the knife, causing her to crumple to the ground. "How many times do I have to tell you that no one cares?"

Shit. Shit. Shit.

Even Kyle seems freaked out by his sister at this point. She tightens her grip on the knife and turns on me, but he steps forward. "Emma, we can still figure something else out. Gigi won't tell anyone. We can pay her off."

Emma sighs. "With what fucking money, Kyle? Did you not forget that Dad basically lost everything? Even if we did have something, I doubt that will work now."

While the two are arguing like I'm not here, I back against the tree so I can have my hands against it. There's nothing really to cut the zip ties. Maybe if it had been rope, I could've broken free with friction alone, but I'm stuck without my hands for the time being.

Instead, I try to move my body so my phone can fall out of my pocket.

"What about the rest of the Mystery Club?" Kyle asks. "They're already suspects; everyone thinks they did it. Let's leave it at that. You can't just kill the whole club."

"I'm not saying *the whole club*. I'm saying Gigi. She's the perfect option. She just joined Mystery Club, so she could've turned on them. Besides, Sean's too strong for us, that freshman's still at home, and Mari's Hispanic so we'd look racist."

I can't fucking believe them. I don't even have the energy to clarify that Mari's family is from Spain and therefore European.

"Maybe you can consider murdering less and studying actual antiracism and allyship more," I suggest. "Happy to send you sources."

Emma doesn't even acknowledge me, which is probably for the best, because my phone is half hanging from my jacket pocket. I quickly move to the side and it falls onto the dirt. Almost there.

"Okay, but Gigi's queer, so isn't that still a hate crime?" Kyle asks.

"She doesn't even look that gay; it's not like anyone will care," Emma snaps. "Besides, I'm doing this for you. You're the one that fucked everything up when you promised we'd leave Dad. After how he treated our moms? After ignoring me my whole life while he gave you everything when he had it? You owe *me*, Kyle, and yet I'm the one doing this for *you*."

There's no way in hell I'm reaching my phone with my hands. Keeping an eye for when they both seem distracted, I twist onto my knees so I can peck at the screen with my nose like a bird. It taps to life, but Jesus Christ I've never regretted having a passcode more. Thankfully, it's just a pin number.

"I know, Emma, but Mr. Ford was one thing. This is another student, and there's people around. What if someone sees something?"

Six . . . Fuck, too high, I hit three. Delete. Okay. Six, four, eight . . . I glance back up to make sure they aren't looking at me before my vision fills with the close-up light of my screen and I hit the final two.

Unlocked. I could cry.

With one more nose tap, I hit the phone icon. Now I just have to press literally anyone to call.

"What the hell are you doing?" Emma snaps.

Startled, I fall onto my side and try to scramble back to a seated position as she snatches my phone. She glares at Kyle. "You didn't take her phone out in the club room? Can you do anything right?"

She throws it, where it smacks against a tree and falls somewhere in the bushes. This bitch. I'll never be able to afford a replacement. Not that it will matter now, when she likely kills me.

"I've had enough of this," Emma snaps. She walks back up to me, pointing the knife in my direction. "Time's up, Ricci."

My heart pounds wildly in my chest. My skin feels like gooseflesh. This can't be the end. It can't.

Emma looms over me, and I don't have my arms, but I'm desperate.

I kick up and hit her right in the chin. Something pops, and she falls back onto the dirt. I scramble, posting on my head so I can inch myself up and manage to find the balance to get to my feet. It's still awkward with my arms behind my back, but it doesn't matter.

I start running.

For a moment, it really feels like I can get away, like everything will be fine, until Kyle grabs onto me from behind and I tumble into the dirt.

"I'm sorry, I'm sorry, I'm sorry," he repeats.

I spit out pieces of leaves from my mouth. "Well, you're not fucking forgiven, Kyle."

I'm flat on my stomach with little ability to move, but I can still see Emma appear behind me. She's holding her jaw and her lips are bloodied and eyes are wild. She straddles my back and grabs my hair to yank my head up. She holds the knife next to my throat, which pulses with my racing heart.

Fear has frozen me. I know I could beat the shit out of her normally, but in this position, with my hands painfully tied, I have nothing. I am nothing.

I'm going to be killed by the freaking president of Peace Studies Club.

"I'll enjoy your death even more than I did that prick math teacher's, you trashy bitch," she snarls.

I brace for pain, but she's suddenly off me. I roll around to see Aimee standing over her with a discarded beer bottle. Some of the shattered glass hit me, but I can't even complain. Emma dropped the knife, which Aimee picks up to cut my hands free. I try not to think about the zip tie painfully peeling away and how gross the cuts look where it dug into the sides of my wrists.

Well. Maybe I don't completely hate Aimee Rhodes.

Before I can thank her, Emma manages to clutch on to consciousness and pulls Aimee back by her hair. I scramble to grab the knife from her before Emma can. Holding the weapon, I dart over to Kyle.

"Sorry," I say, perhaps a little ironically, as I grab him and hold the knife up to his throat.

"Let Aimee go," I shout to Emma, "or I fucking stab your brother."

There's no way I'm going to stab anyone, but she doesn't know that. The last thing I need is for one of the under-classmen members of the Mystery Club to be killed on my watch. Even if she is mostly terrible and joined as a mole, Mari would never let me hear the end of it.

"Do it," Emma snaps. "At least if he's dead, he can't be a bigger freaking disappointment. It'll just make it easier to put this all on you."

Holy shit, she's the absolute worst. Even Kyle stiffens at this one.

"What the hell? Stop! All of you!"

I've never felt happier to hear that voice in my life. Principal Daniels runs up to us with Mari and Cedar in tow. An excited laugh erupts from my throat as I back away from Kyle and drop the knife.

Emma's entire expression shifts. "Oh my gosh, Principal Daniels, thank goodness. I was so scared. Gigi was coming after us with a knife for no reason!" She bursts into actual sobs. "I thought she was going to kill me."

My heart sinks. Is Principal Daniels going to fall for this?

I know I'm not his favorite, and sure, I've gotten into fights before, but I've never used a knife.

"Save your fake-ass white girl tears," Mari snaps. "We have a recording of you and Kyle when Mr. Ford was killed."

That's when I notice that police officers have arrived behind them. Two move forward to grab both Kyle and Emma.

"It was all my brother!" Emma cries out. "I'll prove it once I get my lawyer."

Kyle complies as he's read his rights. "I'm going to tell them everything," I think I hear him say. It's hard to tell, since Cedar and Mari rush up to me at the same time.

They both pull me into a hug, pressing me against them, and it's probably horrible to think but I'm so thankful I did not die before being sandwiched between two hot senior girls. Truly almost makes everything worth it.

"How did you find us?" I ask when we all break apart.

"Benji noticed your location was weird and called us while Principal Daniels was giving the recording to the police," Mari answers. "We all rushed over."

Benji continues to be my hero. I have to buy him flowers or a cake after this one.

"Where is my sister?" a voice angrily yells, before turning into a shriek that kind of sounds like my name. I'm practically knocked over by Luca's hug. "I thought you died! What's wrong with you? Do you have to do everything by yourself?"

I wave at Sean, who trailed behind Luca. He smiles in return.

If not for the people around me, for Benji, and hell, even Aimee, I wouldn't be alive. There are some things I can't fight my way out of, not without help. That much is pretty damn clear now.

"I thought I did," I mumble into his shoulder, "but not so much anymore."

He's crying, looking me over. "What happened to your wrists? Jesus Fuck, Gigi, I'm so sorry. I feel like this is all my fault. I'll confess to everything and turn over all my records and . . ."

I put my hand over his mouth, even though it's covered in dirt and bending my wrist hurts like a bitch. "I don't really give a shit about that, Luca. We already have evidence and it seems like Kyle and Aimee will give full confessions." I move my hand to his shoulder since he stopped talking. "Honestly, no one cares that you sold answers. I almost died."

"Sorry," he says. "I'm just glad you're okay."

"You too," I say, hugging him again.

"Now let me call Mom and Dad before they actually kill us," Luca says. He steps away to place the call. Oof. I didn't really think about how my parents will react to me going off in search of the killer on my own. Again. And nearly dying. Again.

Hopefully the trauma is punishment enough.

Mari and Sean stay close to me.

"Well," I say to them. "How does it feel?"

They both give me looks.

"What?" Mari asks.

I give my best smile given the circumstances. "The West-bridge High Mystery and Thriller Literary Scholars actually solved a mystery."

I swear, the two of them almost start crying. I can't tell if it's out of excitement for having this be over or out of excitement for me using the correct name. Either way, I can't blame them.

Not giving a single shit who sees, I start crying too.

# TWENTY-NINE

## The Second (and Still Somehow Scarier) Confession

**AFTER MOM AND** Dad arrive and my wrists and other cuts are all disinfected and bandaged up by paramedics, the police take a few minutes for questioning. By the time everything is said and done, it's still pretty early. Despite the chaos and arrests of two of the most promising seniors at Westbridge, Spring Fest managed to keep going strong.

Apparently almost dying builds up an appetite, and I managed to convince Mom and Dad to buy me both a bowl of cavatelli and pierogies from different food stalls. I don't even care if I'll be in the bathroom for a while later. I'll chug an Alka-Seltzer and hope my IBS will chill for a night. Since the actual threat is over, Mom and Dad allow Luca and I to have fun at Spring Fest, especially since they are staying as well. I'm just not allowed to go on my own, since Emma smashed my phone.

Still at one of the food tables, I'm watching Sean win a goldfish for Luca that I know he'll cry over once it inevitably dies in a few days. They are cute together, though. I check the digital clock on the scoreboard for the thousandth time.

Thank god Spring Fest took over the field. It's about five minutes until I'm supposed to meet her.

Darting around people, I toss the food containers into the trash and head over to the meeting spot. It's one of the more relatively quiet areas, next to the Peace Studies Club booth. With news out about Emma and Kyle, no one's lining up to make donations now.

It's not exactly romantic, with the smell of sausage and peppers from the food stand next to it, but at least it's far enough away from the music and rides.

I swear, my heart's pounding more than it has been all night and I've narrowly escaped a murderer.

"You wanted to talk?"

It really isn't fair how good Cedar looks right now, with her hands in her pockets and tote bag casually slung on her shoulder.

*I want you to step on me,* I don't say.

"Yeah," I actually say.

I take a deep breath. "I'm sorry about what I said the other day. I was scared. I realized that there was someone good I really wanted and I guess a part of me thought I didn't deserve it while another part of me was already afraid of losing it." While I want to look away, I force myself to keep my eyes on hers. I need her to understand how much I mean what I'm saying. "I'm not the person who likes being vulnerable, and I'll probably continue to make bad jokes when things get serious, but I want to get to that point where I accidentally ruin some of our romantic moments. I want to show you

314

the sides of me that aren't tough and are super messy, and I want to see the sides of you that are bitchy and annoying and piss me off because it's all perfect and I love all of it." I don't blink away the tears that start to form, just breathe into how uncomfortable I feel. "I'm terrified that you'll break my heart, but I want to give you the choice to anyway. You can ruin my whole fucking life, Cedar, because I like you so much it scares the shit out of me." I crack a smile. "And I don't scare that easily."

There's a whole lot in the pause between us, and even more in the way she looks at me. There's the whole damn sky in that gaze.

"Well," Cedar says, drawing out the sound and casually wiping a tear of her own. "I'm totally not crying." She shifts on her feet. "Not to take advantage of the moment, since you almost died and everything, but you brought it up first technically and . . . I won this for you." She reaches into her bag and pulls out a cat plushie. It's a black cat with bright blue eyes and a pink bow around its neck. "Until you can get the real thing."

Cedar hands it to me, and I melt a little. It's so cute and so soft, and I might be tearing up along with her. I hold the cat to my chest.

"I don't mind."

"What?"

"If you take advantage," I say. "Help yourself to whatever you want."

She looks at me but can't hide her smile.

"In that case," Cedar says. "It's been a dream of mine to kiss a girl on the Ferris wheel. Since it seems like we both like each other . . ."

My breath catches. Our eyes are looking right into each other's. Although it takes an immense amount of willpower not to fill the moment with glances down to her bright lips.

"Too soon?" she asks.

I'm smiling too much. "Not soon enough."

I gently put a hand on her shoulder and stand on my tiptoes so I can kiss her.

Her lips are as soft as I imagined, and they push back against mine. They taste like candy and feel like fireworks.

When we break apart, our faces are practically frozen into huge smiles, like laughter paused.

"We can still go for the Ferris wheel," she says.

I'm still cradling the cat in one hand, but I reach to grab hers with the other. "Of course, I won't take away your sapphic *Love, Simon* moment."

"Two girls, sitting on a Ferris wheel zero feet apart because they're totally gay."

I snort. "Am I a loser if I ask if we're girlfriends now?"

"Yes, but you're my loser girlfriend."

My heart flutters. Both of us are messes, smiling and tearing up and letting our emotions all over the place. I have a stuffed cat cradled in my bandaged arms and can't possibly look anything close to my best. But nothing outside of this moment matters. Not what happened earlier, not all the possible bad things that might happen in the future.

"Since we're dating, does this mean I have to join your homoerotic fighting cult?"

Maybe I'm not the only one who will ruin romantic moments with jokes.

I glare at Cedar. "Are you talking about jiu-jitsu?"

I mean, she's not right, but she's not *wrong*.

"Well, I don't know much about jiu-jitsu, but I'd sure like to mount you."

"I hate you," I say through laughter.

She rolls her eyes and holds out her hand. "You love me."

I take it and squeeze her palm, loving the way it feels against mine as we walk in the direction of the Ferris wheel. Because she's basically right.

It might not be *love* yet, but who am I kidding?

I'm hopelessly on the way there.

# THIRTY

## The New Westbridge High Mystery Club

**"I'M SO EXCITED."** I wipe at my eyes. "I've been waiting for this day for so long."

Luca looks over at me, popping the car door open. "I'm not leaving yet."

"Oh, this is better than you leaving."

I open my side door, and Mom and Dad also funnel out of the car. I glance at the slightly run-down building in front of us, but I've never seen a place more beautiful.

*East Side Animal Shelter.*

"You're going to miss me," Luca teases.

"Exactly," Mom agrees, "the cat is to help ease the pain."

I roll my eyes and elbow Luca. "Don't pretend you aren't excited to be here. We see you all dressed up."

His blush confirms everything, but he still slaps me in the arm. It's true though. He's wearing his nice button-up shirt with little birds all over it and he even steamed his pants. I saw him, and I don't think I've ever steamed pants in my life.

"Why can't we get a dog?" Dad asks, and the rest of us glare at him.

Mom crosses their arms. "Who the hell has time for a dog?"

"Besides, I'm the one taking care of Replacement Luca, so I get to pick," I say.

Luca stops walking to pop his hip. "You can't name him Replacement Luca."

"What part of *I get to pick* do you not understand?"

Sure, I'm probably not going to name him that, and Luca will find that out eventually. But I like messing with him.

We step into the shelter, greeting the person at the front desk. They look nice, like a smile is their go-to expression and they'd call everybody *sunshine*.

"Hi, how can I help you!" they ask. It really is more an exclamation than a question.

"I'm Sean's friend," I say. "He was going to help us find a cat."

"Oh, Gigi!" They clasp their hands together.

"Did he tell you we were coming?"

The smile doesn't falter despite the words. "No, but you aren't Mari, and he doesn't talk about any other friends."

Even his coworkers know he only has two friends? Both of us need to get out more. Mari's off to Columbus soon, and then what? I'm not smart enough to go to the same college as Sean. Although he is poor enough to go to the same college as me.

The receptionist walks off to grab Sean, and Luca noticeably fixes his hair.

Sean walks back, looking hilarious in a polo shirt tucked into blue jeans. It's not hilarious, really, but it is so unlike him.

"Looking good," I tease.

He pushes up his glasses. "You're just jealous because my butt looks better than yours in these jeans."

Luca practically chokes on his own spit.

"Hi, Sean!" Mom greets as they walk in with Dad. "How are you doing?"

"Great. I really appreciate you coming here to adopt one of our cats."

"Of course," Dad says, like he didn't just suggest we get a dog.

We follow Sean through the door where the animals of the shelter are kept. We have to walk through the dog section first, and Mom has to keep pushing Dad's back to get him to stop looking at every option.

"It's Gigi's pet," Mom reminds him. "She almost died."

I don't know how long we can play the *Gigi almost died* card, but it's only been a week since everything went down, so I should have a solid month or so left.

"Now, you are more than welcome to look around," Sean says. "But I do have a cat I think will be a great fit for you. He's a sweetheart, but nobody has been wanting him because he has a ton of energy."

"Sounds like a perfect Replacement Luca," I say.

Luca glares at me and Mom stifles a laugh.

We follow Sean back into the cat section. Most of them are sleeping, but Sean walks us to one of the cages. The cat takes one look at me and starts meowing and pawing and biting the cage. It steals my heart.

He's a small black cat with big green eyes. And he's so cute.

"Oh my god," I say. I'm tearing up. "I love him."

"His name is actually Luke," Sean says. "Leia was adopted."

"Holy shit," I say. "It's a sign."

Sean opens the cage and Luke bounds right out. He stares right at me, meowing. I reach down and let him sniff my fingers. He rubs the side of his mouth against my fingers, so I try to pick him up.

He chills in my arms, purring loudly and drooling a little. Now I'm crying.

"I will kill all of you if we don't adopt him," I say.

"I'd like to see you try." Mom smiles. "But we can adopt him."

"He's like Cute Luca," I say.

"Let me see Cute Luca." Mom reaches out, and he's all too happy to be passed over. He keeps purring, sniffing them.

"You are not going to name him Cute Luca," Luca whines.

"He can have nicknames," I say. "Cutie. Luca Jr. Whatever."

Even though Mom holds him, Cute Luca reaches a paw out to my dad and places it on his arm. He blinks slowly.

Dad looks at the cat seriously before looking at the rest of us.

"I will kill a man for Cute Luca."

Luca looks ready to be that volunteer. "I'm so done with all of you."

I hold a hand out to him. "That won't be his actual name. We're just teasing you now because we're going to miss you so much."

I'm working with Mrs. Goode on being more honest about my feelings, which includes telling my brother I will miss him and not *just* teasing him. Not that I won't still tease him. I mean, I've only just started seeing her. We're also getting through dealing with anger and panic with everything that happened, but you can't fix everything in a week.

I'll get there.

And really, she's not so bad.

Not to mention, Luca owes me for not telling Mom and Dad about the whole Big Willy thing. They would've been *pissed*. But I don't want him to have to refund the money or anything. He already did all the work, and most of his clients were happy with it. Besides, compared to literal murder and attempted murder, selling some essays isn't that bad.

And I'm not a freaking saint or Boy Scout, I don't really care. But it should give me the right to tease him, at least.

"For real," Mom agrees to my earlier point of missing Luca. "Except you're going to text every day, right?"

Luca doesn't respond. "Let me meet Cute Luca," he says.

Mom reluctantly passes him over.

I haven't seen Sean look this happy since he caught a shiny Espeon, although the sight of my brother holding a cute kitten might be a lot for him, as his blush rides up to his glasses.

"I'm so glad you all get along," he says. "Randy up front can get you started on all the paperwork."

Mom and Dad go to fill that out, and Luca shifts on his feet. He looks at me like he wants help with something, but I don't understand what he's getting at. He finally sighs and then turns to Sean.

"Want to get dinner with me later?" he blurts, the words tumbling over each other.

Sean blinks. "Does your mom want me over again?"

Luca's jaw drops in disbelief. "No, like with me. Just me."

"Did you need help with something?" Sean asks.

My brother doesn't know what to say, and I swear I can see the Just Give Up flicker in his eyes. I can't handle these two. A summer of awkward interactions and sexual tension is not okay. This has to end here.

I throw my hands up before taking Luke away from these two. "He's asking you on a date, for fuck's sake! You two obviously like each other, just please, *please*, date already and let the Lawn ship sail!"

Both of their faces turn bright red and neither of them can look up.

"Lawn?" Luca asks.

I glare at him.

"Um, yeah," Sean says after a moment. "I'd like to get dinner. With you. On a date."

I didn't think it was possible but my brother's blush deepens. "Okay. Cool. I'll text you. Thanks. Cool. Um. See you then." He smiles and then runs off after my parents.

"Thanks," Sean says. "I think we needed that."

"Break his heart and I'll kill you." I frown. "But if he breaks your heart, I'll kill him."

"I hope it works out, then."

His voice has a joking tone but I can tell by the light in his eyes that he actually does.

Sean and I sit on the floor and pet Luke.

"How are you holding up, by the way?" Sean asks.

"Nice subject change. I'll allow it." I shrug. "I'm chill. Glad all this is over."

I take a picture of Luke—he's extremely photogenic—and send it to Cedar.

**Cedar:** asjkahjakdhsjbf

**Cedar:** SO CUTE

**Cedar:** I LOVE HIM

"You two are clearly doing well, though." Sean nudges me. Now my face heats. "We're good, yeah."

My lips practically buzz at the thought of her, so I go for a quick subject change prompted by me also sending the picture to the Mystery Club group chat.

**Mari:** AHH BABY

**Benji:** Congrats! So cute! *cat heart eye emoji*

Even though Mari won't be part of the club next year and the members will change, we decided to keep the group chat as is to remember this year. Well, aside from Aimee, although when my contacts were recovered, I didn't delete her number.

She redeemed herself enough to maintain status as

That Annoying Former Member of Mystery Club. Yeah, she isn't my favorite person ever, but who knows if I would have made it out alive without her help? Not sure that will keep her out of legal trouble, but hey. It's something.

Sean's phone buzzes with a new message. He tilts it so I can see the notification. It's to the mystery club inbox, with the subject **You might want to take a look at this . . .**

"Weird. Open it up, President," I say.

"Okay, Vice President," Sean mumbles. "Please don't let it be another crime scene location. I'm honestly ready to spend the majority of time going back to talking about cozy mystery or suspenseful thriller books."

We scan the message, Luke sitting in a cute little loaf between our legs.

> Hi Mystery Club,
> So cool you all solved Mr. Ford's murder. I totally can't believe it was Kyle Sinclair and Emma Galligan. Wow. I hate it when evil people have to be hot :(
> Anyway, there's this new IG account that was set up. Willy Westbridge. I think it's a play off the whole Big Willy thing.
> But instead of helping people get better grades, they seem to be leaving weird messages about planning something?
> It's suspicious as hell. Maybe you all can look into it.
> —A New Fan

Sean clicks on the Instagram account. It does look like a parody of Luca's Big Willy logo. The posts don't really make any sense, just different pictures of Westbridge High. The captions are more concerning. The first picture is captioned with *JUST YOU WAIT*.

The rest of the captions seem to be a countdown. The most recent photo is just an artsy close-up of the floor with what looks like a blood stain.

*July 23rd*. The caption reads.

"This isn't Luca," I say. "He would have told me."

"And the bio would have some *Hamlet* quote that is supposedly queer as hell."

Sean certainly knows my brother well.

But what does this mean? And why are they counting down? What the heck is supposed to be happening on July 23 and why must it seem so creepy?

I hate to admit that my curiosity is piqued, but it is.

"You think we should look into it?" I ask, excitement coloring my voice.

Sean smiles. "I mean, it's kind of our thing now."

And he's right. Even if it doesn't always seem that way.

The Westbridge High Mystery Club has many talents, but solving mysteries is not one of them.

Sometimes, though, we might just surprise you.

# Acknowledgments

**EVERYONE ALWAYS SAYS** that second books are hard, and they would be correct. (Although it is starting to seem like every book is hard.) It turns out writing the initial draft of your second book before your first book even sells doesn't make it all that much easier. It has been many months (and many near total rewrites) since I first fell in love with Gigi's voice, which makes it all the more special to be writing this and makes me all the more thankful for everyone who helped along the way (as there are many of you).

First, I would like to thank Cottonelle flushable wipes, for truly saving my ass more times than I can count during this publication process. (If you thought you were safe from IBS jokes in the acknowledgments, you thought wrong.)

A huge thanks to Lily Kessinger for first believing in this project and to my awesome editor, Alice Jerman, for taking it on. Lots of love and cat-pun floral gift sets to the extremely talented team at HarperTeen for getting behind this book and my sense of humor: Erika West, Clare Vaughn, Jan de la Rosa, Gretchen Stelter, Mary H. Magrisso, Chris Kwon, Jenna R. Stempel, Audrey Diestelkamp, Anna Ravenelle, Danielle McClelland, and Melissa M. Cicchitelli.

A major shout-out to my incredible agent, Patricia Nelson, for taking on this project (among others) and believing in me as a writer. You are the absolute best and I'm so, so grateful to have you in my corner!

To the initial members of the Mystery Club: Madeleine Gunhart, Elle Gonzalez Rose, Britney S. Brouwer, Kay Choo, and especially Birdie Schae, who supported this project even in the times I wasn't sure if it was working—this would truly not be a book without you.

Honestly, one of my favorite parts of writing (aside from making myself laugh) is the community. Book people are the best people, and I am lucky to have an amazing group of talented and wonderful writers in my life. I couldn't possibly name you all, so if you think you are included, yes, you are, friend, and I adore you. However, I will name a few people who have especially helped me throughout this process: Caroline Huntoon, Jen St. Jude, Ronnie Riley, Kate Fussner, Edward Underhill, Alex Brown, Lizzy Ives, J. L. Comes, Hannah V. Sawyerr, and still many more!

Thomy, I couldn't do any of this without you. You always support me in the exact ways I need (buy me plushies and cake) and love me in a way I didn't think was possible for someone like me. Any bit of romance in anything I write is because you made me believe in it. Te amo siempre y con todo mi corazón. And to my actual true loves, Jasper and Twinklepop, nuestros gatos más guapos, you are both purr-fect.

To all the librarians, teachers, and booksellers that have supported me along the way. You are all my heroes and absolute rock stars. The work you do to champion queer books truly saves lives, and you are all such a wonderful part of mine. Thank you, thank you, thank you.

More than anything else, even my flushable toilet wipes, I have to thank you, the reader. Of all the gay books in all the libraries/bookstores in the world, you took a chance on mine, and that means the absolute world to me. The fact that we get to share this story, in this moment, wherever you are and whenever it is happening, is something truly beautiful. I love the book community so much and I simply cannot thank you enough for spending some of your time in this story I created. I hope you enjoyed it, or at least got a good laugh out of it, but I am grateful for you regardless! You are what makes this a dream come true, dear reader. Everything I do in my career is for you. Especially if you are queer. Then it's extra for you.